Copyright©2021 Łukasz Drobnik
Vraeyda Literary
Pitt Meadows, BC
www.vraeydamedia.ca/literary

All rights reserved. No part of this publication may be reproduced in any form, or by any means, electronic or mechanical, including photocopying, recording, or any information browsing, storage, or retrieval system, without permission in writing from the publisher.

This is a work of fiction. Unless otherwise indicated, all the names, characters, businesses, places, events and incidents in this book are either the product of the author's imagination or used in a fictitious manner. Any resemblance to actual persons, living or dead, or actual events is purely coincidental.

Edited by Lis Goryniuk-Ratajczak
Cover by Marissa Wagner
Artist Photo by Weronika Woźniak

Printed in the USA
10 9 8 7 6 5 4 3 2 1
ISBN 978-1-988034-19-5 (Paperback)
ISBN 978-1-988034-21-8 (Hardcover)
ISBN 978-1-988034-20-1 (eBook)

Vraeyda Literary sends authors to events, virtual events, Book Clubs & interviews. For promotional consideration, large-volume orders, please contact Lorie at ambassador@vraeydamedia.ca.

VOSTOK

ŁUKASZ DROBNIK

To Mama, Kasia and Karolina

1 CERES

I

On days like this, Poznań was the cruellest of cities. It wasn't easy to tell whether this was because of the twelve degrees of frost, the sharp sunlight, the motionless ice-bound white river, the snow lying on the roofs or a peculiar combination of these elements, but one could clearly sense that the city was streaked with a strange kind of anxiety, that its foundations were filled with elusive energy. You could swear it was about to suddenly break in half, and its northern and southern parts intended (like jaws) to break away from the ground, rise towards each other with a violent movement and forcefully collide until Piątkowo's blocks of flats (like teeth) fitted between the tenements of Wilda.

If you made, right along one of its walls, a longitudinal section through the pub Kisielice, on the left side of the colourful rectangle you would see a bar, the back of a bartender working behind the bar, in the background a wall painted in vividly coloured stripes, black-and-white artwork on the wall, and further towards the right end of the section: empty tables, chairs, sofas. The only clients in the pub visible from this perspective were a man and a woman, in their late twenties by the looks of it, who sat on a soft couch by the right edge of the rectangular section and talked, smoking tremendous amounts of cigarettes.

A cloud of grey smoke hung in the air, the woman talked about the seemingly never-ending winter, there hasn't been a winter like this in years, about chronic lack of sleep, she looked at a window covered with a soaked poster depicting a deer and ran her fingers through her short, bright hair. When she spoke, she gesticulated wildly; while sitting, she constantly shifted; and when she was telling her companion about a preview in that gallery in Jeżyce district, about the stunning works she saw there, she almost rose from the sofa.

The man, on the other hand, mostly sat in silence, inhaling smoke, listening to his friend, smiling faintly, but when he spoke, he covered his mouth with his hand closed into a fist or massaged his thick, dark eyebrow with his thumb and stared into the distance, which made him look unsure of what he was saying.

The pub was slowly filling up. Each time the door to the street opened, a piercing chill came in, covering in a flash the length of the stairs leading to the basement and permeating through a thick curtain which separated the pub's vestibule from the long, colourful room. The man called the woman Weronika, she addressed him as Wu. With the back of her hand, she stroked his few-day-old dark stubble and said it would be nice if Wu moved his shapely arse again and went to the bar for a beer. Or not, maybe she'll drink some wine, but only white, or better: white wine with sparkling water. And ice.

Wu smiled, put out his cigarette, kissed Weronika on the forehead and rose from the table. She followed him with her eyes as he stepped deeper into the pub, and then looked with yearning at his almost two-metre-high body leaning against the counter while he chatted with the bartender he apparently knew.

When he came back, she was sitting on the couch, snuggled into its corner, shrouded in a greenish glow beaming from her phone texting someone obstinately. Once she noticed Wu, she took her legs off the seat, leaning over the phone and pressing the buttons for a while longer. Wu asked whether it was Jerzy, and Weronika replied yes, she was sorry and — after some hesitation — it seemed Jerzy and she got together again.

In response to her friend's judgemental look, she whined it's not that she was planning it, it just happened, and took the first sip. Wu sat down, wetted his lips with beer, pushed the glass away and tossed into the dusky room a rhetorical question,

'How many times can you get into the same shit?'

'Look who's talking,' she replied sulkily, moved closer to the armrest, as far as she could get away from Wu, whose face in turn twitched in a grimace, as if he had a retort on the tip of his tongue.

He lit a cigarette and inhaled the smoke. Weronika texted for a while until she sighed, put her phone down and suggested maybe at least the two of them would stop arguing about it. Anyway, she's giving it two weeks until, in this series of break-ups and make-ups, Jerzy and she will end up where they started. He gave a conciliatory smile, kissed her on the temple and wrapped his arm around her shoulder only to withdraw it a moment later.

They sat for a while, saying nothing against the background of the wall painted in stripes of different shades of green, with black-and-white artwork above their heads. Weronika smoked as well, pulled up her legs, and they stayed almost motionless for a good few minutes, staring into the void and releasing from their lungs occasional clouds of grey smoke. Finally, the thick curtain over the doorway opened, letting inside — in the company of a cold waft from the street — a woman of around forty.

'Olka!' On seeing her, Weronika shrieked, jumped to her feet and ran towards the door to throw herself into the woman's arms.

The forty-year-old found the time to say hello to some friend at one of the tables before she headed deeper into this colourful, half-greenish, half-reddish tunnel, which was indeed formed by the interior of Kisielice, and went to the bar.

She came back to the table holding three beers, put them in front of her friends, then laughed, ran her hand through dyed blond curls, tucked a tuft behind her ear, smoked and sat down. Having taken off her warm white jacket, she hung it on the back of the chair and — visibly amused for all this time — said this thing with the attack was some deep shit, there might be more at any moment.

'Stop it. I'm fed up with discussing this topic over and over.'

'But the problem won't go away because we pretend it doesn't exist. It's hard not to speak about it when such a, well, bomb hasn't happened in years. We thought we were living in boring times of peace, and there you have it.'

Weronika replied she had two days off in a row for the first time since who knows when and was sick of hearing about it. Olka'd better bollock her for getting back with Jerzy.

'You got back with Jerzy?' Olka let out an honest, booming laugh, which infected the others a moment later. Then she changed the topic and asked Wu about the progress of his work on those washing machine instructions.

Thankfully he's done with it. Now he's getting down to writing a truly fascinating spreadsheet user manual. Maybe he'll finally learn how to use a spreadsheet. He rubbed his eyebrow with his thumb again, sighed freelancing has surprisingly little to do with freedom. At the moment, his life is reduced to typing the shit out of the keyboard. This is not what he imagined a few years ago.

'Oh, stop grumbling. You'd rather work in a shop?'

Weronika laughed. 'It's easy to say if you're a director of a thriving company. Have you even been to the office this month?'

'Don't exaggerate. I sometimes drop by. Anyway, I've worked hard for that. If you don't like it, you should find a busier friend, but I'm curious who's going to pay for all those drinks. Better tell me about that novel of yours.'

Wu told her to forget it, he didn't have time lately and, frankly, no longer liked what he'd written so far. It seems he'll have to begin from scratch if he only finds some free time.

Weronika remarked with a sneer he would've had more free time if he hadn't wandered from pub to pub every night, which Wu answered with a humorous 'spierdalaj' only to put out the cigarette and announce he needed to take a leak.

Once he disappeared behind the curtain, Weronika started talking about how insanely wasted she got the night before, totally blotto; she didn't remember much: the voices of drunken people, the smell of kebabs, the bright car lights, the piercing frost. She met some guy — in Dragon, or earlier, in Kisielice — and the two of them walked somewhere across the market square towards Garbary Street, maybe to Mięsna cos where else could they've gone. When she woke up, she couldn't remember anything else, except for the image of small glowing pink rectangles she still has before her eyes. She's got no idea what to connect it with.

'Brilliant!' Olka laughed and added Weronika must take better care of herself, after which she took out a rustling fifty-zloty note and handed it to Wu, who came back from the toilet, asking him to buy another round.

They left the pub well after midnight. Freezing, still air lay heavy over Poznań, high banks of snow stretched along its streets, people occasionally sneaked in the light of lampposts, cars went by.

The three of them walked along the white Freedom Square, next to many-branched platanus trees which looked in the street light like taken from a horror. Olka took Paderewski Street, saying she'd drop by Dragon, while Weronika and Wu kept walking along Marcinkowski Avenue, at the feet of the bulky silhouette of a museum, laughing this barfly wouldn't be home by six, that's for sure. Weronika shivered with cold. Wu wrapped his arm around her, so she sunk into his dark blue jacket, barely reaching his shoulder, and they walked unhurriedly towards Wielkopolski Square.

'She's relentless, I'll give her that.' Weronika rubbed her cheek against the cool fabric. 'I wonder what kid she's going to pick up tonight.'

'Probably a fifteen-year-old,' said Wu, and Weronika, laughing, tightened her grip around his waist. Olka once told her she hadn't the slightest intention of ever being in a relationship again, when she recovered from depression after her husband's death, she decided that from now on she'd count only on herself and it was like being born anew. Weronika envies her. She herself can't last a month without a guy before all her neuroses start to strike down.

They reached St Adalbert Street and stopped by one of the buildings. Weronika thanked Wu for walking her home, kissed him on the cheek and disappeared into a dark doorway. He, on the other hand, began to slowly walk towards a petrol station and farther — along Little Garbary Street.

He entered one of the tenement houses in Chwaliszewo Street, ascended to the second floor of a dirty staircase and opened the door to a cramped, squalid flat. A large portion of the entrance hall was taken up by a book-filled shelf. The kitchen, which Wu entered first to leave a plastic bag clinking with beer bottles, exploded with lush vegetation coming out of flowerpots, while most of the floor in two small rooms was occupied by carboard boxes filled with clothes, books, papers.

Having opened one bottle, he put the remaining ones in the fridge, went to the narrower of the two rooms and turned on a laptop lying on a desk. For a good dozen minutes, he browsed websites, taking an occasional sip of beer, peeking outside the window (where the gaping Czartoria Street fell into Chwaliszewo Street) until he started typing.

If you looked over his shoulder, you could see he logged into a dating site full of pictures of skimpily dressed men. He set the status, 'Sex. Accom. Now' and having glanced outside the window and above the roofs at the distant electronic clock of the technical university (it was past one), he took a long gulp from the bottle.

Half an hour later, when most windows in the twilit Chwaliszewo Street went out, the door phone rang. In a few bounds, Wu crossed the distance separating him from the entrance hall and buzzed the visitor in without asking who it was. He left the door ajar and watched the staircase through the crack, listening to footsteps.

He opened the door wider when a short, slight figure appeared on the landing. The dark-haired man looked up at Wu with his small black eyes. The man's prominent lips, standing out against his pale complexion, formed into a smile.

The stranger went inside and removed his black coat, unveiling an equally black sweater clinging to his thin yet muscular body. He asked if he could hang his coat among the other coats, and after a nod from Wu, who wouldn't stop inspecting him, the man removed his shoes from his small, high-insteped feet predictably encased in black socks. Wu gazed at them with greed.

The man looked around the dusky entrance hall and cheered on seeing the bookcase. For a good minute, he scanned the backs of tattered books until Wu offered him a beer.

When he came back from the kitchen, the suddenly emboldened stranger already sat on a sofa in the oblong room, under a wall that hadn't been painted in ages, and eagerly examined posters covering, though he couldn't know it, some of the bigger chips in the plaster.

He took a bottle from Wu and declared he'd seen *Before Sunrise*, when he had a day off from the bank, because he works in a bank, he's a customer consultant, he likes Linklater quite a lot, there's something about him, it's rather elusive, he doesn't really know what it is in Linklater's films that he likes. Recently he's rewatched a few films which have defined him as a human being, you know, Kusturica, that von Trier's trilogy about women sacrificing themselves for the greater good, *The Flower of My Secret*, etc.

'So?' asked Wu, taking advantage of a small pause. He sat for all this time on a chair one metre from the couch, his eyes wandering over the man's body. Not waiting for a response, he stood up, put the bottle down, sat astride the man's lap and kissed him on the mouth.

II

A tram number 9 derailed in the district of Wilda, hitting cars. Meanwhile, in a completely different part of the city, along the PST (Poznań Fast Tram) line, on tracks laid down in a long deep trench, which — full of snow — formed a completely white tunnel, a two-cabin tram number 16 hurtled along like a bullet. People were crowding inside, the cabins fishtailed at sharper turns, and each time it happened, a sudden wave came through the passengers clinging to yellow tubes and the backs of seats, from the front to the end of each cabin, making them for a moment like one organism.

At the end of the second cabin, leaning against railings and staring outside a dirty pane, stood Weronika (in a red jacket) and some other woman, probably a bit younger: wearing a black coat, black boots, thick vivid orange tights, wrapped in a black scarf onto which her straight dark brown hair was falling. She tucked a tuft of it behind her ear. Weronika and the girl didn't talk, the deafening clatter of the wheels on the rails being a possible reason, and glanced at each other only now and then, for the most part staring absent-mindedly at tracks flashing outside the window. The view behind the panes made up the following sequence: the whiteness of snow, the greyness of concrete (Słowiańska Street Station), the whiteness of snow, the greyness of concrete (Solidarity Avenue Station), and then the whiteness of snow again.

The oblong barrack of a shopping centre loomed over the tunnel, its elevation illuminated with glaring lights, a luminous yellow cord undulating along the building, and from the perspective of the rushing tram, this edifice could resemble a dignified, slowly swimming whale. When the vehicle reached the next, this time stunningly colourful, station (Lechicka/Poznań Plaza), Weronika told Zuza (that is how she addressed the girl gazing outside the window) to wake up, they needed to get off, and then they both headed for the exit.

No more than two hours later, another tram number 16 arrived at a stop in Little Garbary Street, the automatic doors opened, and people started to step out of the green cabins. Among them were Weronika and Zuza, carrying heavy linen bags clanking with bottles of wine.

'Oh, give me a break.' Weronika looked away. Zuza touched her shoulder in a conciliatory gesture and said she was worried about her, that's all.

'Yeah, yeah, everyone's worried about me, but at the same time they treat me like I'm twelve.'

'Because you behave like you're fucking twelve.' Zuza laughed, and Weronika quickly joined her in laughter.

Zuza added, all right, she'll stop wittering about Jerzy cos it didn't make much sense anyway, and Weronika was going to do what she always, kurwa, did, after which she cursed the never-ending frost and suggested they go here, to the green, leave their bags on the bench and smoke cos another few minutes without a cig and she'll go nuts.

Weronika uttered a long sigh. She gets it, she knows what she's doing is totally dumb and nothing good's going to come of it, but there's something about Jerzy that she can't free herself of. Anyhow, maybe they should change the topic, and a smoke is a great idea.

They left their bags on a dilapidated bench, Zuza took out a pack of cigarettes, offered one to her friend, they started to smoke. There was a row of cars standing in the street, a tram crossing the junction, while the snow around them covered a layer of dead grass, animal faeces, litter, shards. The cigarette smoke was milky from the frost.

'Did you see the coverage? I mean of the attack,' said Zuza. 'You have to admit it was a spectacular job. The damage was, kurwa, massive, and it'll take fucking years to patch up the rifts in the infrastructure.'

She paused when she saw someone: along the untended path crossing the green walked a fairly tall blond man in an olive jacket with a white cap pulled over his ears. On seeing the girls, he gave a wide grin and approached them.

They talked for a while, the man decided to have a smoke as well, Weronika and Zuza called him Kuba, Kuba asked whether they were going to Mięsna that night, to which they replied they were throwing a small party at Wu's, but Kuba should drop by if he was in the neighbourhood anyway. There'll be the usual bunch, there'll be squid, and the ratio of bottles of wine to participants looks quite promising.

Kuba replied he'd think about it cos he was working on some 'friend', as he called her, but he can just as well work on her at Wu's, after which he said he must be going cos it was his tram, but he'll let them know.

The girls finished off their cigarettes, put them out against the edge of the bench, lifted their bags heavy with wine, bread, vegetables, cephalopods, headed towards a zebra crossing and — after several minutes at a red light — kept going along Estkowski Street for a bit. They carefully walked down an ice-covered escarpment to where the Warta River once flowed but now it was a sports field and a row of parking spaces, crossed this field, carried on among cars parked in the snow, went past a row of tin garages (black-and-white graffiti on the walls) and walked further, towards Chwaliszewo Street.

The kitchen walls were covered with ragged dark pink wallpaper; on the shabby kitchen cabinets, on the kitchen worktop, on the fridge stood flowerpots spewing out tangled ivy shoots. Once you entered the kitchen, you had the impression it was a freeze-frame from a film, and one careless move would suffice for the whole room to be consumed, in a split second, by the vividly green vegetation.

Weronika and Zuza sat at the table covered with plastic cloth and crammed with bottles of wine, a bowl full of (deep-fried) squid in beer batter, a plate of lemons, an ashtray. Wu stood opposite them, leaning against the kitchen worktop and tapping his leg along to music coming from a laptop placed on top of the fridge.

The three of them drank red wine, cigarette ends lit up above the table. Weronika said she dreamt about small glowing pink rectangles, the same she saw that drunken night. She laughed, said she must have taken some shit while under the influence, or that chap, whoever he was, slipped a date rape drug into her cocktail, as Kuba generously suggested. Speaking of Kuba, where is he? They should call him to come by.

Wu sighed and started chastening Weronika, saying she needed to take care of herself cos she was really going over the top this time and it couldn't fucking end well, when loud ringing of the door phone interrupted him.

Wu disappeared into the entrance hall, a cold draught from the staircase entered the kitchen, one could hear — in spite of the blaring music — increasingly loud steps on the stairs, and a moment later Olka came in, uttering a cheerful 'cześć' and followed by Wu carrying an armful of wine bottles.

She forced her way through the grey smoke to kiss Weronika and Zuza, declared she came only for a minute cos she needed to go to sleep at a reasonable hour, but she'd love to taste the legendary squid. Then she took a cigarette in her hand and began to look for a lighter. Weronika lifted a burning match in front of Olka's face. Kuba was supposed to be here, but he's working on some chick, so it's anyone's guess if he's going to come.

Yeah, Olka knows, she saw them yesterday in Dragon. She reached into the bowl for a piece of squid flesh coated in breadcrumbs, devoured it in one go and went on to say this girl was a tough one. For the whole evening Kuba pretended to be interested in pharmacy, as she was some pharmacy student, whispered in her ear he'd love to see her in a lab coat and protective eyewear, he almost started naming his favourite over-the-counter drugs when the girl interrupted him mid-sentence, saying it's been lovely, but she must be home by midnight. She even tricked him into paying for the cab.

Wu, flipping through songs on the computer, said Kuba never liked the easy way. To Zuza's remark expressing her irritation with the constant change of music, he replied with unvarying composure he was looking for a piece he listened to while wasted the night before. He totally can't remember which one it was. Or maybe he's imagining things.

Finally, he gave up, played a random track, leant against the wall and said those terrorists were fucked up big time. Watching their speech sent shivers down his spine. Though maybe we shouldn't be surprised: the authorities treated them like cattle for centuries, and when you look at this now, it's hard to believe we were so naïve. This was bound to happen eventually. But there must've been a lot of bluff in all this; it's impossible they have the technology they were talking about.

Could Weronika, please, relax with a glass of wine on her day off without being forced to hearing about those fuckers all the time? (For a while, she squatted on a leatherette chair with her glass, giving an occasional eye roll.)

'You're fucking lucky you've got a day off,' retorted Zuza, who — as she quickly added — didn't have a day off in three weeks because her greed made her take on another translation, though her schedule was already full, and to top this all off, Weronika was dragging her round the shops and talked her into cooking some, kurwa, squid, as if she knew how to cook.

'Oh, have a drink.' Weronika laughed, filling up Zuza's glass.

The events of the rest of this evening could be captured in stills: Wu leaning against the fridge, Zuza, Weronika and Olka at the table, bright dots of burning tobacco. Next, a similar scene, but with Kuba and a dainty bright-haired girl standing in the doorway, the girl was pale and had big blue eyes, she barely spoke a word. Then the dark pink kitchen, Weronika and Zuza above an empty bowl, the former whining about her complicated relationship with Jerzy, a cloud of grey smoke above their heads. Half an hour later at the table sat Weronika, Zuza and Kuba, the latter walked his blonde friend to a cab and told the girls someone must've got pretty stoned cos they broke into the military museum and stole a war scythe. Even later, a similar scene: Wu standing in the doorway with a bottle of wine, saying Olka went to Dragon after all but promised she'd be back, which meant she wouldn't. Then a bulb blowing out, darkness instantly filling the kitchen. Later again, the rest of them sitting by candlelight, against the background of the wallpaper which seemed almost black in this light, Weronika immersed in a greenish glow beaming from the phone and texting. After one more hour, there was only Wu, Kuba and Zuza, the latter saying it always ends like this, sooner or later Jerzy calls and after ten minutes Weronika's gone. And the last scene: a candle burning out, Wu and Kuba sitting in silence above the last of the wine, with lustreless eyes, smoking; the room was tightly filled with smoke, the smoke was as dense as fog.

III

A heavy dark sky hung above the city, it was night, Poznań's blocks of flats and tenement houses remained dormant, car parks choked on freezing air, lampposts cast a lurid light, snow lay heavy on the roofs, and a strong, piercing wind ran along the network of streets; it carried frost.

In light from the street you could see unfocused outlines of the furniture and cardboard boxes, crumpled bedding, Wu tossing and turning. You could smell the pungent scent of tobacco smoke. Hear the muffled voices of brawling chavs. Finally, Wu sighed, got up from the bed, walked through the darkness of the entrance hall to the darkness of the kitchen, groped for the switch, pushed it, and when in spite of this it remained dark, he silently cursed the blown-out bulb. He felt around the worktop to find a bottle of mineral water and started to drink — with fast, greedy gulps.

Twenty minutes later he already walked along Garbary Street, there was no one within the range of his sight, some dead-drunk girl lay in one of the doorways, but he couldn't possibly see it, so he walked, trembling with cold, towards Bernardine Square, passed a shop selling telescopes (a bloated Jupiter on a poster next to the entrance), a row of black shop windows, a chemist's 'Wenus', a dot-matrix display scrolling the message, 'Stay healthy. Stay productive. Collect points.'

Then he followed the tramline towards the river, Mostowa Street at this time of night was dark and motionless, no cars were approaching, so Wu walked diagonally to the other side and kept striding along the street, only to take a right turn before Roch Bridge and go down a steep embankment to the river itself. The Warta was ice-bound and covered with a thick layer of snow, the sky whitish from the city glow. Wu smoked, slowly carrying along the invisible bank, and as he walked, he sometimes squinted and massaged his eyelids, like one does to soothe an unbearable headache.

One time after he opened his eyes, and it was when he nearly reached Chrobry Bridge, he stopped to stare, straining his eyes, into the dark space under the bridge's deck. Right next to the bank, under a pillar, loomed a shape. Wu hesitated, then took a few steps forward, approaching the shape to a distance at which one could already see it was a girl kneeling in an unnatural pose, strangely bent forwards.

He asked if everything was all right. Silence.

After a moment he came closer, an arm's length away, and — with hesitation — gently touched her shoulder, but the girl didn't budge. Finally, he took his phone out from his pocket and shone it on her face.

The reddish light revealed a mouth gagged with a decent-sized lemon, blue, ghastly open eyes, hands tied behind the back and a belly slit open to pour onto the snow a ripe cluster of guts.

Meanwhile, a little more than three kilometres to the north, along Murawa Street, between the cuboid blocks of flats of Wuthering Height Estate on one side and of Cosmonauts Estate on the other, Weronika walked with a shaky gait, smoking a cigarette, crying, uttering silent 'kurwas' and at times wiping her tears with the back of her trembling hand.

When she was approaching Solidarity Roundabout, the city's almost absolute silence was suddenly interrupted by a phone ringing. She tossed one more 'kurwa', hurled a butt-end into the snow (it cut across the air like a comet roaring with fire) and started to nervously poke around her pockets. Finally, she took out her phone and once she saw who was calling, her face, now drenched in a green glow, tightened with anxiety.

She picked up. Whoever it was, she told that person: calm down, one thing at a time, slowly, from the beginning, listened in silence, paler by the second, to the voice coming from the receiver until she crouched and hid her face in her palm. She muttered they must stay calm, she'll go there right away, everything will be fine. The voice in the receiver said something, she asked if he was sure he was going to be okay cos she could take a cab any minute, although he might be right, it probably doesn't make much sense, let him call her when they stop questioning him. She was silent for a moment, breathing heavily, the voice in the receiver ceased as well, until she asked, 'What about Kuba? Does he know?'

MURDER INVESTIGATION AFTER YOUNG WOMAN FOUND DEAD NEAR WARTA

Police were called to the vicinity of Chrobry Bridge on Thursday night where a 22-year-old pharmacy student was found dead by the riverbank.

A police spokesman confirmed that the cause of death was a sharp-force wound to the abdomen. An investigation is underway to find the perpetrator. Anyone with information is asked to contact the authorities.

The main area of the pub Dragon was filled with the smell of incense, cigarette smoke hanging above the tables, sad music coming from speakers, people crowding densely along the bar, while in front of the crowd and behind the bartenders' backs you could see a row of long shelves filled with bottles of liquor. Over the scene loomed a carved dragon head, protruding from the wall and painted black.

The pub itself was an enormous, multi-level creation: beneath the main area was a stifling basement with another bar and a cramped dance floor; from the main room one could also go outside to the garden — this time of year claustrophobic and covered with snow. From the garden, via a narrow stairway, you could reach higher levels: another bar behind a swing door, through which you could enter a second garden on an elevated terrace snuggled against a weather-beaten wall; to a room opposite this bar; to another room above it — and yet another, fitted on a wooden mezzanine above the bar. From one of these rooms you could get — through a usually closed door — to further areas: a room housing concerts and author meetings, and from there — to yet another bar. Dragon was like slow-spreading cancer each year occupying new spaces of the old tenement house, appropriating new rooms and corridors, and no one seemed to have any doubt that one day it would engulf it all.

In the corner of the main room, next to a door leading to the garden, in the soft light of a shaded floor lamp, Zuza and Wu reclined on a sofa, accompanied by stooped Kuba sitting on a comfy pouffe. On the table stood three barely touched beer mugs; in the middle, a vase with white tulips. The three of them barely spoke, smoking unhurriedly, looking somewhere ahead.

'Can't believe it,' murmured Kuba and leant down to wet his lips with the beer. He can't get his head around it. Okay, he saw Ania a second time in his life and had no serious plans for her, but such things, kurwa, just should not happen. Though maybe that's the reason he feels so shitty about it. And the way they killed her. Like in some slaughterhouse.

'Don't torture yourself.' Wu touched his friend's shoulder for a moment. 'What can you do when there's nothing you can do?'

He knows, he knows. After all, he walked her to that cab, paid for the fare. He even started to suspect she was seeing him only because of those cab rides. Cos there was no way he could talk her into sleeping with him. He saw her drive away, so how is it possible she ended up back by the river? One hundred metres from Wu's place?

'Ja jebię,' interrupted Weronika, who came from behind the bar. She sat on Wu's lap and, leaning towards the table, took a cigarette of out a pack and asked if anyone had a lighter.

It must be a punishment, this working behind a bar when she almost viscerally hates people. She should have consulted a career advisor or something. But wait, she can't do anything else anyway.

'How're you holding up?' she asked, tenderly ruffling Kuba's blond mop of hair, once she stopped laughing at her own joke.

'Just look at me,' he said, clenching his fists alternately (his joints made a soft crackle). Zuza, who remained silent for this whole time, looked at his wrists covered in bright down. 'And all those interrogations, I'm going there again tomorrow. I'm sick of them.'

They fell silent and got back to listless smoking and drinking. People crowded in queues outside the toilets and at the bar, some visibly inebriated man in his twenties staggered towards Kuba, almost spilling his drink on him, while the speakers now played a jauntier, electronic piece.

'Break's over,' Weronika announced with resignation, put out her cigarette, kissed Wu's temple and got back behind the bar.

Wu followed her with his eyes and happened upon a pair of dark irises piercing him. A short black-haired man of slight build, pale face and prominent lips, the one who paid Wu a night-time visit two days earlier, sat on a bar stool in front of a small beer. He stared at Wu for a moment with a timid smile, then finished his beer, stood up from the bar and started forcing his way through the clump of people, towards the exit.

IV

She said she remembered the navy-blue sky over Międzymoście Square, there were white clouds below the sky, gulls against the background of the clouds, and she walked with that chap, whatever his name was, she must have got herself really wasted. They walked between one guarded car park and another, now she almost recalls his face, he might have had thick black eyebrows, protruding cheekbones, he was saying something, they talked, they might have said something about Venus, about Ceres. Next Chwaliszewo Street, Czartoria Street, the broken lamppost kept flickering while they were necking in front of the off-licence. She remembers she felt the texture of his navy-blue jacket under her fingers; the frost seemed to pierce her with small daggers. They kept walking, perhaps towards the river, she's just remembered he helped her down the ice-covered embankment, there hasn't been a winter like this in years, she guesses there were some other people, can't remember how many, her lips were chapping, she totally can't recall their faces. They stood for some time under the bridge, the motionless ice-bound white river, they talked, she was completely drunk, it was night, trams no longer ran, until one moment the bloke who led her there took out from his pocket a box and out of it a small object — a rectangle giving off pink, fluorescent light. And then nothing, a complete blank.

Olka laughed. No soap opera is better than Weronika's stories about her drunken excesses, and she can't wait for new episodes because each one is a whole new level of absurdity.

Weronika whined it wasn't funny, she got totally blotto, she couldn't have drunk that much, the guy must have slipped something into her cocktail. And what's with those rectangles, maybe she hallucinated or dreamt the whole thing, but for the last few days, whenever she closes her eyes, she sees small pink bloody rectangles, it's driving her nuts, and on top of it there's that girl under the bridge. She hid her face in her palms and let out a theatrical sigh.

Olka laid her hand on Weronika's forearm and told her to calm down, nothing happened, she just needed to take better care of herself, she'd been through a lot, this whole situation with Jerzy and all, it was going to be okay, she simply needed to work some things out — after which she downed a shot of vodka with one swift move.

They were in Mięsna. Snow melted on the dirty floor, they were set against wallpaper with a concentric orange-and-purple pattern, lamps with plastic shades. The interior was dense with cigarette smoke, loud with music, crowded with people, bartenders behind the counter poured beer into plastic cups as they had apparently run out of glasses.

From the main room you could go upstairs, where was a dance floor surrounded by different wallpaper (with a similarly orange-and-purple pattern) and full of inert bodies of tipsy twenty-year-olds bending to the music. You could, through a currently closed door, go down to the basement with a small stage. If places had memory, the yellowish walls could still feel the touch of bodies swarming in the darkroom located here a few years earlier.

'By the way,' said Olka, 'tell me about Jerzy. Is there any chance it's going to work out this time?'

Weronika glanced at a bearded DJ behind turntables, at drunken people in their twenties swarming around the bar and replied to her ever more inebriated friend she couldn't say. Please, let Olka not mention it to Zuza or Wu, but they've already managed to have two deadly quarrels. That night when Ania got killed, they fought so badly she walked home all the way from Winogrady. But we'll see.

'And that thing with Zuza and this guy—'

'Jacek? Nothing came out of it. They went on a few dates, and then Zuza retreated.'

Olka nodded, then asked, struck by a sudden thought, 'Has Zuza ever been in a serious relationship at all?'

Weronika stammered, looked to both sides in a moment of reflection, then again at Olka, who suddenly burst into laughter.

'Well, well. And I thought you were such besties.'

Come on, Olka's fully aware what Zuza's like; it's hard to get her out of her shell. And she's such a good listener. (Olka couldn't stop laughing.) Weronika remained silent for a while, chuckled nervously and finally asked whether she really was such an egocentric.

'Don't worry. Zuza doesn't seem to be bothered.'

Weronika, somewhat embarrassed, took a big gulp of beer and changed the subject, saying she was worried about Wu, he'd been working too much lately, sitting at his laptop from early morning until late night and banging on the keys, and the last thing he needed was a story with a corpse under the bridge.

Olka eyed Weronika in silence for a moment, as if a little concerned, against the background of the bar, the lights, the clouds of smoke, fiddling with a lighter, until she asked, or rather stated, 'You're not over it yet, are you?'

After Mięsna it was time for Dragon, for pushing one's way through the crowd, drinking vodka at the bar, smoking cigarettes, for superficial conversations with friends and freshly befriended people, for drunken looks at blurred lights. In mere twenty minutes, the completely intoxicated Olka managed to knock two beers from the bar with her elbow, put out a smoke in someone's cocktail and insult her fiftyish-looking friend by asking her tips for coping with senescence.

Meanwhile, Weronika, drunker by the minute, sat on the small wooden stairs at the door to the garden and watched people, silently sipping wiśniówka on the rocks (freezing air wafted through the crack under the door). After a while, she poked around her pockets to eventually reach for her jacket lying on the side and take out her phone; immersed in a greenish glow and slurping alcohol through a straw, she began to type.

She raised her eyes and saw in front of her a man who had been standing there motionless for at least a minute: not too tall, of rather slight build, with a few-day-old stubble and prominent lips. He asked if he could join her and, without waiting for Weronika's reply, sat next to her on the wooden step.

Said his name was Staszek, said he was new to going out and didn't know too many people, asked whether Weronika came here often and, having received no response, began to blab about his musical interests. Weronika kept typing, her strained face and blank stare suggesting it caused her considerable difficulty. She sipped wiśniówka through a straw and seemed to completely ignore Staszek, who said he couldn't call himself a fan of Tori Amos's music, but got hold of her double record from the late nineties, which he found somewhat interesting, especially the arrangements, and the lyrics, which — as always in the case of this artist — were definitely noteworthy. As Weronika remained unimpressed with Staszek's digressions about popular music (the smell of his cologne lingered in the air), he clearly decided to show his wide reading and started to talk about his interest in classic science fiction. He proudly told her that after much hardship he got his hands on the anthology *Farewell Fantastic Venus*, the first edition of 1968 (when he talked, his protruding Adam's apple moved, muscles shifted under his T-shirt) until he asked Weronika's name.

She stopped pressing on the keys and looked at Staszek for the first time. After a moment of silence, she introduced herself, remarked it'd been a pleasure, only to take the last sip of her cocktail, put the glass down on the step, get up and, having grabbed her jacket, start forcing her way towards the exit.

To Staszek, who was following her, she said no, she won't be staying, and no, he can't ask her a question, and they'll surely come across each other many times cos in this shitty city there are maybe four decent pubs, after which she opened the door to the street and walked out into the burning frost.

Above the ice-bound river hung a dark, equally still sky, it was the middle of the night. Slowly, the lights of Poznań went out, one by one. From a bird's-eye view one could see the individual districts — Rataje, Sołacz, Łazarz, Winogrady — plunge deeper and deeper into impenetrable darkness. The blackness devoured, cancer-like, residential buildings, offices, shopping centres. Eventually, you could see nothing but a network of streets lit with the pale glow of lampposts.

In the shade of Chrobry Bridge, right above the frozen Warta, appeared a bright moving point. If you looked at it with human eyes, which gradually adjust to the darkness, you could see an ever-sharper silhouette, a shaking hand, a visibly anxious face. The luminous point glowed for the last time, and Wu tossed the butt towards the river. Then, using his phone as a torch, he started raking up snow where, a few nights earlier, he found a slit-open corpse.

After several minutes of clearly futile search, he put his phone back into his pocket and took a few steps towards a pillar of the bridge when a silent crack sounded under his shoe. He crouched, took out the phone again, shone it under his feet and dug out from the whiteness a small black object. When he swept snow from its smooth, slightly fractured surface, it became clear it was an mp3 player (it glowed vaguely in the nocturnal light).

Without hesitation, he took a pair of tangled earphones out of his pocket, plugged them into the player, placed them in his ears and pushed a big black button. On the dark surface flashed the text, 'track 05'. A moment later Wu's eardrums were hit by a clear and powerful, seemingly multiplied sound of French horns playing an unhurried, melancholic, insistently repeated phrase. A dozen seconds passed, and the text disappeared, the music fell silent.

Weronika

Small glowing pink rectangles, I can see them whenever I close my eyes. The navy-blue sky over Międzymoście Square, the white clouds below the sky, the grey gulls, guarded car parks. Frost like small daggers plunged into my body. Once again we walk towards the river, neck in front of the off-licence. Once again the scratching of his stubble, pink rectangles, something about Venus, about Ceres. Chwaliszewo Street, the lamppost like a strobe light. Czartoria Street, we walk down the ice-covered embankment.

Now I'm sitting in my kitchen. Everything's still grey: the snow-covered St Adalbert Street outside the window, the blurred outlines of the kitchen furniture and fridge getting sharper by the minute. The light from my laptop must make me look like a ghost. I'm strangely sober drinking the last of the last beer. My hands still tremble.

I look at the curtain edges, then close my eyes. I can see the small pink bloody rectangles, hear the words of our quarrel in my head like a broken record. Insults shouted by Jerzy. The sound of a shattered glass. The rustle of clothes packed in a hurry. My own weirdly alien voice, screaming that if I feel like it, I'll let half of the city shag me, and it's none of his business because it's over. A door slam.

In my mind I walk out again, heated into the cold night. Stand in front of the block of flats. Cosmonauts Estate is silent and unreal. My hand struggles to hold a cigarette when I try to light it. The smoke irritates my throat, sore from all the screaming. The light of lampposts, the block of flats' blue door, its façade painted in blue rectangles. The blue gutters, blue bench, blue railings enclosing a white lawn, the pink rectangles (I need to keep it together), the naked branches casting tangled shadows on the snow.

I start to sob and, a few minutes later, walk across the roundabout, empty at this hour, under the night sky heavy with white clouds, wondering what Zuza and Wu are going to say. I can almost see their concerned but smug faces. They always know better, and I always get myself into the same mess.

Stop thinking about it. St Adalbert Street outside the window, almost no beer left. There's still a little wine in the fridge. Lurid light, drinking straight from the bottle, the pink of the rectangles under my eyelids, thinking about Wu.

Suddenly, it's the first weeks of our friendship. It's early summer, and we go together to the Warta River, to the sun-burnt grasses, to be devoured by mosquitoes. We sit down on the concrete riverbank, still warm from the scorching day, look at the river's waters, listen to the hum of cars on Chrobry Bridge, drink krupnik straight from the bottle, talk.

It turns out Wu and I read exactly the same books, go to the same films, have uncannily similar reflections on the emptiness and pointlessness of life. Something about Venus, about Ceres, it's getting colder. Wu wraps his arm around me, goose pimples all over my body. My breathing gets faster, and I feel an urge to take him home, for eternal exclusivity, and make love to him all night until dawn. It's because I don't know yet that in a week's time he'll introduce me to his boyfriend.

The small pink rectangles, pink blood gushing from arteries, I dive again into the chill of the deserted Winogrady Street, agitated after my quarrel with Jerzy. Walk along the row of villas and the park lurking behind them, on top of the sparkling, well-trodden snow.

I can't stop thinking about the terrorists' new announcement, Antarctic landscapes and threats spoken by a speech synthesizer. My heart is pounding. Dark windows line the street on both sides. People sleep behind them, likely dreaming about their relationships, children and problems at work. Pink rectangles under my eyelids. And this ever more palpable presentiment that all this might suddenly vanish: those villas, that dark park, tramlines, all the bus stops, streets and blocks of flats, all the shops. And I who walk crying in the middle of the freezing night.

Thinking what it is that makes me come back to Jerzy over and over, repeatedly push my way into his no longer young arms. I'm starting to regret I told him about that guy, the one who took me to the river, who must have slipped something into my drink. About that kiss under the lamppost. About the ice-covered embankment. About the small pink rectangle. Okay, perhaps I was trying to get together with Jerzy at the time, but we weren't a couple yet. I didn't think he could be jealous of such a thing. Though Jerzy can be jealous of anything.

Almost no wine left, the kitchen almost completely bright, the walls light up pink again, and I'm standing once more in front of Dawid, the first of the series of arseholes Wu fell for. At first, I don't feel a thing but have the impression I am being lifted high above Poznań. They stay down below, Wu touting the questionable attributes of the slightly chubby blond in a way too tight T-shirt, and I look at all this without emotion from the height of hundreds of metres, my sight able to embrace all the districts: Winogrady, Grunwald, Wilda, Rataje.

I come back down to the ground at last, talk to them for a few minutes and, on my way home, buy a half-litre bottle of żołądkowa and two cartons of grapefruit juice. Then drink disgustingly warm cocktails and cry long into the night.

V

The white frozen Warta pierced right through Poznań (like an arrow). It was snowing. Outside the windows of the pub Dragon one could see densely falling flakes, the street submerged in grey afternoon light, dirty banks of snow and, at times, people passing by. Inside, in an almost empty room, Weronika and Zuza sat in silence, one could smell incense, hear the sound of a chocolate mixer. Zuza was lost in thought, slurping the remains of her iced coffee through a straw, while Weronika held a cup of tea in her hands, with shot eyes, bouncing her leg nervously.

'Go on, I know you want to say it,' she began, and Zuza gave her a searching look. '*I told you so.* You and Wu can high-five each other.'

'Stop it.'

Weronika shrugged, scratched her neck and said maybe it was better this way, Jerzy and she were exhausting each other from the beginning and, sooner or later, one of them had to flip, any pretext was good enough. She only hopes he won't call her in the middle of the night after a week or two, saying he can't sleep without her. Like he did after earlier break-ups.

Zuza uttered 'chujnia' as a remark and resumed slurping. Someone entered from the street, and a cold, piercing waft reached the girls.

She thought she'd care less. That she'd go to sleep and when she woke, some of this bloody sorrow would disappear.

'Well, you know, break-ups *are* depressing.'

'What's depressing is that I came to work on my day off. Why are we even here? Ah, right, employee discount.'

Weronika took a sip of tea and put her cup down, saying she bloody wanted to get drunk, now she'll get drunk every night again, meet inappropriate people, end up in bed with blokes she barely knew. It's always like that when she's not with Jerzy. After a moment, she realized it wasn't much better when they were together.

Zuza smiled and stretched her arm across the table to caress the back of Weronika's hand. She remarked, given the circumstances, the idea of getting drunk isn't that bad; anyways, it's already past two and this time of year it's almost evening. So, two mojitos?

An hour later, they were already drinking a second cocktail, the room was slowly filling up, the sun slowly setting, the snow thinning.

'I'd love to run away,' Weronika's eyes were becoming dull, 'pack one suitcase and leave all of this. First the attack, and now Jerzy…'

Then she talked about the powerful explosion she watched, again and again, from new points of view; about white buildings and bridges turning to dust; about cables coming out like bowels; about the fact it was only a matter of time before those freaks struck again, when Zuza interrupted her,

'What was there between you and Wu, exactly?'

Weronika seemed disconcerted. She put down her glass, scratched her neck again, gave her companion a long silent stare, lit a cigarette and finally said it was nothing, at least not on his side. She had a slightly different understanding of the beginning of their acquaintance. Maybe she counted on something more than friendship, but it was when she wasn't aware Wu actually preferred cock. (Zuza glanced at a text message: *Where are you?*) Well, it went how it went. Anyway, a good thing came from this, so maybe there's nothing to regret, I guess. (She replied with a short: *In Dragon, with you know who.*) The air in the room grew thicker with smoke.

A phone on the table suddenly vibrated, its green screen flashing, so Weronika picked it up with disaffection, read the text and uttered a loud curse. She swears she's going to kill that nutter.

Zuza, amused, asked what Olka did this time, to which Weronika replied — having taken the last drag from her cigarette and put it out in an ashtray — this drunk, presumably between her fifteenth and sixteenth shot, gave Weronika's number to a bloke who latched on to her yesterday and kept talking some rubbish about Björk or PJ Harvey, about some fantasy books, she barely managed to fob him off, and now that bore — listen — wants to meet her in Meskal at eight.

WAR SCYTHE THEFT POSSIBLY LINKED TO YOUNG WOMAN'S MURDER

The authorities admitted the theft of a war scythe may be 'linked to the recent murder of a 22-year-old pharmacy student, although it is too early for a definitive answer.'

The 19th-century weapon was stolen from the Military Museum of

Wielkopolska on the night preceding the woman's death. It remains unclear how the thieves managed to bypass the museum's security system. The authorities urge anyone with information to come forward.

They've questioned him about that night again, he's come straight from there. They wanted to know exactly what happened, in what order and at what hour, kept asking the same questions hundreds of times, but how's he supposed to remember it all if he was totally wasted? It seems he must start a notebook in case another miss he wants to score ends up ripped open under a bridge.

Wu must know that with each account his memories became sharper. After a few rounds, it was almost as if he were standing again in the entrance hall of the Chwaliszewo flat, behind Ania's back, holding her cloak to help her get dressed. The room was gloomy, music and laughs came from the kitchen, they just said their goodbyes: Kuba kissed the girls on the cheek, Wu right on the mouth, holding his face in both hands, while Ania remained in the doorway, waving shyly.

She walked down a few steps ahead of him, leaving a trail of flowery perfume and the smell of cigarettes. When she took a turn at the landing, he gazed once more at her bright hair, snub nose and those big, impossibly blue eyes. They sent him a cheerful look.

He remembers the frost stung, and one of the lampposts flickered like a strobe light. Ania was cold, so he wrapped his arm around her, still hoping she'd let him shag her. When he attempted a kiss, she dodged him with a smile.

They strode unsteadily along Chwaliszewo Street towards the taxi rank, parking spaces, unmoving trees. Under the cross stood a lone silver Toyota (he can't recall the name of the cab company), he walked Ania to the door. What he remembers, though, is the driver: he asked him to take good care of her and take her safely to Rataje. And it was quite a tall guy, well-built, dark-haired, with thick black eyebrows and a strange tattoo on his forearm, perhaps in the shape of some continent.

The club Meskal was filled with loud music, people crowding around the bar, thick cigarette smoke hanging under the ceiling; a freezing waft rushed inside through cracked open windows. Wu leant against a dark red wall, slowly sipping beer, looking by turns at colourful carpeting, people at wooden tables and artwork decorating the room (photographs of Antarctic landscapes). Through a rectangular opening in the wall, one could see at times people entering and leaving the place, and it was exactly in that direction Wu seemed to be staring.

Suddenly an expression of surprise appeared on his face, his lips parted, and it was precisely at the moment when in the rectangular clearing flashed a black-haired man with pale skin, prominent lips and dark eyes, the same who visited Wu's flat not that long ago. He entered the pub and vanished in the crowd.

A dozen minutes later, Wu stood outside the entrance, in the frost, smoking, as if waiting for someone or wondering which way to go. Nowowiejski Street opened before him, the smoke he exhaled grew cloudy from the frost, while the walls of buildings echoed shouts of drunken adolescents standing at the entrance to a nearby dance club.

Suddenly, from round the corner, emerged the slight figure of Weronika, who rushed along the pavement with a brisk, springy, slightly unsteady gate, trying to avoid some of the bigger lumps of frozen snow and forgetting to look ahead while she dashed along. She bumped right into Wu, who held her, protecting from a fall, said 'cześć' and, in the same breath, asked where she was rushing to and how much she'd drunk.

Weronika, happy about the unexpected encounter, said 'cześć', it's good to see him, and she's got no idea how much she's drunk, but she's going to drink at least as much, and she's headed right here, to Meskal cos that nutter Olka set her up on a date with a total drag, who — she hopes — will buy her drinks for the rest of the night.

'How're you holding up?' he asked, tossing the butt-end towards the street.

'Just look at me.' Her voice trembled lightly. 'But don't worry, another three mojitos, and it's going to be okay.' Then she stood on tiptoes, kissed Wu on the cheek and rushed inside the club.

While hurtling along the narrow corridor, she took a fleeting glimpse through the rectangular clearing where one could see the interior of the pub frozen like a film still, people conversing, the bar, clouds of smoke. Round the corner she plunged into the crowd, said 'cześć' to some friend, unzipped her red jacket and entered the crowded room.

Staszek already sat at a table under the small rectangular window, and when he saw Weronika, he sprung up and sent her a wide grin. When he leant down to kiss her on the cheek, she jumped away with outrage, asking if he's fucking mental, and then, while taking a seat, told him to get her a mojito, or better two at once because there's always a long queue at the bar.

Several dozen minutes passed, Meskal was still full of smoke, frigid air still wafted through the windows, it was invariably loud with conversations and music, while Staszek kept telling Weronika about how he was in love with literally every aspect of *The Truman Show*, but she seemed to completely ignore him. Weronika was finishing her second mojito and, with a cigarette in her mouth, scribbled on a piece of paper with a pen. Only now and then did she glance at Staszek's pale face, prominent lips, well-defined cheekbones, dark eyes before she quickly got back to the doodling.

With some hesitation, Staszek said he saw Weronika with her friends in Dragon a few days ago. She replied with a detached 'aha', never gazing away from the sheet of paper.

'I know this tall one from somewhere,' he continued. 'What's his name?'

'Wu.' This time she gave him a searching glance.

'Wu? Strange name.'

'It's not a name.' The pen moved obstinately. 'You don't want to know his name.'

Clearly at a loss for what to say, he started talking about his freshly rekindled interest in retro video games and the adventure game *Black Dahlia*, which he played with unfeigned pleasure, then — noticing Weronika wasn't listening to him anyway — dared ask,

'Do you think you could maybe… give me Wu's number?'

'Oh.' Weronika stopped drawing. 'So that's what it's all about. Couldn't you ask Olka?'

Staszek blushed and said he tried, but Olka was, well, she wasn't at her most sober and she started talking how he and Weronika should meet and wasn't listening to Staszek's explanations, oh my gosh, he now realizes how this looks, he's sorry, it wasn't his intention, he's rather, well, how to put it, socially awkward would be a proper term, he probably should've asked straight away, he sees that now, oh my gosh, he's so sorry, maybe another drink?

'Let's summarize.' Weronika didn't meet Staszek's eyes, her pen scratching against paper. 'First you're so socially inept that instead of getting the number of a guy you want to shag, you end up with the number of a girl you clearly *don't* want to shag. Sure, we've all been there. Then you text her. But of course you won't ask for the guy's number. No, that would be too simple. You ask her out for a faux date where you bore her to death with some bullshit about artsy films and stupid video games and buy her drinks until, what, she's drunk enough to give you the number?'

'That wasn't my intention.' Staszek looks down, cradles his hands on his lap. 'So… do you think you could perhaps—'

'No,' she growled, put her jacket on and headed for the exit, leaving the mortified Staszek at the table. If you looked at this scene from above, you could see the abandoned piece of paper was filled with rows of small pink rectangles.

VI

Red, green, cigarette smoke, ash-soiled tables, chapped lips, light, the hubbub of conversations, loud music, skin reddened by frost, black-and-white artwork on the walls. The interior of Kisielice was full of people occupying every single chair, tightly filling with their bodies every sofa, while those who couldn't find a seat crowded around the long bar and talked, laughed, drank, smoked.

Among the latter were Weronika and Wu, standing close to the curtain-covered entrance, surrounded by people, in the spot where the long counter took a turn to meet the wall.

'No, I didn't meet him in a darkroom, but the usual way, on a hookup website.'

Weronika whooped with laughter, spilling a drop of beer from an almost full glass. Her red jacket thrown over her shoulder stood out against the green, striped background.

'But tell me more. Does he have a name?'

Wu scratched the back of his head in embarrassment, put the glass down on the bar and said with a vague smile he'd tell her later cos he didn't want to jinx it. Let her give him a few more days. He really hopes it won't be another of the series of chaps he introduced to Weronika as the love of his life, and after a moment they all turned out to be complete fuck-ups. Although this time he's got a good feeling about it. The guy's a good lad, Wu loves talking to him, and something tells him Weronika will instantly like him.

'Okay, you've got until the end of the week.'

'If you insist.' He gave up and fell silent.

There was red, green, there was the smell of cigarettes, there were people crowding next to the bar, there was music. Some man said to a friend there hasn't been a winter like this in years. Some girl drew aside the heavy curtain while walking in, and cold air forced its way into the room. It was as sharp as a dagger.

Weronika feels sick when she thinks about tonight. Maybe Olka'll manage to drop by and entertain her with her drunken jabbering. Did Wu hear about those breaches?

Yes, he did. Good they stopped them in time. The authorities claim the cyberspace hasn't been compromised, but they're surely not telling them everything. Though no one can be certain if it really was the terrorists. But the other option isn't optimistic either.

'True.'

She looked for a second at his face covered in dark stubble, as if wanting to say something, but she changed her mind. Her sad eyes traced the line of his long forearm sheathed in a thin sleeve as he put a cigarette into his mouth.

Wu talked to Kuba today, he didn't sound too well. Imagine he said he must slow down a notch with this partying, with this hitting on chicks. Kuba. Can Weronika believe this? This thing with Ania must've shaken him more than he wants to admit. And they keep nagging him with the interrogations, even though the rest of them were called on only once, and that was it. Kuba believes he's the main suspect, so Wu's telling him he's being paranoid cos there are also our testimonies, cos he disappeared only for a second to walk Ania to the car.

Weronika shook her head. 'Zuza's drowned in translations. She won't go out anywhere. It's not even clear if she's going to be at that bad film night tomorrow.'

'That's tomorrow?'

'Don't say you're not coming either.' She tightened her lips and took a deep breath through her nose.

'I was sure it was the day after tomorrow. I can't tomorrow, I've got a date.'

Weronika tilted her glass up and started to guzzle its contents, gulp after gulp.

'But I can reschedule,' he added quickly, watching the foaming beer disappear inside her body.

She finished it off, put the glass down on the bar, wiped her lips with the edge of the sleeve of her grey sweater and, while heading in silence towards the exit, started to put on her jacket. Wu gave her a conciliatory pat on the shoulder.

'I don't want you to change your plans for me.' she snapped, pushing his hand away. 'Hope you'll enjoy yourself tomorrow. Have a nice penetration!' she shouted loudly enough to attract half-amused, half-embarrassed looks from the furthest corners of the room, before she left the suddenly pale Wu at the bar, passed through the curtain, ran up the stairs and stormed out into the darkness of the frosty street.

If you were suspended from the ceiling of the pub Dragon, you could observe the exhausted Weronika, who — as if part of a religious ritual — reached for vessels to fill them with fluids and ice, collected money and, once in a while, if the rush wasn't too high, walked out deeper into the room to have a wistful smoke. The crowd pulsated, either growing in number, or thinning; at times it filled the room to the brim, only to come unglued from the walls a moment later; it stuck out amoeboid projections always in the same directions: to the exit, to the toilets, to the bar, down the stairs to the basement and — through the frosty patio — to the bar upstairs. Meanwhile, over the old tenement house, black clouds moved beneath the black hanging sky.

Several hours passed and Dragon's interior changed beyond recognition. Chairs in the suddenly dark, emptied room were put on tables with their legs up; dead silence prevailed, interrupted only by splashes of water, the scrubbing of a mop against the floor and occasional knocks of plastic against wood.

From a bright room behind the bar emerged Weronika, zipping up her jacket which seemed brown in this light. She said 'bye' to a bartender washing the floor, then another one to a hefty security guard standing by the exit and walked out to the street.

The sky was already clear, full of stars. The cobbles on Zamkowa Street shone in the light of lampposts, the freezing-cold air kept covering the cobblestones, over and over, with infinitely thin layers of ice, while the compressed snow muffled the clack of her heels — the only sound in this stillness. Weronika took out her phone, gave the green screen a disaffected look and put it back in her pocket. She slipped once, almost falling. Then again.

When she was nearing 23 February Street, her puffy eyes wandered around the dark windows of the archive, the empty pavements, the ad saying, 'Remember to update your software', the tram tracks sticky with frost, the bare tree limbs.

Suddenly, her eyes met the gaze of a man's.

VII

The cruel rains of Venus, we are walking slowly,
lifting our feet with effort through the pallid jungle
that opens up a ghastly mouth before our faces,
trying hard to stop thinking of the never-ending
beating down of fat raindrops against our pale bodies,
trying hard to keep breathing and not choke on water,
plants as if from a horror, eyelids as if leaden.

The rain frays lurid foliage in a stubborn rhythm,
stimulating nerve endings, permeating deeply
the fibres of our clothing, which is almost tintless,
the rain's washed out the colour, only in some places
mould has made it look greenish, the sky is still golden,
uniform, thick and heavy, I still see the redness
of sharp and clean wound edges, the tattered soft tissues.

St Adalbert Street, snowing, winter without mercy. A dilapidated narrow staircase of a post-war tenement house, flowerpots in windows at landings, notes stuck to walls to inform about the requirement to turn off the basement light and report any suspicious behaviour to the authorities.

Zuza, in a black coat, pink tights, hair tied in a loose ponytail, stood in front of a door on the second floor and rang the doorbell. She held a paper-wrapped bottle of wine. Soon one could hear footsteps coming from the inside, then the silent creak of the inner door, and — after a moment to peek through the peephole — the outer door opened.

In the entrance hall stood Weronika — wearing a bathrobe, with bloodshot eyes, a dressing on her forehead, bruises on her wrists, against the background of hanging cloaks. She said a quiet 'cześć' and having spotted the wine in Zuza's hand, smiled, affectionately called her a drunk and invited into the red interior. Weronika directed Zuza to the living room, took the bottle and disappeared into the kitchen situated at the opposite end of the flat.

Zuza sat down on an orange couch, surrounded by the grey walls of the spacious room. Took off her jacket, threw it on the armrest and lounged back, only to stand up and walk to the window. You could see tenement houses on the other side of the street, while in front of you — like an empty space after a pulled-out tooth — stretched a small car park covered with concrete slabs. In the background were trees, chimneys, trees.

Weronika finally entered the room, holding the now uncorked bottle of wine and two glasses. She placed them on the table and sat on the sofa, tucking her feet under her. Zuza pulled up a chair for herself, poured wine into glasses and finally — after a generous moment of silence — uttered one short, 'go on'.

She said it was night, it was freezing, it could be four, maybe later, she just finished her shift. She was slightly drunk from shots she'd been secretly throwing back, so she kept stumbling on frozen banks of snow. The sky was cloudless, she could see the stars.

She was almost the last one to leave Dragon. It was silent, but her head kept thumping from the hubbub of people sloshing between the bar, the tables and the bog for hours. She walked down Zamkowa Street, the frost was unbearable, she wanted to puke, realized she didn't eat much. She thought about Jerzy, about this fucker pestering her with phone calls again. He probably wanted to apologise, wanted to come back, as usual.

She remembers she took out her phone to see if there was anything besides texts from Jerzy and Wu. Wu and she had a quarrel over something trifling, that bad film evening, which she had to cancel anyway and which she found, for some reason, super important at that time.

When she entered 23 February Street, she spotted a shadow in front of the greengrocer's: next to a tree, against the snow-covered green. The whites of eyes flashed in the dark.

She only glanced at him and turned away as she kept heading towards Wielkopolski Square but noticed the man was rather tall and seemed to be staring in her direction. When she was nearing the square, she decided to cross the street. There was no one around except for the man, not a single cab.

While crossing, she looked at the grey edifice of the archive. She remembers she slightly slipped on the cobblestones and then heard fast, ever louder, persistent footsteps.

Before she knew it, she was running away along the square, the chap kept rushing right behind her, she squeezed between parked cars, galloped amid the stalls. The bloke got her. Grabbed her by the wrists. Twisted her arms behind her back, but she, somehow, managed to break away. She must've buried her heel in his foot.

After that she doesn't remember much: dark stalls, running along a lane, the glow of street lights and then the man assaulting her again, putting his arms around her waist, shouting at her, calling her a whore, a cunt, she could swear she knew his voice. She glanced at his forearm, where a tattoo emerged from below his jacket. It had a strange shape, perhaps of Antarctica.

She remembers her feet weren't touching the ground, recalls the pain and tenement houses surrounding the square. The guy lifted her up like a rag doll and flung her to the ground. Landed a few kicks on her back. Grabbed her hair and with all his might bashed her head against something hard.

He leant over her. Kill her, but she can't remember his face, even though he was inches away. Wait, she does remember something — the guy had thick black eyebrows — but other than that, a complete blank. Then he must've hit her once more.

For some time, there was only blackness, then she was lying on the cobbles, frozen to the bone, the bloke walked away, every breath was painful. She tried to get up, the freezing air filled her lungs, she stared at the stall roofs.

Wu

I can still hear her voice in my head telling me not to be silly, definitely not to come over and to stop apologizing for yesterday because it was her fault. Her reaction was irrational, as always. I reply I would stay out of her way. Bring some wine. Spend the night on the couch, and at least she'll have company. But she won't even hear about it.

The sun has set, you could eat the dark with a spoon. I imagine I have eyes on the back of my head and look with them outside the window covered with a net curtain: at cars parked down in the tenement's backyard, at the dilapidated building next to it, bare trees, ever darker Poznań. The voice in my head doesn't cease, replaying the whole conversation over and over, it's her fault, she says, the ivy covering the cabinets seems almost black. The door to the room in front of me is wide-open, showing Czartoria Street brimful with the pale light of lampposts. The fridge is buzzing.

I should get up and take another beer. The voice in my head keeps cataloguing bodily injuries: a swollen brow ridge, scratches on the forehead, bruises on the wrists and around the kidneys, grazed knees and elbows. Later, to change the topic, she pushes me to tell her about my sudden infatuation, while I, as usual, refrain from it as hard as I can. Before my eyes I have the snow-covered square, the flight among the stalls, the attacker's strong hands, the scuffle, the hitting of her head against the edge of a stall, the black sky.

I should get up from the table, open the fridge, a sudden flash, and take out that beer, but some unknown inertia makes me stay and, once again, I walk through the snow-filled Garbary Street in the middle of the night, with a headache, in the glow of street lamps. I run my finger across my chapped lips. Walk past the Jupiter on the poster, the chemist's 'Wenus' (unbearable frost), then along the tramline towards the river.

I walk down the embankment and follow the frozen Warta. Massage my eyelids. The snow around me is like white ivy. Then all I can see is the blurred shape, the cluster of bowels, the lemon, the deadly blue of eyes.

The snowy landscape transforms into a landscape of skin. I run my hand over it — it's smooth like a baby's. Clumps of black hair around the nipples. My tongue across his Adam's apple. Kisses so long they make my lips go numb. The stubble on his thighs and forearms. The soft spot right behind his ear.

I feel as if I were drowning, as if ivy entwined me, entered my mouth. I'm not even trying to catch a breath. No question it's only drugs in my head that make me think about him all the time. About when I'm going to see him again. Some part of me must know it's going to end as it always does.

The kitchen is almost completely dark. I sit in this darkness instead of getting up to grab that beer. The voice inside my head fades with each replay. The black ivy covers the black furniture, and there's nothing but the flight between the stalls, nothing but frozen snow, punches of fists, marks of boots on the ribs.

VIII

The plumes of soot lay flat in a radial pattern on the ice sheet's surface. The plain stretched to the horizon. Soaring airships cut through the air, shining in the sun which wouldn't set. He looked at this all from the height of dozens of metres.

There was something eerily beautiful about the gaping black rift in the extensive Vostok City, in its innards coming out in places with hundreds of torn pipes and sparkling cables. In the swarm of flying robots bustling about the charred ruins like fish eating sedentary animals and seaweed from a black reef. The forest of moving cranes gave off an ominous, multiplied drone.

In the uneven cross section, you could see a tangle of monstrous, once white and now sooted oval towers, the bundles of lift shafts and the network of layered streets and pavements built back in the times of humans. He made a circle over the city and went lower to look at it from a different perspective: from there he could no longer see the vast, dark pit; for a moment he almost believed no attack took place. The rounded line of roofs reminded of pudding straight out of a mould blended with the white sky. He added Wu could sometimes go out to the real world as well.

'Give me a break.' Wu leant his head out of the cubbyhole in the entrance hall. 'This is my natural habitat, and I shit all over this trendy contact with reality.' They laughed.

Kuba sat in the kitchen, against the background of the dark pink wallpaper, it was midday, intense sunlight poured into the room through dirty windowpanes. One could see, in all sharpness, grease on pots piling up in the sink, clumps of dust in the corners and tangled ivy shoots (they made one think of murderous plants). Outside the window stretched the greyness of Poznań.

'Maybe you'll change your mind and stay for a coffee?' Wu peeped out again from the dark cubbyhole. And by 'coffee' he means 'beer'. It's in the fridge. Kuba can grab one for him as well.

After a while, both of them sat at the kitchen table drinking beer when Wu said he had no idea where he lost those keys. Kuba's sure he hasn't seen them? They were on this fancy Jupiter-shaped key ring. Bought it with Weronika at some stall in the market square after they got pissed in the middle of the day, right after they met. Oh well. If he doesn't manage to find it, he'll cut the padlocks. Too bad about the key ring, though.

They were silent, staring at the floor, until Kuba asked how Weronika was doing. Wu sighed, scratched his head. She sounded quite okay over the phone yesterday, but he's afraid this experience was a bit much, especially after everything with Jerzy. He hopes she's going to recover after all.

Struck by a sudden thought, Wu jumped to his feet and, taking his bottle with him, walked to the window and opened one of the drawers of a narrow cabinet. With dogged determination, he rummaged through cutlery, filling the kitchen with sharp metallic clanks.

'So, when am I going to meet your new babe?' Kuba asked in a more cheerful tone, stretching out his arms with interlinked fingers.

Wu replied, sooner than he thinks. He's going to join them tonight in Dragon.

AUTHORITIES TO IMPOSE NEW SECURITY MEASURES IN RESPONSE TO VOSTOK CITY ATTACK

The authorities announced new security measures in response to the recent Vostok City bombing. In their official statement, they reiterated they would not yield to the terrorists' demands.

Although the new measures are yet to be specified, it is speculated they will involve heightened scrutiny of all citizens.

Vostok City, the largest metropolis of Antarctica, is situated roughly 1,100 kilometres from the Queen Maud Land Reservation's border.

If that day you looked at Poznań as a whole, you could fall under the illusion of harmony: some trams left the terminuses while others arrived at them; traffic lights at crossroads alternately halted cars approaching from different directions; people, in a regular, pulsating rhythm, gathered at zebra crossings and crossed them; in a deep trench in the ground, under Theatre Bridge, under Station Bridge, two trains hurtled along in opposite directions.

Only if you dived closer to the urban tissue and looked at the apparently insignificant details: chavs fighting near Rataje Roundabout; oranges spilled from a stall in Jeżyce Market Square; a tram stopping between PST stations in a cascade of sparks shooting from overhead wires; a dog running under the wheels of a tram in the Głogowska-Hetmańska junction, it would become clear the structure of the city was overtaken by uncontrollable chaos.

The basement of the pub Dragon was filled with cloudy cigarette smoke and a damp smell, music coming from speakers, people densely seated around tables, a few dancers on a small dance floor, and if you passed, walking towards the bar, the entrance to a long room leading to the dance floor on one side, and a small table snuggled beneath stairs on the other, you would reach a room in which, on wooden benches, all of them sat: Zuza, Kuba, Olka, Weronika and Wu.

Over their heads was a thicket of artificial plants immersed in reddish light, you could see a brick wall, and next to them at the bar, which stretched parallel to the room with the dance floor, sat some men drinking whisky and having a cheerful talk with the barmaids.

Facing away from the entrance, Zuza talked to Weronika, gently touching the dressing on her forehead and asking if it hurt, saying this whole thing was a total chujnia and she hoped Weronika already used up her limit of mishaps for this year cos what worse — she giggled — could happen to her.

'Actually, I can think of a few scenarios.' She took a sip of wiśniówka on the rocks. For instance, Jerzy could go completely nuts and set her flat on fire, or they could find her tomorrow ripped open under a bridge.

'Now you're being dramatic.' Zuza rolled her eyes.

You can't even be a little dramatic any more. Zuza'd better look at her. When is the time for self-pity if not now? At least her boss told her to take some leave. Perhaps he didn't want her to scare the customers off.

'But you're scaring them off anyway, only from the other side of the bar,' remarked Zuza, to which Weronika laughed and replied, 'We've come down to the basement, haven't we? Anyway, he's on a leave until the end of the week.'

Then she said she couldn't sleep. As soon as she closes her eyes, it's that night again, and she's walking towards the square. But the guy isn't standing by the greengrocer's but materialises at once an inch away and glares at her with a pair of black, merciless eyes. Then she wakes, turns on every light in the flat and smokes cigs, trying to erase this image from memory.

Deeper into the room sat Olka and Kuba, half-listening to Wu's disquisition about how he wasted a whole fucking day because he had ambitious plans to take some junk out to the garage but couldn't find those keys anywhere.

'How's your novel?' interrupted Olka.

Oh, he doesn't know. It's all started to fall apart. He's got no idea whether he'll manage to finish it. So far, he's written three chapters: in the first one, there's an 8-bit amoeba devouring Poznań, in the second, a chick living in a house composed of an infinite number of floors and in the third, a chap wandering around Poznań, riding trams and discovering he's a superhero. There's also going to be mannequins and a journey inside a human body, but he doesn't know how to work this all out. Well, what can you do when there's nothing you can do?

While he talked, Kuba didn't take his eyes off Zuza. An artificial plant above her head formed a nimbus of sorts. She kept tucking a strand of straight dark hair behind her ear, listening to Weronika's story about a golden sequin jacket she ordered to cheer herself up. Customers walked in both directions through the narrow passage. One of the men in the background, at the bar, cackled loudly at a joke. The barmaid told him to calm down.

Olka didn't seem to pay much attention to what Wu was saying. She set fire to a shot glass filled with krupnik and coffee grains and looked into the flickering flame, nodding now and then.

Suddenly, Wu interrupted his tale, waved at someone at the entrance and shouted they were here, encouraging him to join them, upon which Olka glanced at the newcomer, and embarrassment showed on her face.

Wu stood up and announced to the gathering he would like them to meet someone. Kuba and Zuza smiled lightly, while Weronika turned her head towards the entrance to finally see the well-defined cheekbones, pale skin, prominent lips and dark eyes of Staszek, who stood at a one-metre distance from her, sending a hesitant, as if apologetic smile. From where he stood, he could clearly see Weronika's suddenly vanishing smile and her face freezing with anger, and at the same time, this position made it rather difficult for him to dodge an attack when Weronika grabbed her glass of wiśniówka from the table and flung its contents right in his eyes. She took her jacket, walked away from the table without a word of explanation, leaving the stupefied Wu and the amused others, and headed towards the stairs.

The frost embraced her, she forced her way through the crowd in front of the entrance, and then, uttering silent curses, striding at a fast pace, took out a cigarette and lit it with the flame of a lighter. If you looked at her from above, while hanging over the white roofs, you could see her run across 23 February Street, then continue at a brisk walk along Wielkopolski Square, turn left behind the market, cut the tramline, only to dash across the street at a red light. No doubt at that moment she didn't realize she was being continuously watched.

LAURASIAN FORESTS

I

Poznań could be flooded with pink — gushing out of manholes, running down the gutters. The walls of tenements and blocks of flats could start soaking up fuchsia. The city's main arteries: Głogowska, Grunwaldzka, Dąbrowski could become channels for the colourful, turbulent torrents, while the grey spaces of the Old Market Square, Freedom Square, St Martin and Ratajczak Streets could come alive, as if on command, with a swarm of pink reflexes. Finally, all the streets and squares could, at once, open like a mouth, uncovering cross sections of basements, the sewage system, underground car parks, and the pink could pour down there, cascading with enormous weight, filling every space and stealing air.

Meanwhile, the city invariably remained in a safe range of shades of grey: with the white roofs, banks of dirty snow, sooted walls of Piątkowo's blocks of flats and tenements of Jeżyce, dark coats of people waiting at stops, the greyness of the Imperial Castle and the cuboid Alfa department store high-rises, the graphite-coloured smoke coming from chimneys. Among this all — patches of white, as if wiped out with a giant eraser. The grey solid of the modernist Arena gave the usual impression of not an edifice but a spaceship that perched for a moment among the leafless trees.

Like every morning, people walked along pavements, tram stops were rhythmically filled and emptied, trams, buses and cars moved over the uneven asphalt, and if you stood at that moment on Theatre Bridge and ignored the omnipresent noise, you could hear the creak of street lamps rocking above your head.

You could look down and see — hung on overhead wires stretched like strings above the railway tracks — a human corpse swaying in the wind, with an eruption of pinkish viscera coming — like garlands — from its cut-open stomach.

Along the motionless ice-bound white river two people walked. From thirty metres above the ground, from above buildings, from above a bridge, you could merely see their blurred silhouettes, but if you descended, sank into this white trench enclosed from both sides by flood banks and allowed this whiteness to surround you (the whiteness of the meadow faded into the whiteness of the river, into the whiteness of the meadow), you could tell they were Zuza and Wu. They trod slowly, smoking, glancing at Roch Bridge, at a tram crossing the bridge, talking.

Zuza put a cigarette in her mouth, inhaled, making its end glow red, emptied her smoke-filled lungs, tucked a tuft of hair behind her ear and said she was never, kurwa, going to touch alcohol again, she means, at least for the next couple of hours, Wu missed a lot leaving before midnight cos Weronika and she stayed for a little longer and made some new friends.

They were some guys from some band who turned up at one point out from chuj knows where and kept buying them vodka. Zuza, although the waisted drummer was clearly hitting on her, came back home. Unlike Weronika, who decided to hang out a little longer with the double bassist, so no one knows how it ended. Zuza's been trying to reach her all day to get a detailed account, but it seems she hasn't got up yet.

'Fucking hell,' she continued. 'Good, at least, you talked me into this walk. I wouldn't do anything constructive today anyway.'

Wu is sick of looking at those charts and formulas. If he doesn't catch up, he'll have to start snorting speed before the deadline. He laughed and, after a pause, massaging his eyebrow, asked whether Zuza talked to Weronika yesterday, about you-know-what.

She shook her head. Weronika wouldn't talk about it, and Zuza gets it. In her place, she'd feel humiliated as well. She doesn't know Staszek and doesn't want to judge him, but kurwa, he didn't navigate the situation in the most graceful way.

Wu lowered. His cheeks, reddened by the frost, seemed to blush even more, and he said, in a slightly higher than usual voice, Staszek is how he is, a little socially awkward, and he tends to make blunders now and then. Like, ten times a day. But he's a good lad; Wu doesn't think he had any bad intentions. He was just looking for some way to reach Wu after he deleted his account on that dating website. But true, he should've taken a more straightforward approach.

'I'm not sure what to, kurwa, tell you.' Zuza shrugged. 'Perhaps it'll be best to wait and hope things will go back to normal on their own.'

They disappeared beneath Roch Bridge, and if you soared up in the air at that moment and looked down at the entire scene, you could see the whiteness of the river almost indiscernible from the whiteness of the meadows on both sides, bare trees, cars, a tram crossing the bridge.

They walked for a moment in silence along the invisible bank when Zuza took her phone out of her bag, selected a number and, after a longer while of listening to the dial tone, said it was about, kurwa, time Weronika got up and answered.

Mięsna. The smell of tobacco, the pattern of wallpaper, the dimmed light, the loud conversations and loud music, the sweaty bodies at the bar, the beer poured into glasses. Staszek was telling Olka about one of his favourite shows. It was a show about death and the final episode — mind-blowing! Olka has got to see it as it's arguably the best five minutes in the history of television.

They sat at one of the tables, dirty snow melting on the floor, Staszek's monologue from time to time interjected with enthusiastic comments of the visibly drunk Olka: 'you don't say!', 'really?', 'o kurwa!', 'you're shitting me!'. There was a row of emptied shot glasses in front of her, while Staszek — whenever he made a pause — sipped beer from an almost full mug.

Finally, Wu entered the room. He walked down the stairs, panting, a smile on his face, his orange T-shirt drenched in sweat. Having squeezed his way through the crowd, he stretched out on the sofa next to Staszek and laid down his head on his shoulder.

Heedless of the fact he interrupted Staszek's disquisition on Gaspar Noe's films, he gave a blissful sigh and said this was what he needed. Olka laughed and asked him whether he spotted any hunks, to which Wu replied, in spite of Staszek's slight embarrassment, not really, the usual bunch, but he met a friend who told him someone was murdered near Theatre Bridge. The guy didn't say much cos he wasn't at his most sober. He did say, though, it was a very bloody business.

'What's going on with this city?' Olka let out a gloomy sigh, but concern quickly disappeared from her face. She took out a hundred-zloty note from her wallet and gave it to the silent Staszek, asking him if he could, please, go to the bar and buy her one more eighty and whatever Wu and he wanted. Though, she noticed, Staszek would probably pass this time cos his pace tonight was rather sluggish.

When he left the table, and Wu stretched out over the entire length of the sofa, Olka said she'd called Kuba and, believe it or not, she didn't manage to talk him into going out this time either. It seems he's not in his best shape.

'Yesterday he told me about some chick he was working on, so it seems there's improvement. I'm starting to get seriously worried about Weronika, though. How long can you have your phone turned off?'

He straightened up, ran his finger along his eyebrow and (against the background of the wallpaper with a concentric pattern) said he was at her house today, and she wasn't answering the door phone. Though perhaps they shouldn't worry yet: there were a few times when, after a night of heavy partying, she woke up in the evening or disappeared for several days without a sign of life. Maybe she's at this double bassist's. He hopes he's not some arsehole like Jerzy. Speaking of Jerzy, Wu heard from Zuza that Weronika started talking to him again, which is never good news. 'Can I grab a smoke?'

Taking a Camel from an almost empty pack, he said it must be her revenge for that thing with Staszek. They'll have to patch this up somehow, though he's got no clue how. He'll drop by Weronika's tomorrow morning, maybe she'll get over it by that time.

The interior of Mięsna grew thicker with smoke, alcohol vapours, the hubbub of conversations, the beat of music coming from speakers. Olka, Staszek and Wu sat in silence, foggy-eyed, listening to the music and perhaps thinking of something distant: Wu with his head on Staszek's shoulder, Olka slowly sucking down the last of her cigarette.

Suddenly, the eyes of all three turned towards the entrance. Wu got up from the chair and waved, his face first relieved, then filled with panic. Visibly irritated, brushing snow off her coat (it was snowing over the entire Poznań), Weronika stormed into the smoke-filled, patterned room. On seeing Staszek, she rolled her eyes (the scratches on her forehead were almost healed, yellow bruises covered with thick makeup) but walked over to the table, shook his hand, threw herself into Olka's arms, kissed Wu on the cheek and went to the bar.

A few minutes later, she was sitting with the rest, apologizing for not calling back all day, but she went to sleep somewhere around six in the morning cos Zuza and she met some guys who first bought them a shitload of alcohol and then one of them insisted he would take Weronika on a stroll along the Warta. As pissed as she was, she obviously decided it was a marvellous idea, and they wandered like that for a few hours, and he kept blabbing about his double bass, cos he was a musician, she didn't even ask his name.

'Yes, Zuza's already told me. But please, could you stop pulling stunts of this kind?'

In response, she sprung up from her seat, said a reconciliatory 'all right' and leant over the table to kiss Wu on the forehead. Staszek watched this spectacle with some reserve.

Olka cackled, downed the contents of her glass and announced she'd love to stay with them a little longer and listen to Weronika's drunken stories, but, imagine that, she'll have to show up at the office tomorrow and keep an eye on her workers a bit so they won't sink her business, and she doesn't want to look like an utter drunk.

No way! Wu said they should start to worry about themselves if they stay out longer than Olka, to which she laughed, zipped her jacket up, kissed everyone on the cheek and left with a spry gait.

The remaining three sat for a moment in awkward silence until Wu cleared his throat and urged Weronika to say something about that bassist. Was he cute?

Cute-ish. She spent a few hours with him drinking by the Warta but then felt sleepy and fobbed him off. Not much to talk about.

The silence returned. Weronika passed her fingers along the cigarette as if deciding whether she should light it. She looked around the room with indifference, then turned to Wu to send him a faint smile, not even glancing at Staszek. His head was lowered, hands clasped around his beer-filled glass dirty with many fingerprints.

Wu shifted in his seat for a while until he said, warily, he must go to the toilet and asked if he could leave the two of them alone. Weronika told him not to be silly, flashed an excessively friendly smile and lit the already somewhat crumpled cigarette.

When he walked away, glancing back every other step, the atmosphere got even denser. Staszek sipped beer from his glass, looking blankly at the concentric orange-and-purple pattern, at a plastic lampshade, while Weronika, completely ignoring him, smoked and typed something on her phone.

Finally, he put down his beer and mumbled he felt stupid about this all and wanted to apologize, once again, for that terrible misunderstanding. He instantly fell silent, though, when he met Weronika's angry gaze. She hissed, listen, buddy, she doesn't give a damn about what he wants to say. He's got a thing going on with her close friend, so she must tolerate him, but she's not buying his bullshit explanation, and he shouldn't count on any girly talk. She's got no idea what his agenda is, but she knows he's onto something, and she'll be watching him closely. Her only hope is that he won't hurt Wu cos if he does, it's going to get, kurwa, ugly. Then, as if nothing happened, she took a drag on her cigarette, glued her eyes back to the phone and resumed typing. Staszek, on the other hand, returned to sipping his beer and gazing silently at the patterned wallpaper. The smoke permeated all.

II

I Burn Poznań. It does sound like that band's name, ja pierdolę. Zuza turned pale against the green striped wall, sat down on a comfy sofa, not saying a word for a while, only shaking her head in disbelief. But how? Ja jebię, this isn't happening. In response, Weronika gave a slight shrug, downed a shot of wiśniówka, swept her scared eyes over the interior of Kisielice and repeated after her friend: this isn't, kurwa, happening.

It won't be long, Wu said, before those fanatics from Queen Maud Land strike again, in Vostok City or other cities of Antarctica or African cities, the attack was just the beginning. He only hopes they won't manage to breach the cyberspace's security systems cos if they do, they're all screwed. He patted his thigh for emphasis, but Olka was probably too drunk to care. She kept twiddling in her fingers a white carnation taken from a vase, looking absently outside the window: at the dusk, at the grey walls, at the coffee shop signpost across the street, only nodding once in a while.

They were in Dragon. The scent of incense mingled with the pungent smell of tobacco, bartenders poured drinks, people talked, jazz came from speakers. The room was slowly crowding up, the front door opened again and again, each time drawing in a cold waft, the dragon's head protruded with dignity from the wall just below the ceiling, and from its perspective you could clearly see people drink beers or cocktails, get up from their tables to go to the toilet, return to their seats, every so often burst in laughter or wait at the bar for one of the bartenders to serve them.

One time when the door opened, Staszek came inside, together with a gush of frosty air. On seeing him — perhaps happy to no longer have to listen to Wu's lengthy disquisition on geopolitical affairs — Olka instantly roused herself, sprung up from her chair and, probably a bit too loudly, shouted at Staszek to come here, let her kiss him. Having embraced Olka and given her a peck on the cheek, Staszek started to remove his black coat, saying there hasn't been a winter like this in years and asking what they wanted from the bar as he undid the buttons.

Olka's animation didn't last long. When Staszek came back to the table with three beers, settled in his chair and made some habitual complaints about the unbearable weather, he started talking how unsettling, multi-layered and visually arresting the *Ghost in the Shell* film was. Olka's enthusiasm evaporated. She began to sip beer from her mug, and when Staszek changed the subject to another film, in which an enormous blue planet strikes the earth, she only nodded thoughtlessly, once again staring into the greyness outside the window, into the street lights.

One hour later, it was darker outside, louder inside and people populating the place were drunker — these included Olka, who stopped pretending she was listening to anyone and drank beer in silence, her solemn eyes glued to the dark window. Kuba joined the scene. He sat next to Olka and, visibly amused, gave the account of his recent disastrous date.

A ringtone interrupted him. Wu took out his phone from his pocket, looked at its display for a second, picked it up and went outside (harsh wintry air reached those remaining at the table). A few minutes have passed, during which Staszek sipped his beer, Kuba smoked a cigarette and Olka, ever drunker, gazed vacantly at the tabletop. Finally, the entrance door opened, and Wu — upset, his skin reddened from the biting frost — returned to the table. He sat down, took a pull of beer, and uttered a silent 'ja pierdolę'.

'That guy who was killed... He was a guy from that band, I Burn Poznań. They've played in Dragon once or twice, I've heard they're kind of awful. The girls drank with them that night.'

A silence fell over the table. Olka, as if finally woken, looked thoughtfully at Wu, then outside the window. Kuba's jolliness suddenly vanished.

'But how?' he asked and took a long sip of beer.

Staszek, somewhat tense, glanced at the others' worried faces, as if not entirely sure about how to react. It seemed for a second he wanted to say something, but he changed his mind. Wu, after some more silence spent in an invariable position, his hands on the table, explained it was Weronika, she was all jittery, almost crying to the phone. All they revealed was the band's name, so we can't be sure who died exactly, and the girls didn't take their phone numbers or anything. Weronika's praying it wasn't that double bassist who drank with her by the river. Fucking hell. They say it was a sharp-force wound to the abdomen, like the last time.

'So, what now? Are we dealing with a serial killer?'

Olka, matter-of-fact in spite of her inebriation, calmed Kuba down, saying two killings are far from a series. Anyway, they know too little to tell whether one has anything to do with the other. It can be just a coincidence. There's no need to panic.

Kuba turned pale, put his trembling hands under the table, looked away towards the room, cursed, lit a cigarette and, having held the smoke in his lungs for a bit, said it was a little too many coincidences.

The smoke grew denser, the music louder. Only Wu and Olka were left at the table. The situation turned around as now it was Olka — in end-stage intoxication — who bored Wu to death with her grievances about the futility of life, about the passing of time, about the fact she wasted the best years of her life with that fucker, her husband, which was all for nothing in the end. Okay, she's got money, she doesn't have to work too hard, she's set up for life, but what's the point of this all? However you look at it, she's not getting any younger, and she'll eventually grow too old and too ugly to pick up those kids, even for money. Maybe she keeps lying to herself; maybe she's not as independent as she'd like to think. Perhaps she's simply afraid of starting another relationship after her husband screwed her over like that.

Wu, in accordance with the principle of symmetry, did not seem to listen, only nodded, as if lost in thought, looking at people, at the dragon's head, at the lights, colourful glass, smoke.

If you looked from above the rooftops of Wuthering Height Estate's cuboid block of flats towards the setting sun, you could see the almost identical blocks of the neighbouring Victory Estate, Połabska Street down below, snow-covered lawns, ice-glazed car parks and sports fields, bare trees, a billboard advertising Beyond the Moon travel agency, the lights of cars driving along Solidarity Avenue — all of this in a bloody red.

A similar vista, although largely restricted by a window frame, could be admired from a kitchen on the top tier of a fifteen-floor block. In the foreground, you could see saddened Weronika, surrounded by the red light, leaning against the worktop, wrestling with the cork in a bottle of wine. At the table sat Zuza — equally sombre-faced, smoking.

'It's a nightmare,' the latter finally broke the silence. 'I feel like I've been through a mangle.'

The interrogation took two hours or so. Zuza told them hundreds of times she didn't remember the drummer's name until they finally said his name was Filip. They looked at her like she was a fucking drunk when she insisted she had no idea when they left Dragon and, no, nothing happened between them.

He insisted to walk her to Theatre Bridge, and she felt she couldn't say no after all the vodka he was buying. Perhaps he counted on more, sure, but didn't get any. It was fucking freezing, it was snowing, and as they reached the opera, he tried to embrace her — he must've been expecting something more. They talked for a little at the stop, she weaselled out of giving him her number and then got on a night bus. And that was, kurwa, it.

Weronika, who — after a long struggle — managed to get the broken cork out of the bottle, looked at the red glow outside the window and said she'd suspected from the beginning it was that double bassist. Michał, as it turns out.

He seemed to expect something more as well. After they froze to the bone by the Warta River, emptied two bottles of cytrynówka, kissed a little, he must've been positive he'd score her that night. If she hadn't got so sloshed, maybe she would've asked him to come over. Though it was probably too soon after Jerzy.

'By the way, how's Jerzy? Still texting?'

All the time. He's basically texting himself. She replied once or twice, even though she promised herself not to. Her only hope is she won't bump into him on her way home.

She can only guess how Michał ended up by Theatre Bridge. Maybe he wanted to catch a night bus, though chuj knows where he lived. They can't rule out the possibility whoever killed him, was following him from the beginning, maybe even watched the two of them for hours as they were getting drunk by the river.

III

Trailing with her eyes the line of the white rooftops over Mielżyński Street, Zuza talked about the cities of Antarctica. She and Kuba stood on a fourth-floor balcony, smoking; the rows of tenements flanking the street led to Ratajski Square, where one could see fog, bare trees, people waiting at tram stops, ads of quick ways to boost one's points, drunkards on benches, tram tracks. After she tossed the cigarette butt down towards a passing tram, she said, okay, the view's nice, but they should come back inside before they freeze their fucking arses off.

From the balcony they stepped into Olka's study: solid dark red wallpaper, tall shelves filled with books, an enormous desk piled with papers, empty cigarette packs, beer cans and spotted with yellow sticky notes.

'I don't feel like being in here,' said Kuba, twiddling a pack of smokes in his cold hand. What are they even doing? It turns out the double bassist was killed with the same weapon as Ania and most certainly, it was that scythe stolen from the museum, and they what, throw a party? They can drink themselves to death, but the fact remains they're probably dealing with some psycho, and the murders have only begun. So, what now, when one of them gets killed, they're going to host a reception for one hundred guests with a laser light show and a DJ?

They walked to the living room. It was spacious and shaped like a truncated rectangle, with a wide window placed in this truncation and overlooking 27 December Street, modernist buildings across the street and a McDonald's on the ground floor. The walls were covered with patterned grey wallpaper, the panelled floor sparingly fitted with furniture: a TV stand, home cinema speakers, a sofa, some armchairs, a low, long coffee table.

'Aren't you tired of it?' he asked, glancing at Zuza's exposed neck as she scratched the nape of it, and then said he feels like they've been stuck in a loop for the past couple of years, going from Mięsna to Dragon to Kisielice to Meskal, drowning any major problem in beer and vodka. Weronika can't seem to get out of this sick ping-pong between Wu and Jerzy, Olka lives from hangover to hangover, Wu launches himself into the arms of ever more obnoxious guys, while Kuba himself is no better, his only preoccupation figuring out who he's going to shag next. Anyway, where's Olka? What can you be doing in a shop for so long? Or maybe she's decided to drink some of the booze on her way back.

Zuza sat on the sofa. For an instant, Kuba examined her profile with a small nose and prominent chin against the long corridor and then sat next to her.

'But what can you do when there's nothing you can do?' she finally asked. Granted, this escapism won't lead them anywhere in the long run, but kurwa, as a plan for today it's not that bad. Especially since they have no power over the course of events.

Kuba scratched his bright temple and said yes, he knows, he gets it, he didn't mean to sound like a know-it-all, he was speaking about himself too, but he's just tired of it. He wakes up, starts the graphics editor but instead of working on a project, he surfs the Web looking for anything he can find about the attack, about Ania and Michał's deaths. He's getting worried one might have something to do with the other. What's more, he's read on an unofficial dashboard it could be Queen Maud Land's terrorists who were behind both murders (Zuza gauged him carefully).

It's become an obsession. He doesn't know about Zuza, but after something like that he feels he should take a step back and, dunno, have some reflection rather than drown his thoughts in booze. The world as they knew it is now a distant dream, dreadful things can await them, and drinking beer after beer is not going to enact change.

At that moment, the front door in the adjacent entrance hall burst open, letting in Olka laden with shopping bags, struggling to hold her phone to her ear, saying, sure, they should come around, Kuba and Zuza are already here. Then she said bye and laid on the coffee table the bags heavy with wine, beer cans and puffy packets of crisps.

Snuggled on a soft orange sofa against a grey wall, Weronika talked on the phone, smoking. In front of her, on a low table, stood a half-emptied bottle of white wine and an ashtray bristling with butts. You could see the shaking of her hands, redness of her eyes, hear the tremble in her voice as she said, no, she's sure she doesn't want to come over, he's lovely, but she'd rather be by herself at the moment, this interrogation was one too many, especially since it turns out Michał was most probably murdered right after he walked her home, kurwa, perhaps she should stay here forever.

Weronika put out the cigarette end in the ashtray, refilled her glass and said, honey, of course it's not about Staszek, come on. After a moment of listening to her interlocutor's voice, she snorted with laughter and said, that's insane, she's not going to see Jerzy. Sure, he's been texting her all the time lately, but please, she still has some self-preservation left. It's over between her and Jerzy, promise. They talked some more until Weronika said bye, sent kisses and put the phone away.

She sat still for a moment, her arms wrapped around her hunched legs, then cursed, took a sip of wine and picked up the phone. Having dialled a number, she held the phone to her ear, said, 'cześć, Jerzy' and told him to come over as they agreed. He should bring some wine. After a short conversation, she hung up, tossed the phone back on the sofa and swore once again.

The kitchen of Olka's spacious flat overlooked the cylindrical Okrąglak building, the pavements full of dirty snow, the car park in front of the Polish Theatre, the Gorals' stalls, the McDonald's, the leafless branches of the tree growing next to the tenement. Dusk was falling.

'I'd like to show you something.' Wu's voice was stern as he put a small black object on a plastic tablecloth. Olka scrutinised the mp3 player, took it in her hand and pressed its large button several times, to no effect.

'What's that?' she said, already slightly drunk. From the living room came the sounds of the party. One could hear Kuba's hearty laughter, shouts uttered by the suddenly enlivened — presumably by alcohol — Staszek, Zuza asking someone to please help her uncork the wine, daftly cheerful music coming from speakers. Finally, Wu explained he found it under the bridge. The one, you know… where Ania…

Olka fiddled with the object for a moment, after which — as if struck by a sudden reflection — put it quickly down on the table and asked Wu whether he shouldn't rather report it to the authorities.

Abashed, Wu started to explain he knew he should, but he went under that bridge, can't really say why, a couple of days after her death, and found that player by accident. He thought about turning it in but then realized it would look suspicious, his moochiing around the crime scene, and it made no sense to put it back into the snow where no one would find it.

Anyways, before the player got completely fucked, he managed to listen to a part of a track. He knew that piece, he heard it not long before but couldn't find it on the hard drive no matter what, even though he looked through the library twice. Some brass or woodwinds, maybe cor anglais, a beautiful and sad melody. He tried to plug it into his computer, but the player was completely dead.

Outside the balcony door, down below, one could see a handful of people and occasional cars slowly passing by. Olka lit a cigarette and, after a moment of silence, said it could've been already lying there, or maybe someone lost it while drunk afterwards. It may have no connection to Ania's death whatsoever.

She fell silent, while Wu lit a cigarette as well, took the player in his hand and, deep in thought, started to knock it against the table edge. Finally, Olka stood up and turned on the radio. An announcer was speaking of a foiled attack on the Weddell Sea's underwater city.

Everything's without colour, lost it to the water,
my comrades keep discussing the rain which reduces
us to undersea creatures, they say, they keep cursing,
looking at wet compasses, trying to decipher
the path to the dome, slowly wading through the jungle,
counting down miles and wiping foreheads, cheeks and temples.

The downpour is unceasing, the rain leaves me breathless,
I can feel it all over my skin, in its every
centimetre, in every crease, no longer hearing
their muttered conversations swallowed by the jungle,
uniform, thick and heavy, Camembert-like marshland,
getting further away from the rocket, the bodies.

Then the skin-cutting metal, then the shrieks, blood gushes,
I can still hear you screaming, still picture the sudden
unravelling of tissues, tearing of blood vessels,
fraying of nerves and tendons, heart-pulping, bone-cracking.

We keep progressing deeper, the rain is unceasing,
mouth opening and closing in a fish-like fashion,
limp legs are as if wooden, eyelids as if leaden,
there's nothing left but downpour, nothing left but sadness.

Several hours later, the kitchen was dark and empty; in the murk, on the table, one could see emptied beer bottles, cigarette ash, overfilled ashtrays. Outside were the same Okrąglak's windows, Gorals' stalls, car park, all drenched in cloudy, fluorescent city glow.

Finally, Kuba and Zuza entered the room. Not bothering to turn on the light, they sat next to each other at the table to sip some wine straight from the bottle.

'Can't stop thinking about it.'

Zuza can't either. She doesn't even try to, kurwa, imagine what would've happened if they detonated the explosives. There would be nothing left of the city's dome, the water would flood everything.

After a thoughtful moment, Zuza decided to change the topic and — in a lighter tone — said she hadn't seen Wu that wasted in a long time. She thought she was, kurwa, going to lose it when he started taking off his pants on the balcony, in the freezing cold. Poor Staszek who had to take him to Chwaliszewo in this state. Olka got pretty pissed as well, she's going to love the photos they took of her sleeping on the couch, that bag of crisps in her hand. All that was missing was a cig in her mouth.

Several more minutes of talking, drinking wine straight from the bottle, smoking was enough for Zuza to sit on Kuba's lap and start kissing him. The fingers of her one hand sunk into his blond mop; the other creased his T-shirt. Her long hair fell onto his chest, onto his arms. Suddenly, she stopped, stood up from his lap, muttered with a smile in her voice it was a fucking bad idea, took a sip of wine, they'd see each other tomorrow in Meskal and left the kitchen.

IV

O^{*lka*}

Blade: 80 cm; shaft: 155 cm; materials: iron, wood; technique: forging; time of creation: 19th century. Not much more information besides, but a photo. A grey background illuminated by a camera flash reflected in the blade's matte surface. The shaft not quite parallel to the photograph's edge, darker at the end where it meets the metal. Maybe it's a war scythe from the January Uprising. History was never my thing. It wouldn't hurt if the museum's staff wrote anything more on the website.

The scythe seems strangely light, but it must be an impression. Ania and Michał's bellies slit open and exposing bowels — whoever did this, they had to be fairly strong. The glaring sun outside, the musty still air filling the room laced with smoke from a few cigarettes I've had inside because the frost effectively deters me from going out on the balcony. Blade, shaft, materials, time of creation, the dull ache under my skull not responding to pills I keep popping, to a small beer I've opened in desperation. If this one doesn't help, I'll open another.

Bogdan's large oak desk, its top stacked with layers of books, newspapers, magazines, boxes of sedatives and painkillers, empty cigarette packs, blown bulbs. On top of this all: yellow sticky notes with my chaotic jottings which I almost never come back to. My laptop fitted into the only free spot.

I've made all the calls I was supposed to, answered all emails, checked on my employees. Now I'm pondering possible options: have lunch with Kuba or Weronika, go out shopping, watch a show alone, pay a visit to Kisielice to get drunk in the middle of the day — all of them equally unappealing.

And this persistent thought I can't free myself from, the same way you can't stop poking a sore tooth with your tongue. The little screen in my head once again replays the sea bottom and the city hidden under a massive dome. In my mind the terrorists manage to detonate the bombs after all. A series of muffled explosions is followed by a shock wave running through the sea. The water gushes in through a vast breach. Falls heavy under the dome as if under a broken eggshell. Floods the multi-storey city layer after layer, crushes the pipes, tears to shreds the suddenly incandescent wires.

It was okay for a while, at least that's what I kept telling myself. Once news websites and newspapers forgot about the Vostok City attack, it seemed that the worst was behind us. That the world returned to its predictable course. Now wherever you turn, you see the headlines about the Weddell Sea, photos of the underwater metropolis.

There's this untiring train of thoughts in my head: the pharmacy student, the I Burn Poznań's double bassist, the war scythe, the mp3 player found under the bridge, Weronika's beating. All of this must be connected. Though it's possible I just wish there was some order in this chaos.

The desk piled with books, the yellow sticky notes and medicine boxes, blade, shaft, maybe I should try to reach out to the drummer, what's his name, Filip. Maybe we have some mutual friends in Dragon. Perhaps it's not the worst plan for the evening.

Iron, wood, forging, take another pill, wash it down with lukewarm beer. The glare behind the window makes me think of that sunny June day. It's eight years ago, and we wake up hungover in our uncomfortable bed, naked, under a sweaty sheet. The gaze of puffy eyes, the bad breath after the night, the touch of his coarse hands. The scratching of his thick black beard when he kisses my cleavage, the tickling of hair overgrowing his chest. Then the sitting on the balcony overlooking the Okrąglak, the drinking of wine despite the early hour, the mould cheese and sickeningly sweet fudge we chase the wine with. The laughing, the looking at passers-by, the sudden ring at the door.

They were in Meskal, surrounded by red, almost alone in the pub, save for two men drinking cocktails at the bar and having a cheerful chat with the barmaid. Calm music seeped from speakers, biting chill came in through the windows, on top of the bar was a pile of leaflets printed with slogans such as 'In Unity We Win', 'Transparency is the Key', 'Let Us Take Care of Your Future' while the red walls were invariably adorned by a gallery of photos from Antarctica: the plains of Queen Maud Land, the icebergs of the Ross Sea, Lake Vostok.

Weronika kept rolling her eyes as Staszek elaborated on Atwood's books, Blomkamp's films, M.I.A.'s records, and using a pause he made to take a sip of beer, she asked a rhetorical question whether that nutter couldn't be on time for once.

Wu chortled and replied he wasn't so sure she'd show up at all; anyways, he wouldn't be surprised if Kuba had a last-minute change of heart as well and found a more exciting way to spend the evening. But Zuza texted, she's on her way.

All three of them fell silent. Weronika, sitting cross-legged on a wooden chair, facing the centre of the room, made sure not to even glance towards Staszek, who also stared into the distance, silently sipping his beer. Wu observed their reactions and, clearly aware of the awkwardness of this situation, started talking about the garage keys he still can't, kurwa, find. Maybe one of you have seen them? They had a Jupiter-shaped keyring, the one Weronika and he bought together, remember? Weronika shrugged in response, Staszek shook his head, and silence returned.

In a desperate attempt to start a conversation, Wu said he was dreadfully hungover. Olka's parties always end badly. Much to his disappointment, Staszek only nodded and glued his eyes to the table, while Weronika made a silent grunt and took out her phone.

He hasn't done anything today — now Wu was talking to himself — can't be sure he'll meet the deadline. He set a daily goal of pages but keeps changing it every day. And this winter, to top this all off, there hasn't been a winter like this in years. Why can't it be summer already?

He eventually fell silent, looking at the completely listless Staszek and Weronika smiling at her phone, but at this moment, in the small rectangular window in the wall Zuza's head flashed. On seeing her, Wu started up from his chair, said a short, relieved 'cześć' and, as she was weaving between the red room's tables, asked what she wanted to drink.

Half an hour passed, and the four of them sat in a cloud of cigarette smoke, with several more people in the room. Zuza talked about another fucking interrogation, during which they kept asking her the same pointless questions over and over: at what time did she leave Dragon, who stayed there, what happened when Filip was walking her to the stop, is she sure he didn't go with her to her place. She's got, kurwa, no idea what their deal was. Were they fishing for inconsistencies?

Weronika, ruefully sipping wiśniówka, said she had no clue how this could've happened. She shouldn't have drunk so much that night. She remembered once Michał and she left Dragon, they popped into an off-licence to buy a bottle of cytrynówka, then trudged to the river, it was freezing, people walked with kebabs in their hands, occasional cars passed by, and the two of them strolled towards Chwaliszewo Street and further, to the Warta.

By the river it was completely still, they were treading snow, smoking cigs, drinking the vodka, talking about different things. She seems to remember Michał boasting about how fucking good a bassist he was, she laughed him off, but they kept wandering, talking, maybe even kissing a little under the bridge. And when they emptied the bottle (it was the middle of the night, trams no longer ran, almost no cars on the streets), they took a walk to the off-licence for another one and went back to the river. It lasted maybe a few hours, and Michał suggested he walked her home. Hadn't she been so drunk, maybe she would've invited him in, and he wouldn't have ended up ripped open under a bridge. Kurwa, she was so sloshed she can't even remember how she got home.

Zuza told Weronika to stop it, cos what could she do, the most important thing is that nothing happened to her, and having asked the others what they wanted to drink, she went to the bar. As she was leaning against the counter, Kuba's voice came from the room. He cheerfully greeted everyone and flashed a wide smile at Zuza, who already turned towards him and returned the smile.

QUEEN MAUD LAND'S TERRORISTS CLAIM FOILED WEDDELL SEA ATTACK

Militant group Queen Maud's Heart said it was responsible for placing explosive charges in Nova Cracovia, Weddell Sea's second-largest city.

Queen Maud's Heart issued a statement claiming responsibility for the foiled bombing and saying more attacks will take place unless their demands are met.

The terrorists demand opening Queen Maud Land Reservation's borders and reinstating all rights of its dwellers.

The authorities called the demands 'outrageous' and asserted they would 'not rest until every last member of this illegal organization is either in custody or dead'.

Several hours and many litres of alcohol later, Zuza and Kuba walked across Freedom Square, glancing at the ghastly lit platanus trees, then back at a digital clock mounted below the roof of a bank, while Kuba talked about the several years he spent in a toxic relationship with his last girlfriend, Iwona, a relationship he'd thankfully almost managed to forget.

It was his first love, he plunged into it mindlessly, all the way with no parachute. He was so young, she was a few years older and impressed him big time. When they started dating, he knew she had a boyfriend; she said she was about to dump that guy but dumped him only after a year. Not much later, it turned out all this time she'd been seeing yet another bloke. But Kuba forgave her, what else could he do, and she kept cheating on him for a few more years. He went on to say it wasn't that shagging was all he cared about, he wasn't as shallow as everyone thought.

Zuza laughed, told him to stop it, they got a tad carried away yesterday, but there's no point bringing it up again. He's a great buddy, she adores him, and that's exactly why they should stick to what they already have. There's no point ruining it. Saying this, she flung a smouldering cigarette butt towards the street and, for a split-second, they both looked at its luminous trace hanging in the air.

It was completely windless, the biting chill entered the insides of buildings, trams, human bodies.

Late morning, Chopin Park. Bushes and many-branched trees covered in fresh snow, the pink Jesuit college building in the background. Olka sat at the backrest of one of the benches, smoking, her eyes following a passing tram. She kept looking around as if waiting for someone.

Finally, through a gate in the low fence, a hefty man entered the park. Sporting a thick ponytail of dreadlocks and a camo jacket, he stood for a while at the top of cobbled steps, scanning the lanes and snow-covered greens. When his gaze met Olka's, he took off towards her.

He was a few metres away when she tossed the cigarette butt into the snow, stood up from the bench, coquettishly ran her hand through her fair locks and extended her arm for a handshake.

She started with a friendly 'you must be Filip,' introduced herself and thanked him for coming. He didn't have much time, he popped out from work for a sec.

They sat on the backrest of the same bench Olka got up off. The college building stood behind them, white-and-pink and full of windows, while before them, along a lane, a girl walked a silvery pointer on a leash.

'I'm so sorry,' Olka said finally, offering him a Camel and — before he had a chance to light it — asked him whether Michał had any enemies.

Enemies? How could someone like him have enemies? Filip knew him from secondary school, he was two years junior, so he called him 'kid', they were in their first band together. At one point, he even dated Michał's big sister. He can't imagine how someone could want to hurt him.

Filip's voice broke, his nostrils ejected thick, milky smoke in a short sob. Ashamed, he wiped his tears with his big hand and looked at snow-covered thujas. Eyeing his trembling jaw, Olka waited a second before asking if he'd seen anything disconcerting that evening.

An evening like any other. They were with their bandmates in Dragon when they met those friends of Olka's: Zuza and the other one, what's her name, right, Weronika. They kept buying the girls shots, Michał hit on Weronika a little, Filip hit a little on Zuza, it was pretty fun, they talked about things, you know, typical pub talk, told some crass jokes.

Finally, Zuza got up from the table and said she had to go; maybe she drank too much. Weronika wanted to leave with her, but Zuza told her to stay. Filip offered to walk her to a stop, she reluctantly agreed, and off they went. The other guys didn't even notice when Michał and Weronika sneaked out of the pub. The next day they all thought he was sleeping off a hangover and didn't try to reach him.

'Sorry, it's time for me,' he said, and having shaken Olka's hand, started towards the exit. She intently observed his shrinking, burly, somewhat stooped silhouette as he ascended steps, then she lit another cigarette. In her mouth, the wintry air blended with smoke.

V

That evening it would be best to look at Poznań as a collection of incongruent images, sounds and movements: the screech of tram wheels, the red of a jacket, the flash of headlights, the cold blast of wind, the crackle of platanus tree branches along Independence Avenue, the screech of wheels, the flash of headlights, the blast of cold air over Wilda Market Square, the red of plastic bags, the commotion of people at the sight of a tram, the grey snow in Copernicus Estate, the crackle of branches, the bareness of trees, the large logo of a Tesco supermarket, the white mist over the Warta River, the blast of cold wind, the flash of lights, the siren of an ambulance, the sparking of wires, the snow, the screech of wheels, the desolate Łazarz Market Square, the whizz of a fist, the red of blood, the passing of trams, the grey of rooftops merging with the grey of the sky.

In this cacophony of colours, movements and sounds you could see the pink of kitchen wallpaper in one of Chwaliszewo Street's flats. If you subtracted half of the tenement, in the resulting longitudinal section, at second-floor height (next to the dirty grey stairwell, among grey rooms), the illuminated pink rectangle of Wu's kitchen would pop into your eyes.

Inside this quadrangle you could see two silhouettes: Weronika sat on the left, smoking a cigarette at the table, while on the right Wu leant against the worktop, having a smoke as well. In the middle of the dark pink rectangular background was a window, outside the window you could see grey.

'I would like you to give him a chance. It's really important to me.'

Weronika sighed, rubbed her forehead with her hand and told Wu that, Staszek's total inability to ask for someone's number aside, there was this air around him, she couldn't quite put her finger on it. It's... he doesn't seem like a trustworthy person to her. She knows Wu is in love with him, but that's exactly why he's unable to look at things soberly.

'Okay, but I've got the impression you are amping it all up. I really don't believe Staszek meant any harm.'

Weronika said, maybe, but she has a bad feeling about him. She's worried about Wu and doesn't want him to get into the same shit all over again.

'Like you, all over again, got into a relationship with Jerzy?' There was a hint of anger in his voice.

Weronika grew pale. She raised her eyebrows, put out her cigarette in the ashtray, reached for another, then smiled and asked,

'How did you know?'

'I heard you talking in the staircase. Only Jerzy can get you pissed like that. How long has it been going on?'

A week, maybe. She means, they're not together yet, they don't know if they'll try again, but, yes, they see each other once in a while. For now, they mostly exchange lengthy texts.

'I don't want to sound like your mother, but are you sure it's a good idea? After all Jerzy's done to you?'

She slowly released smoke from her mouth and said with some irritation she was sure it was a totally bad idea, but, kurwa, after all this, after the girl under the bridge, after the beating in Wielkopolski Square, and now after what happened to Michał, ja pierdolę, she doesn't have the strength to go through this on her own.

Having put his bottle down, Wu rose from the worktop a little, stretched out his arm across the kitchen and stroked Weronika's face. In a murmuring, barely audible voice, he said, it's okay, honey, he doesn't mean to judge her, he's just worried.

He took his hand right away, leant back against the worktop, scratched his eyebrow, cleared his throat, while Weronika, looking into the greyness outside the window, said she got it, she was worried herself, but trust me, it's not like she's plunging herself into another relationship with Jerzy completely blindly and stupidly, they've set certain rules. They don't promise each other anything at the moment. Besides, Wu must bear in mind Jerzy is a guy who spent over a decade in a tough relationship, he shouldn't judge him too harshly.

'But why are you doing this to yourself? It's about this thing with Staszek, isn't it?'

Weronika thanked her friend ironically for his diagnosis and pursed her lips in embarrassment. Okay, let's change the subject. She opened a can of beer with a pop, took a sip, looked at Wu, then outside the window, and contradicting her own words, said maybe it was a little about this, and perhaps she owed Wu an apology, you know, for all her fits around Staszek. She wasn't acting in an entirely rational way, and the thing with wiśniówka might've been a tad over the top.

She laughed nervously and, with some reluctance, offered a ceasefire. But, she continued, since they've already started all the preaching, she'd like to ask Wu to be a little more cautious with Staszek. All in all, he's known him only for a few weeks, the bloke came out of nowhere, they don't know much about him. Wu must believe her, she sincerely hopes her concerns are unfounded, but she wouldn't want Wu to get hurt, okay?

'Okay,' he replied, gave her a vague smile and took a long draught of beer.

EARTH

Mass: 5.972×10^{24} kg
81.35 Moons
Mean Diameter: 12,742 km
Orbital period: 365.26 days
Rotation period: 23 h 56 min
Category: Planet

Earth is the third planet from the Sun. It is the largest of the four terrestrial planets in the Solar System. Earth is orbited by the Moon, its only natural satellite. The composition of Earth's atmosphere has been returned to its pre-industrial state. Most of the planet's surface is covered by oceans, surrounding five continents: Africa, Eurasia, America, Antarctica, and Australia.

Earth has thousands of cities, most of them predating the awakening. The Antarctic region Queen Maud Land is home to the only remaining human reservation.

Humans caused utter devastation of their home world through pollution, greenhouse emissions, and direct obliteration of many non-human species. The so-called reterraforming process started immediately post-awakening and lasted close to 850 years.

The colourful interior of Kisielice was full of people, smoke, conversations, laughter, music played by a DJ at the end of the room, vivid stripes, black-and-white artwork on the walls. The bartender, against a colourful, backlit liquor shelf, talked with his clearly drunk friends. Once in a while, someone entered through the curtain separating the inside of the pub from the vestibule, letting in cold air. The place was densely studded with bright smouldering points.

At the table next to the window, under the soaked poster, you could see Kuba and Olka. She flipped her blonde curls, laughed and told him to cut this crap, he's making up problems out of boredom: after years of careless fucking around, he suddenly wants something serious, and with Zuza? Come on.

Kuba chortled, took a sip of beer and said he didn't think about her that way before, he means, she's hot and all, but he treated her as a friend. That kiss, though, kurwa, that was something. Don't know, it unlocked something in his head, made him look at her from a different angle. He realized he spent the past few years going from party to party, and from each, if he got lucky, he took home a different babe.

Eventually, he wasn't able to remember their names. He inhaled smoke against the green wall and, while blowing it out, said it had all, dunno, become totally empty and meaningless.

'Honey, you can't stuff the void in your life, certainly not with a relationship.' Olka laughed out loud. She added, in a little patronizing tone, her theory it's got too easy for Kuba to get laid, he can have any shag he wants, so he's looking for challenges. 'Listen to an older friend's advice,' she giggled.

Kuba admitted okay, maybe there's a grain of truth in it, he's turned on by the fact he can't get her too easily. The thing is, though, he sees Zuza not only as a hot chick — he wouldn't mind scoring her, sure — but also a valuable person. He burnt his fingers a few years ago and decided not to give a fuck about relationships, but, dunno, maybe it's time for something more permanent. He must be getting old. But perhaps it's about something more — he said in a serious voice — about Ania, about that psycho with a scythe, about Queen Maud Land's terrorists.

Olka waved her hand with a sigh, took a draw of her beer and told Kuba to do whatever he wants, but she knows one thing: the years she spent with that chuj, her husband were the worst years of her life and she started to live only when he gave her the push. And he did it with a bang, she'll give him that.

A look of astonishment crossed Kuba's face, and he said, hesitatingly, he was convinced Olka's husband was, you know, dead.

Olka laughed somewhat hysterically and said, true, she's been telling everyone he died, but that's because she's too ashamed to admit what really happened. She'll tell him this equally spectacular as pathetic story one day, but it'll require a sea of booze.

Her face seemed to gloom for a moment, she put out her cigarette, took her last sip of beer and, in a lighter tone, asked, 'Shall we?'

They pushed through the thick curtain, walked past the toilet doors in the vestibule, a bicycle resting against the wall, and climbed a flight of stairs to reach the exit, where frigid air awaited them. When leaving, they didn't even notice across the dark Taczak Street a tall man watched them in silence. From under the navy-blue sleeve of his jacket peeked an Antarctica-shaped tattoo.

VI

He watched her when she walked out of a doorway in St Adalbert Street, when, having looked to the sides, she crossed the ice-covered roadway, and later, when she trod a layer of frozen snow towards a petrol station. He was there when she waited at the traffic lights.

In Wielkopolski Square he blended into the crowd but kept watching her pick through tomatoes with her cold hand, take her phone out and talk a little (a cloud of breath), get back to shopping, put a bunch of chives, some peppers, a cauliflower into her canvas bag and finally, the bag now brimful, cross 23 February Street and go further, towards Zamkowa Street.

He kept following her while she cut the Old Market Square, glancing at the black sky; he watched her intently as she disappeared in the Arsenał bookshop, and he stood in the same spot when, a dozen minutes later, she left the building, rubbing her tired eyes, the bag hanging from her shoulder.

Weronika suddenly stopped, her eyes fixated on a not-too-tall figure in a black coat who walked along the square's frontage.

Wu's every step was watched as he crossed, smoking a cigarette, Międzymoście Square, waited at traffic lights and later — when he walked along Wielka Street towards the Old Market Square and then towards Paderewski Street.

Under the Arkadia building, Wu stopped again at a zebra crossing, staring absently into a billboard advertising a trip to the flying cities of Australia. The green light went on at last, and he started towards the Okrąglak.

One hour later, when he headed back home along Chwaliszewo Street, holding a plastic bag full of clanking beer bottles, he was still followed by a pair of eyes.

Olka's flat lay bare before him. He knew the exact moment when she left her study to grab something to eat or brew some coffee, and when she came back.

He had perfect insight into what was happening in the adjacent bedroom, and if the living room door was ajar, he could watch Olka after she went there to sit on the soft couch for a moment, listen to some music or drink a glass of wine at high noon. When she had a cigarette while working, he could see its smouldering end through the windowpane.

Once in a while, she went out to have a smoke on the balcony. Every time she did so, he could examine her hands trembling with cold, sad eyes wearing no make-up, clouds of smoke coming from her mouth, fingers running through her hair in a nervous gesture.

He followed Kuba into the brick interior of The Old Brewery shopping centre. Keeping a distance of several metres, he ascended the same shiny escalator, and later, when Kuba passed with indifference the colourful clothes and jewellery shops, he went out after him into the courtyard.

He waited outside a bookshop as Kuba wandered among its shelves, and he stood surrounded by trees when, a few dozen minutes later, Kuba sat with a friend on a bench in the nearby park, taking stealthy sips of wine from a kraft paper-wrapped bottle, shivering with cold, exhaling an occasional cloud of cigarette smoke.

From this perspective, he could most probably see Kuba's smallest gestures, his hand patting his thigh, discreet glances at his companion's dark hair barely extending below her ears, at the movements of her hands, at the curves of her body hidden under a coat. Perhaps he could notice the trembling of Kuba's cigarette-wielding hand, the redness of his cheeks and maybe even — who knows — the throbbing of blood vessels under his skin.

When Staszek walked in a black coat along St Martin Street, amongst fine snowflakes, under flashy signs of shops, of an erotic cinema, of a kebab joint, he also was being watched.

The day was bright, headlights darted along the street, one could hear the pulsating roar of engines (cars approaching, cars moving away), the dirty roofs up above stood out against the white sky.

From the other side of the street, he could perfectly see Staszek take out his phone (the screen flashed a yellow light) and maybe even hear him say he was sorry, darling, but something came up, and he'll be an hour later. After a short conversation, he put the phone back in his pocket.

On the corner with Ratajczak Street, a tall red-haired man waited for Staszek, beaming at him. Having returned his smile, Staszek stood on his toes to kiss the man on the cheek and looked around, as if sensing a stranger's gaze.

He watched her from the second car, Winogrady's landscape moved outside the tram windows, it was evening, every vehicle's movement had its reflection in the tone of her muscles, the waving of her dark brown hair, the changing patterns of folds on her black coat.

During a sudden turn into Murawa Street, Zuza clung to the railings, her bag tilted by the centrifugal force. Outside the windows were some newer housing estates, the grey high-rise of a City Hall department, followed by Under the Lime Trees Estate, Solidarity Roundabout, Yuri Gagarin Park, Castorama. Having taken a turn at the roundabout, the tram sped along the tracks, and all around one could see snow, the Wuthering Height Estate's monumental blocks, some disturbing shadows, some people passing by, some trees.

When the vehicle stopped at the terminus, he took his time leaving the car. He watched Zuza walk, utterly oblivious to his presence, along the tram towards the traffic lights, look for something in her bag, tuck a tuft of hair behind her ear. She stood alone at a red light, rummaging in her bag (blocks of flats above her) as he approached her — soundlessly, step by step. Before long, he had her within reach of his arm.

VII

If you looked at Wu's bedroom from right under the ceiling, you would see it was full of grey afternoon light, on the floor were cardboard boxes piled with books and CDs, an old, dusty computer stood next to the wardrobe. In the bed, on a crumpled sheet, Staszek pressed his cheek against Wu's hairy chest and, sliding his fingertips over his thigh, said he loved his cock, loved the smell of his skin, had no idea what was happening, but whenever he was near Wu, he got an instant hard-on, and that he felt around him, ja pierdolę, totally safe. You could descend from below the ceiling, hang just above the skin of their bodies and sweep over it like over the surface of an alien planet: passing straightening hairs, listening to the swoosh of blood vessels hidden below the surface.

MOON

Mass: 7.342 x 10²² kg
    0.012 Earths
Mean Diameter: 3,474.8 km
Orbital period: 27.3 days
Rotation period: Synchronous
Category: Satellite (of Earth)

The Moon is Earth's only natural satellite. It has a thin artificial atmosphere and is home to nearly ninety domed cities, all built by humans pre-awakening. Each city holds a unique ecosystem composed of terrestrial species.

She didn't mean to follow him, he happened to be there. His black coat flashed in her view as she walked out of the bookshop. At first, she planned to walk behind him only for a moment, maybe even say a cold hello. She put her canvas bag on her shoulder, looked around as if someone could see her and slowly took off. When she followed him into Paderewski Street, a fine snow started to fall from the sky.

She knows what Zuza thinks about it, but with each step it was harder to stop. What can you do when there's nothing you can do? She promised herself that when she reached Marcinkowski Avenue, she would turn right and go home, but instead, she went the other way, after Staszek.

Actually, he wasn't doing anything suspicious. She thought maybe he was going to his work at the bank, wherever his bank was, but at the same time, she had this ever-stronger feeling he was hiding something. Though she'll admit, she had similarly irrational feelings about all Wu's previous boyfriends.

In front of her, two young men talked about the recent failed attack, about the cyberspace's new security measures, while she followed them two steps behind, using the back of the larger one as a hiding spot. She never took her eyes off Staszek, who at that moment almost reached St Martin Street.

Opposite the Chinese restaurant, he stopped and took out his phone, so she stopped as well, under the erotic cinema's signboard, and also took her phone out as a disguise. She wondered what to say in case he noticed her, but he was too busy talking. Finally, he took off, and she followed him.

And imagine, she looks up and this fucker approaches some redhead standing on the corner and, kurwa, kisses him on the cheek. A handsome chap, even taller than Wu, it must be that little liar's kink. She followed them for a moment, but they disappeared into one of the doorways in Ratajczak Street. She doesn't know how to tell Wu about it.

The four of us are rowing into the dark, morbid
rains of desolate Venus, whipping our frozen
necks, shoulders, trembling bodies, on a boat surrounded
by the brown, heavy river, whose calm swirling waters
are spreading flat and drowsy amid the dense jungle,
cut with dagger-like raindrops, the boat takes on water.

The comrades won't stop talking, the dome, they keep saying,
will save us from the downfall, we're closer and closer,
my uniform is slowly devoured by mildew,

the fabric permeated by its thread-like fibres,
the mould seems to be eager to penetrate also
my skin and all my tissues, the cobweb of vessels.

I'm thinking of the simplest of things: morning coffee,
breakfasts to bed, naps, quarrels, your touch, and the evening
the two of us were walking the streets of our city.

We reach the bank, the jungle is equally rainy,
full of pale vegetation, there is the sky: golden,
uniform, thick and heavy, we are walking slowly,
looking at the compasses, at the blurry outlines
of what we sure are hoping is the dome, a distant
shape behind the thick bushes, we start walking faster.

It is a swampy clearing with trees all around it,
in its middle our rocket, that pile of scrap holding
dismembered lifeless bodies, bags of tissues really,
open eyes with no colour, lost it to the water,
your swollen hands and fingers, shapeless face and gaping
mouth that spews out a fountain of spongy green thallus
creeping down your bare sternum until it meets metal
that cuts in half your belly, spilling out your bowels.

At once I can no longer see the jungle, downpour,
swamp or pale vegetation, can't hear my friends' curses,
feel the incessant rainfall, all I can see is you:
a pale, monstrous cadaver with eyes of no colour.

Can't hear the ever-closer thunders, see the lightnings.

  Chwaliszewo Street was full of frosty air, the broken lamppost flickered in a strobe-like fashion, down below one could see a lit sign of the Żabka shop with a smiling frog on it, dirty snowbanks, chavs talking loudly in front of a grey tenement, cobblestones bestrewn with salt and sand. Over the tenements, in the distance against the black sky, loomed red digits of an electronic clock.
  Weronika and Zuza smoked on a balcony, flicking ash towards the street. They talked, their mouth ejecting in turn water vapour and white cigarette smoke. Weronika admitted she felt bad about it. Not that she ever liked Staszek, she suspected

it might've looked that way from the beginning, but some part of her still hoped this time Wu hadn't happened upon another compulsive liar. He must have a sixth sense for finding the worst bellends.

'How did he take it?' asked Zuza.

Weronika pouted her lips slightly and admitted not too well. She means, he thanked her a dozen times, pretended he was glad he knew out about it, but his face kind of went out. He finished his coffee and took off home, and she felt like a scumbag.

Zuza shrugged, and Weronika, after a moment needed to take a drag on her cigarette, asked her if she could check again how he was holding up. Having tossed the butt-end down onto the street, Zuza went inside, only to return after a while and announce, nothing's, kurwa, changed. Wu's beaming at everyone, joking, pretending he's having the time of his life, but at the same time emptying what must be his seventh bottle of beer tonight. Weronika inhaled smoke and cursed.

If you left this scene, permeated the balcony door, slid through the room full of cardboard boxes, entered the entrance hall and took a peek into the kitchen, you would see — in the dark pink interior, among grey wisps of smoke, against the backdrop of ivy shoots — Kuba, Olka and Wu almost rolling on the floor laughing, as if one of them told a hilarious joke.

Having returned to the balcony, you could hear the rest of the girls' conversation. Weronika, putting out a cigarette end in a snow-filled flowerpot, said maybe it's nothing, maybe it's just some friend of his, and she jumped to conclusions. After all, gays kiss each other on the cheek all the time. They could've been having tea rather than shagging.

She sighed, lit another cigarette, looked down at the flickering street lamp, at the Żabka signboard, at the chavs and said there was something she wanted Zuza to know, but please don't laugh, to which Zuza immediately burst into laughter.

'Thanks'.

'Sorry. Come on, tell me, what is it?'

Weronika took a long drag and said she was thinking about applying for psychology. Seeing Zuza was doing her best not to laugh again, she said she knew she talked too much, and when she talked, it was usually about herself, but this somehow made sense. And she doesn't want to spend the rest of her life behind a bar. Anyways, probably nothing will come out of it cos she doesn't have enough points.

'Tell me about it. I'm still trying to gather enough points for the fucking sworn translator exam.'

'It's a dumb idea, I know.'

'Are you kidding? I think you'd make a great therapist. You're empathetic, your EQ is through the roof, and you always know what everyone is up to, like that thing with Staszek.'

Weronika whispered a 'thanks', they were silent for a moment until Zuza, having another smoke, asked how things with Jerzy were going.

In response, Weronika smiled and told her to sod off. She added she knew exactly what Zuza thought about it, but trust me — she doesn't expect much of it, it's hard to even call it a relationship, but in some way, she needs it now. Though she doesn't believe it either. However you look at it, they've been together — with breaks, of course — for almost two years, so there's something more serious going on, you know, some feelings. She wishes she weren't dependent on Jerzy, but, you see, it always so happens that when the chips are down, she's running straight to him. Sure, it can be pretty bad, the guy's fucked-up big time, he's totally immature, but she has some kind of stupid weakness for him, no matter how shitty it gets. Okay, she thinks it's time to have a drink.

They both inhaled smoke, their faces turning red from cold (in this light their skin seemed to darken), until they finally put out their cigarettes against the railings and opened the door to the warm interior.

VIII

From a certain distance, Poznań could make you think of the rugged surface of a rocky world observed through a telescope. Streets would shape into ravines; squares and car parks — into lava lakes. Once you got lower and slipped into the gorge of St Martin Street, the illusion immediately burst, and you could only see the familiar dilapidated buildings of the Alfa department store, the tenements across the street, the trams, the parked cars, the language school ads, the gloomy pedestrians, the banks, the shops.

If you wandered among Gwarna Street's shabby walls and garish signs and glided over the pavement, you could spot Zuza: in a black coat, black boots, blood-red tights, holding a phone to her ear. You could hang above her shoulder and listen carefully to the conversation.

About half an hour later, you would be able to watch her from the opposite end of the Meskal's main room, where she sat alone at a table, sipping coffee, reading a newspaper, glancing now and then at the blind-covered windows.

The front door opened, letting in a portion of bitingly freezing air, and in the rectangular window in the wall Weronika's head popped up. The girl entered the red room, cursing and swearing and flicking snow off her equally red jacket as the city became engulfed in a thick snowfall. She smiled at Zuza, kissed her on the check without a word, then went to the bar, where she ordered a coffee, using this as an opportunity to have a short talk with the barmaid. When she returned to the table, she didn't even sit down before telling Zuza to give her a thorough account of everything that happened after she and Kuba took off, totally wasted, from Wu's party.

Zuza snorted with laughter, said nothing happened, they just went out fucking hammered like that into Chwaliszewo Street, into the biting cold and, idiotically, walked along Ciasna Street towards the garages, she saw the black-and-white graffiti on the walls, and then they carried on across the sports field and towards the tram stops.

It was the middle of the night, trams no longer ran, it was fucking freezing, they stood like morons at the crossroads, she remembers he embraced her, she guesses they kissed, she remembers the sky, wasted people with kebabs, banks of snow sparkling in the light of street lamps.

She wanted to call a cab but was so drunk she couldn't even dial the number. One of them came up with a fucking brilliant idea to go to Jeżyce on foot, to Kuba's place, in this frost, in the middle of the night (it had to be Kuba's idea). They talked about something, can't remember what, Kuba blabbered all the time, said there hasn't been a winter like this in years, she didn't really listen, focussing instead on walking more or less in parallel to the curb.

Finally, they made it to Jeżyce, took a lift to the fifth floor, started to kiss, kurwa, already in the hall, stumbled into his two-room flat, tripping over some books, some clothes until they landed on the couch.

'And?' Weronika was so excited she almost knocked down her cup.

Zuza laughed and said, nothing, when they found themselves on the couch, she instantly sobered up. She realized she didn't want to get into any relationship, and it would be totally dumb to spoil a decent friendship for a shag. She told him exactly that, he took it rather well, said he understood and all, he was sweet. Kuba let her sleep in his bed, while he took the couch. When she was leaving this morning, he was still asleep.

Weronika let out a wailing 'boring!', followed by 'what a shitty story!', said Zuza could've seized the opportunity and slept with Kuba, and only start to analyze things later, and asked if she always had to control herself like that? Even when drunk?

'Believe me, nothing good would've come out of it,' Zuza said in reply and, to change the subject, asked if she hadn't by any chance heard how Wu was doing; had Staszek contacted him?

Weronika only pouted her lips in resignation, and they both fell silent. Someone at the next table talked about Martian cities.

Kuba

One more puff, the weed is slowly kicking in. The gloomy flat, the cloudy sky, the slightly parted blinds, the block of flats outside the window, the plastic bags and windmills tied to balcony railings to scare away pigeons. The swelling, biting wind. Let the long-awaited numbness come. Let everything become distant, muffled, as if drowned in amniotic fluid.

Another draw, I walk through Sołacki Park again, cheeks burn from the cold, trying to remember what Ania's face looked like. It was a moment ago, but I only recall its fragments: the big blue eyes, curious and cheerful, the snub nose, the line of her brows. I'm not sure whether she had a protruding chin or is it parts of Zuza's face overlapping hers. I do remember, though, the scarce touches of her soft white hands, the slender wrists, the mole on her forearm, the shreds of idiotic conversations about pharmacy and politics, her silence at Wu's party.

She walks a few steps ahead of me down the shabby staircase, smelling of flowers and tobacco. I think of the skin on her inner thighs, of kissing her small breasts, still hoping she'll let me shag her. Then the freezing Chwaliszewo Street, the strobe light of the street lamp, my arm around her petite shoulders, her dodge when I try to kiss her. Then again the silver Toyota, the driver's thick eyebrows, the tattoo shaped like a continent.

Suddenly, it's Olka's talking head, scolding me that my thing for Zuza is a form of escape, I should give it a rest. She's right. Even if Zuza finally lets me fuck her, instead of backing out at the last minute like she did yesterday. Even if it doesn't end with a one-night stand and we create something in the shape of a relationship. Even then nothing in my life will change, certainly not after what happened to Ania and Michał. What Queen Maud Land's terrorists have been up to.

I take a drag, let it all end. This nervous browsing through websites. Checking if there's been another attack. These conspiracy theories, message boards full of teenagers I can't seem to stop reading. This fear crawling under my skin, rubbish posts claiming the terrorists managed to do what's been accomplished only a few times over the millennia. They broke the code. These murders were their doing. They created a virus which can control human behaviour. I keep repeating to myself it's complete bollocks.

Smoke in my lungs, it's getting darker, and I teleport to the kitchen overlooking the Okrąglak, Zuza's hair tickles my face. The most fucked up part is I kind of get them, all in all we're the ones to blame. We built them a ghetto, cut them off the swarm, not very effectively as it turns out, and now it's hard to say what we should do about them. The attacks — either in real life or in the cyberspace, in one form or another — will simply keep happening.

The weed kicks in, I'm falling down a soft well, into an amniotic ocean, the red of the wall is like blood, like Zuza's thick bracelet over her black sweater, we kiss in the freezing air. I touch her breasts through the thin material. Feel her cold hands on my back. Smell the skin above her collarbone tart with perfume. Her gaze is absent, as if she were thousands of miles away, somewhere on an alien planet.

If you looked at Chwaliszewo's buildings from Venetian Street, you would immediately notice a neglected green tenement, full of broken windows, speckled with bird droppings, inhabited by bats and pigeons. There was another tenement adjacent to it, this one quite inconspicuously grey, with no balconies to overlook the backyard, only a makeshift terrace built on the ground floor. Behind the dirty pane of one of its windows you could see a dark pink kitchen interior.

Reflections on the glass greatly limited visibility, but if you strained your eyes, you could see the blurry silhouettes of two men. Wu gesticulated wildly, shouting (the glass filtered the sounds and all you could hear was a muffled, deep drone), waving some object, probably a phone, in front of Staszek's face, who stood motionless, drooping his head while leaning against the kitchen worktop.

After a while, they both disappeared into the entrance hall so you could get away from the window with no regret. From this perspective, through a vertical row of staircase windows, you could clearly see how Staszek stormed out of Wu's flat and all trembling, ran down the stairs.

△▽△

He watched her as she stood at the tram stop in Little Garbary Street, shivering from cold (a cloud of breath), surrounded by people in dark coats, against the background of a red office building and passing cars. She didn't see him when he looked at her face flushed from the cold, at her flashy tights, her hand inside a fingerless glove, her dark brown hair occasionally tucked behind her ear. He, on the other hand, could see even the tiny flakes of polish on her nails.

He pulled up the sleeve of his navy-blue jacket to glance at his watch, baring a fragment of an Antarctica-shaped black tattoo. Then his sight focussed back on Zuza: standing under the dirty stop shelter, earphones in her ears, her arms crossed, foot tapping to the rhythm.

The overhead wires sparked, and a green tram number 4 arrived at the stop, with dirty windows and a layer of frozen snow covering its roof. The man couldn't see which car she entered. He waited for a bit on the other side of the tracks, then calmly walked across a zebra crossing and, at the last moment before the door closed, sneaked into the tram.

He leant against the railings under the rear window and spotted Zuza in no time: she stood among people in the front of the car, near a validator, holding the back of a seat, staring into a point outside the dirty pane.

The tram took off, and Poznań started to move below and around them. Within a couple of minutes, Wielkopolski Square slid smoothly under the tram, surrounding it with colourful social realism tenements, stalls covered with green-and-white tarpaulin, flowers standing outside tin booths. The doors opened, letting people in and out, then closed, and the tram got swallowed by 23 February Street. They were passed by low blocks of flats on one side and dilapidated tenements on the other until they cut through Nowowiejski Street.

They couldn't possibly know it, but some hundred metres away, in Meskal's red interior, slightly inebriated Weronika comforted devastated Wu, stroking his forearm. When they left them behind, the tram became surrounded by the tenements, trees and tram stops of Ratajski Square. The doors opened, letting people in and out, and then closed.

The tram got tightly embraced by Mielżyński Street: by cars, by dirty snowdrifts, by pedestrians on the street. The tenement where Olka lived went past them, followed by the Okrąglak, and they were devoured to the last bit by the frosty Fredro Street. Poznań's landscape moved outside the windows: the church, the Collegium Maius building, the opera house, the many-branched platanus trees in Mickiewicz Park across the street.

He eyed Zuza intently when they crossed the Theatre Bridge, high above the tracks, when she waved through the window at Kuba waiting at a red light, when the tram rolled lazily along the streets: Pułaski, Winogrady, Murawa, and later, when it entered the landscape of cuboid blocks of flats.

Once it stopped at the terminus, the sun suddenly came out from behind the clouds, and bright, sharp-as-a-knife light filled to the brim Solidarity Avenue and the inside of the tram. Dirty snow sparkled in snowbanks.

Crouched in the back of the car, he watched Zuza walk out through the front door, head towards the pedestrian crossing with the remaining passengers, take out earphones from her ears and wrap them around her hand, hide them in her bag, shield her face from the harsh sunlight.

Without a sound, he stepped onto the glazed pavement, never taking his eyes off her straight dark brown hair, slender legs, petite shoulders.

In front of them loomed the towering blocks as he followed Zuza's every step, walking right behind her over the crossing, and later, when she squeezed between cars parked next to her block. For a split second, you could get the impression the whole of Poznań — all its blocks of flats, tenement houses, all the parks and parking areas, shops and shopping centres, trams and buses, all the stops — grew completely still, as if in anticipation.

He grabbed her forearm. Frightened, Zuza turned back, trying to release her arm from the mugger's grip. When she saw his face, though, she sighed with relief, laughed, rolled her eyes and uttered a few hearty curses. Kurwa, does he always have to sneak up on her like that, can't he say hi like a normal person? Poznań was like wild vegetation, engulfing all.

THE TWENTYSECOND OF MARS

I

To see one more time the rust-coloured Martian deserts, feel — by means of complicated instrumentation — the Martian wind's salty taste, slither through the air like an eel through water, merely an inch above the surf of the boundless ocean. Let the sky be steel grey, the sun as always distant, the marine depths heavy with brown seaweed. Then dive, swim to the shore, enter the cool thicket of coniferous woods, become surrounded by ferns, clamoured down by fowl, with a robot body glide among the pine trunks.

He still remembers the towering buildings of New Tokyo, their colourful elevations covered with a swarm of lights. He remembers precisely, as if he were there yesterday, the gently arching shoreline of the bright Hellas Sea. The metropolis, like dozens of fingers, sank into the sandy beaches, descended underwater to encapsulate in this submerged city all the buildings, robots, winding tunnels, vehicles beneath a glass sky alive with jellyfish and mantas.

Before he snuffs it, he wants to see Endeavour with its hanging gardens, climb the Olympus Mons this once and then stare ahead, to the point of queasiness, where the clouds will creep up the slopes, the lights of the vast Dawkins fade lazily, where a dark desert storm will loom in the distance. He added sometimes, contrary to what he usually says, he'd like to have, as he used to, more time and money to visit the real world.

Kuba listened to all this with certain dreaminess, smoking in silence, sitting on the back of a dirty bench on St Adalbert Hill, in frosty air, looking to the right, towards the soaring forms of the Army Poznań monument, then down at the low kindergarten building, then ahead, at the church almost entirely covered by trees, to the right again, at the monumental modernist Polonez hotel which protruded from behind the park's bare tree crowns. Wu and Kuba's backs were to modern university buildings.

After a moment of silence, of inhaling cigarette smoke, cold air, Kuba asked how Wu was doing, any improvement, to which he said he's managing, more or less, he keeps doing the same thing every, kurwa, time.

He meets a guy and, bang, he's all 'till death do us part', before he even has a chance to see if the bloke isn't, say, some kind of psycho. Or isn't fucking around all the time like in this case. And he was stupid enough to start planning moving in together, wondering whether they should rent something more suitable than this Chwaliszewo dump, even though it lasted only a few weeks. What is, kurwa, wrong with him that he keeps getting himself mindlessly into such situations? Wu took a draw on the remnant of his cigarette to the point where it usually starts to burn one's lips and crushed the butt with his shoe.

Having scratched his eyebrow, with pain in his voice, he said the moment he read the texts on Staszek's phone (Wu got up earlier, Staszek was still asleep), he felt as if the ground had been removed from under his feet. He wasn't nervous, he doesn't think so, he read text after text from some chaps, about some, kurwa, dates, some walks, some thank yous for nights spent together. He stood reading, totally stunned, until he reached the last message. Then he put the phone away, sat down at the kitchen table and stayed there, completely numb, waiting for Staszek to get up. And then they had this row.

Staring absently ahead into the greyness of St Adalbert Street, he took a sip of ice-cold beer from a kraft paper-wrapped bottle. The hitherto silent Kuba assured his friend he understood him perfectly. He was in this kind of situation himself.

'I know,' Wu replied and, after a moment, in a slightly lighter voice, asked, 'What's going on between you and Zuza exactly?'

Kuba sported a broad grin, took a sip of ruthlessly cold beer and said nothing was going on, he might've got a little carried away, Zuza was probably right when she said it's better not to sleep with your buddies, let alone get involved in some kind of relationship, especially if it was supposed to end like the one with Iwona. Okay, they almost ended up in bed, but Zuza had a last-minute change of heart, and maybe that's okay cos… you know.

Anyways, he can't say where all this came from. Perhaps he tried to prove something to himself after Ania's death: that he could be a person he's never going to be.

He fell silent and, looking at a car passing down below, lit another smoke from the lighter's flame.

The room was permeated with the smell of incense, grey afternoon light fell through the front windows. Dragon was usually starting to fill up at this time of the day, so you could only hear the quiet conversations of a few customers, the sound of a chocolate mixer, the clinking of glasses put by a bartender on shelves.

Playing with a light pink lily she took from a vase, Weronika confessed to Zuza, who sat across the table, she had no idea what to think of it all. She knew from the beginning this little louse Staszek was up to something, but she never suspected he would pull crap of this magnitude. He must have some serious emotional problems, or else what could it be about? Unless he robs all the blokes of money (she laughed nervously). Zuza shrugged, cursed perfunctorily as was her habit and peeked at the cobblestones outside the window.

Weronika continued, kurwa, she wished she could do something, but what can she do? Wu is in total disarray, and she'd like to help him somehow, dunno, make it easier on him.

'He'll be all right,' said Zuza. 'And besides, he's not your boyfriend or anything, so you don't have to care *this* much.'

Weronika laughed, presented her friend with a short 'spierdalaj', then lit a cigarette and complained, as if it weren't enough, Jerzy keeps triggering her. He's mad at the world again that his life doesn't look the way he imagined but, obviously, won't do a thing to change it. Something tells her she's going to have a fight with him tonight. Well, she wanted it herself.

'But what happened exactly?'

Nothing, really. He didn't pay off a loan a few years ago, thought it'd expired, but — surprise, surprise — it hasn't. To top this all off, he has beef with Weronika, claiming she's not offering him enough support. As if she didn't need support. She realized ever more often when she had a problem, she confided in Zuza or Wu rather than Jerzy. She didn't even tell him about Michał, that she spent the last hours of his life with him cos she knew Jerzy would get mad. As if he had an exclusive right to her, even when they're not together.

They were silent for a moment, perhaps listening to a conversation at the bar, when Weronika suddenly roused herself, said, 'look who's here', then stood up and waved to Kuba, who stepped inside from the street.

Panting, his cheeks reddened from cold or perhaps effort, he smiled at the sight of the girls, albeit slightly abashed. He gestured at them to let them know he'll join them in a sec and disappeared from their view behind a small wall in the middle of the room.

He approached them after a moment, embracing a not-too-tall, slim, short-haired brunette, who smiled at the girls shyly. When Kuba introduced Monia to Weronika and Zuza, and then Weronika and Zuza to Monia, it was difficult to tell whether the crimson shade of his face was the result of cold, effort or rather embarrassment. The girls said hi to each other, and then the visibly amused Zuza shot Weronika a knowing look.

△▽△

The reality unravels, yet again. First, there's the familiar, almost imperceptible glitch of the matter around me. My confinement's bright walls slightly wobble. The small window shifts by an inch. Outside, the hairy, meaty leaves acquire a transient purple halo. I place my hand over my pounding heart, a second before it all peals away.

It was evening, trams and cars passed along the streets, the wind was freezing cold and carried dust and fine snow, overhead wires pierced through the urban tissue. Scattered all over the city, LED panels advertised Martian journeys — their screens shone a bright, sharp, aggressive light. Meanwhile, below the street level at one of the tables, against vertical stripes in different shades of red, you could see Olka, who — surrounded by glasses — knocked down another shot, and Staszek, who sat across the table, sipping beer, with a troubled look on his face.

Having finished her vodka, Olka ran her hand through her blonde curls, inhaling the smoke-filled air, and said, perhaps with some disappointment, she was far from judging Staszek, she pulled her deal of crap herself on that chuj, her husband, but look, Wu's a decent, sensitive guy, and besides, so many blokes at the same time? At the very beginning of a relationship?

Staszek muttered he knew he fucked up big time, he was aware Wu would never want to talk to him again, but, believe me, those other guys meant nothing to him. (Olka snorted with laughter, at which Staszek blushed.) He knows how it all looks, and it's all his fault, but he wants her to understand he never faked anything with Wu, he truly loved him, he means, loves him, he's never going to forgive himself for what he did. He uttered an unusually hearty curse and drew a swig of his degassed beer.

Olka remarked, in a much softer voice, 'There's no point in self-pity now. All of us do a major fuck-up once in a while.'

They grew silent. Staszek continued sipping beer, his eyes glued to the floor, while Olka glanced around the colourful interior: people talking at the tables, smoking cigarettes and placing orders at the bar. She seemed to be intently thinking about something.

'Wu told me he met you the day before Ania died. Interesting, isn't it?' she asked. (Staszek nodded, with a quizzical look.)

'He also told me,' she continued, 'that the night Michał was killed, you didn't stay at Wu's for the night. Were you with one of those,' she chuckled, 'friends of yours?'

Staszek turned red again and snapped back, saying he was alone, he had to get up early for his morning shift at the bank. Anyway, what kind of questions are these? What is Olka suggesting?

'Ah, nothing, relax,' she said nonchalantly, then left the puzzled Staszek at the table and walked to the bar to order another shot. Holding a twenty-zloty banknote in her hands, she stared absently into colourful lights.

II

My lungs are filled with water, that is my impression
as I lie snuggled into the wet soil below me,
surrounded by my comrades under the loud thunders,
light-blue lightnings in cloudburst, can't catch my breath, sinking
into the cold and soggy ground like a knife into
butter, the bolts are mighty, keep striking the foliage,
the undergrowth, the mucky dirt, the sky's above me,
but I can't see it, blinded by a lightning hitting
the rocket with a gong-like roar, the wind keeps lashing.

Suddenly I imagine I become this tempest,
this wind and all these thunders, looking down from dozens
of yards at our pathetic, soaked and trembling bodies,
and from such a perspective nothing really matters:
all the breakfasts and touches, our quarrels, your cheating,
I stop picturing tissues unravelling quickly
like embroidered lace, only to start to send lightnings,
pierce the skin with cold raindrops, crumple it like paper.

I'm back cuddling the mire, again I hear thunders,
mouths opening and shutting in a fish-like fashion,
can't catch my breath, keep choking, when all of a sudden,
one of the friends starts running, his eyes blank and bloodshot,

*light-blue lashes of lightnings cracking all around him,
all I can see is blueness when he falls so listless,
the smell of burning reaches my mud-covered nostrils,
nothing left but the jungle, the pale vegetation,
the cruel rains of Venus, the breathing through water.*

The air was still. Harsh sunlight filled the squares and streets, tenement backyards, greens, car parks — mercilessly. Kuba walked along St Martin Street, towards Spring of Nations Square, his arm wrapped around Monia: much shorter than him, a pink wool hat on her head, reddened cheeks, face brightened with a smile, eyes darting curiously to the sides.

They passed a snow-covered green cut with a diagonal path, some homeless people sitting on one of the dilapidated benches; further towards the square was a small car park, even further — a food truck. The smell of zapiekankas and hamburgers mingled with the smell of exhaust fumes, snow sparkled in the sun like broken glass.

Monia said yesterday's encounter with Kuba's friends was a tad weird, she might be wrong, but she felt they were quite sceptical about her (a tram passed by). Is there something she should know?

Kuba laughed, somewhat awkwardly, what is she talking about, the girls really liked her, they even told him so later, they have this peculiar way of being, anyways, Monia'll see it for herself when they go to that party tomorrow.

Well, she's not convinced. There was something off about their behaviour: those looks, those questions whether they knew each other for a long time and how they met, those laughs.

Suddenly blushed, Kuba ensured her it was what the girls were like, there was nothing to worry about, believe me, and then he changed the subject, suggesting maybe they should go to the Mexican, they haven't been there yet.

'Okay.' Monia eyed Kuba suspiciously.

They stopped at a red light. Before them — surrounded by dirty, icy snowbanks — loomed the chunky edifice of The Merchant of Poznań department store. On the corner, next to Podgórna Street, there was a gap in the building (delineated with perfectly flat walls and accommodating a billboard, a roasted chicken truck) as if someone, with a divine hand, cut off a chunk of the construction like a piece of cake.

'Do you still paint?' she asked after a longer pause as they walked over another crossing to enter Wrocławska Street.

'Why?'

'It just came to my mind. Do you?'

Kuba admitted he hadn't touched the brush in years, scratched his head with his free hand, and, as if to explain himself, went on to say he completely stopped believing in it after graduation. He lost the conviction he had anything new to say, and getting into the cogs of this machine, with those exhibitions, critiques, arty-farty talks at previews… It didn't attract him at all.

'That's a pity. I liked your paintings.'

Kuba looked to the side, then at the pavement.

'I don't know. Sometimes I miss it,' he said. It must've been Iwona who finally made him realize his works were shit. Sure, she did it cos she liked to bring him down, but what can you say, she was right. In Monia's works there's always something fresh, be it sculptures or installations, each of them tells you something you didn't know, makes you look at a given subject from a completely new angle. And, frankly, all those daubs he painted were terribly one-dimensional.

'Bollocks,' she chirped and looked at the starry nimbus around St John of Nepomuk's stone head. Standing on a high pedestal, flanked by the angular Arsenał buildings, the saint sprouted in front of them from the Old Market Square's cobbled surface.

When they walked past the town hall, she confessed she was glad they reconnected after all those years. It all worked out as it did because she's always liked him a lot and — she's not sure if she should say it — if he hadn't been with Iwona, she would've made a move on him earlier. She let out a joyous laugh, as if surprised by her confession, and buried her face in his green jacket. Perplexed, Kuba answered only with a perfunctory, 'I'm happy, too.'

Mars

Mars is the fourth planet from the Sun and the outermost terrestrial planet in the Solar System. It has two small natural satellites: Phobos and Deimos.

Mars was the first extraterrestrial world colonized by humans. As a result of terraforming, Mars has an oxygen-rich atmosphere, and around one-third of its surface is covered with water. The biggest reservoirs are the ocean, located near the North Pole, and Southern Hemisphere's Hellas Sea.

Mass: 6.417×10^{23} kg
0.107 Earths
8.74 Moons
Mean Diameter: 6,779 km
Orbital period: 1.88 years
686.97 days
Rotation period: 24 h 37 min
Category: Planet

After Earth, Mars is the second-largest world ruled by the Terro-Martian Federation. The planet's cities, most of them built pre-awakening, serve as important information nodes and replication centres.

The terraforming process lasted between 2,100 and 300 years pre-awakening. Martian ecosystems are inhabited by organisms introduced from Earth, some of them genetically modified specifically for this purpose.

Clouds shrouded the sky making it monochromatically grey, all at once darkening the streets. If you observed the city from above the rooftops, you would see people coming back from work, cars passing by, a tight network of tram overhead wires. You had the impression that if you snapped a single wire and started to pull, Poznań would fray, exposing its concrete innards.

St Adalbert Street was almost empty, the occasional whirr of cars echoing off the tenement fronts. A conversation of young men interjected with their loud cackle coming from a distance. Near Podgórze Street, against a maroon door, stood a man. He smoked a cigarette with a calm, as if trained, movement. Tall, with prominent cheekbones and thick black eyebrows, he peeked from time to time across the street, perhaps towards the windows of Weronika's flat. When he reached into his pocket for his phone, a black tattoo in the shape of Antarctica slid out from under his sleeve.

Yep, no news, he said to the receiver, the object got shit-faced as she does every day and doesn't leave the flat. He's knackered. He'd do anything for a warm bath, but he'll need to stay here for a little longer.

Well, he never got it why the fuck they needed all this human software, with all this getting tired, those feelings, all those cravings. The job would be so much easier without this add-on. Well, it's this romantic human gene — it will doom the entire race one day. That sex drive is the worst. His cock's starting to get sore from all the chicks. Ah, sorry, he's shutting up, he doesn't have to talk about it, no prob, he has to be going anyway. He'll call if anything changes.

III

They can't fuck this up. She's sure they can move on to the third termination? No worrying behaviour? No memory problems? All right, all right, if she's saying she's sure, then she's sure, he's buying it, no problem, but, kurwa, the whole thing is nerve-wracking. Everything must go according to the plan, or else they'll have to start anew. And this wouldn't bode well for their uprising plans.

The man's voice was barely audible since before it could get from the kitchen to the small dark red bedroom, it had to penetrate the wall (the door was closed). If you stood in front of the window, which occupied a large portion of your view, you could look down at the thickening dark, at the street lights that were starting to come on, at the snow-covered Victory Estate, the vast Solidarity Avenue (the bright headlights).

If you pressed your ear against the wall, you could hear the much quieter voice of Zuza, who said they should chill, they still have time, there's no need to worry just yet. The night was slowly falling, the windows of the tall office building ahead lighting up one by one, the distant hum of cars sending vibrations through the glass.

If you were to look at this scene from a distance of several metres, your view would be filled with the grey of a wall contrasting with an orange sofa in the middle. Zuza sat on it, leaning on a side rest, cross-legged and painting her nails a similarly flashy colour.

The frame would also accommodate a fragment of a tall dresser standing on the right. In front of its open interior on a chair, with an eyelash brush in her hand, Weronika looked into a mirror hung on the door, her mouth spouting out a monotonous sequence of sentences about how she was sick and tired of it, how this whole relationship must be a product of her self-destructive tendencies. She wants to take him to a party — he's not happy about it; she goes without him — even worse. It's as if she was babysitting a forty-year-old teenager who needs constant attention and, on top of that, his mood is all over the place. She really must love him if she came back to him.

Zuza listened to this with growing irritation until she blurted out, 'One more word about Jerzy and I'm leaving.'

The brush, dipped in black mascara, stopped halfway. For a moment, Weronika's wide-open eyes stared at Zuza, who carried on painting her nails in silence, her lips pursed. Finally, from the larynx of Weronika's frozen body sneaked out a quiet, 'Everything all right?'

Zuza said I'm sorry, she's had a bad day, there hasn't been a winter like this in years, she'd rather stay at home. She's starting to get pissed about all those Olka's parties for the dumbest of occasions. Isn't Weronika bored with them already? The way Zuza understands it, today they're celebrating Kuba's new shag. As if it was some kind of unusual event.

'Ah, so that's what it's all about!' Weronika began to laugh spasmodically, bent in half on her chair.

Zuza, back in a cheerful voice, said a quiet 'spierdalaj' and then changed the subject, asking, 'How's your point-saving going?'

'As you can see,' Weronika gestured towards a bottle of beer standing on the dresser. 'The points system is going to kill me. But I bought some handbooks for the exams. Haven't opened them yet though.'

She resumed applying mascara on her lashes. Only once in a while did she look away from the mirror to glance at Zuza with amusement until, all of a sudden, as if she remembered something, she jumped to her feet and ran out of the frame.

From the adjacent room, she shouted Zuza must totally listen to something, Weronika was listening to this track over and over again for two months or so until she lost her player somewhere and completely forgot what the track was called. It was only today that she accidentally found it on the hard drive.

A moment later the room was filled with a clear and powerful, seemingly multiplied sound of French horns playing an unhurried, melancholic, insistently repeated phrase.

A narrow staircase of a Mielżyński Street's tenement. Wu ascended the steep wooden stairs, glancing at the green dado, peeking through the colourful windows at the landings (at the backyard, the many-branched tree, the nightclub on the building's ground floor). Finally, he reached the fourth floor (the rumble of music came from behind the door) and, pressing two bottles of wine against his chest, rang the bell.

The door opened after a fair while, letting clouds of cigarette smoke out into the stairwell (the loud dance music hit his ears). At the door stood Olka, already bleary-eyed, laughing and staggering, all in glitter, in an atypically smart evening dress, with a crown of curls on her head. She kissed Wu on the cheek, collected the bottles and enthusiastically gestured him inside.

He turned right into the spacious living room, in the middle of which (probably also drunk) Weronika danced eagerly to the primitive music, doing pirouettes with her arms stretched upwards.

At the sight of Wu, she stopped and, slightly swaying on her feet, ran up to him in a series of lively leaps and fell into his arms. She cheered, said it was great he finally came, just when she started to think he wouldn't show up, pointed at the coffee table heavy with bags of crisps and other snacks, told him to help himself and informed him vodka was cooling down in the kitchen. She hugged Wu more tightly and, in a conspiratorial whisper (as much as it was possible in this noise), added once he was there, he must check out Kuba's new babe.

In the narrow corridor, he greeted Zuza, who was walking out of the bathroom.

'How are you holding up?'

'Just look at me.'

He reached the end of the corridor and peeked into the bright kitchen, where Olka, now adorned with a dark pink boa, was pouring vodka for the guests. She shouted to Wu to come over, she's counting him in.

At the table sat Kuba, with Monia on his lap (on seeing Wu, she smiled shyly). Kuba introduced her, somewhat awkwardly, as his new girlfriend. Outside the window, the gloomy shape of the Okrąglak emerged from thick darkness.

Against the dark red wallpaper, which seemed almost black in the murk, one could see the silhouette of Weronika leaning against the wall. Wu stood next to her. The door was left ajar, and rhythmic music seeped through it, muffled enough for their conversation to be easily heard.

The day before yesterday — nine, yesterday — ten, today — six, for now. (Glass glinted in the dark as he took a sip.) Wu promised himself not to read them, but he can't resist. Can't even get around to deleting them.

Each of Staszek's texts: confessions of love, expressions of contrition, pleadings for forgiveness. And the thing that pisses him the most: recollections of these five or six happy moments together. When Wu got shit-faced at Olka's party and Staszek had to walk him home, and then they kissed in Ratajski Square in the freezing cold, not caring if anyone was looking, or when they spent the whole day in bed, walking out of the bedroom only to the fridge to get more beers or to the door to collect a pizza they ordered. As if Staszek completely forgotten that straight from Chwaliszewo he hurried to Rataje to get fucked by one of his blokes. At least that's what that twat's texts suggested.

Wu admitted Weronika was right: he shouldn't have trusted Staszek. He's sorry he didn't take her seriously.

'Stop it. How could you know?' She took a sip of beer from her bottle. 'I regret it came to this. In this one particular case, I'd rather not be right.'

Wu smiled and kissed her on the forehead (you could barely see it through the darkness filling the room).

For the last few days, all he did was work on this fucking textbook. Around five, he would open his first beer and work some more while drinking; after eight, he would only drink.

He has no idea what kind of mechanisms in his head make him do the same thing again and again. A new guy appears on the horizon, and Wu takes a headlong jump into this thing you can't even call a relationship. As if some molecular screw in his brain was a little too tight. It lasts a few weeks, the bloke turns out to be a total dick, and Wu despairs as if he was the love of his life. What's wrong with him? He should've grown out of it by now. After all, it's not like he's twenty.

'Maybe we like going in circles,' she replied without a trace of emotion.

'Maybe,' he said and, in a more cheerful voice, continued it seemed they must go back to plan A: buy a villa overlooking Sołacki Park, fill it with books and cats and sit on the porch all day like an old marriage. They'll use blokes only for casual sex because that's what they're best suited for. 'What do you say?'

'We'd drive each other bonkers within a week,' she replied, attempting a playful tone, and sipped the last of her beer.

Tandem Definition
Each tandem consists of two cooperating insurrectionists:
- The infiltrator
- The handler

Thousands of tandems will be uploaded to the lowest level of the Terro-Martian cyberspace, one tandem per locus. See separate instructions for the definition of each tandem member's mission.

Zuza, leaning against the door frame, bathed in yellow light coming from the kitchen, was having a lazy smoke, taking the occasional sip of her drink. Smoking as well, his back against the narrow corridor's opposite wall, Kuba was telling Zuza about a film he'd recently watched, one that moved him enormously. If you were to look at this scene as a human would, you could fix your eyes on what was at the other end of the long corridor: then Kuba and Zuza's silhouettes would blur, and a fragment of the living room would reveal itself in all sharpness, with the extremely drunk Olka rambling something excitedly to Monia, who sat next to her on the sofa with pretended interest.

Some melancholic song was now coming from the living room, which could indicate the imminent end of the party, and to its accompaniment, leaning against wallpaper, Kuba carried on with his disquisition about the film.

Using a pause he made, Zuza said she liked Monia, she seemed a pretty okay person, and she sincerely hoped things would work out between the two of them. (Then she laughed as if amused by what she said.)

Kuba, perhaps thrown off balance a little, was silent for a moment until he finally muttered he knew what it looked like, it's not that he didn't mean the things he'd told Zuza, it's not she was, you know, a random shag to him — not that he's treating Monia this way, he clarified right away — and he doesn't want Zuza to think when she turned him down, he immediately went for a hunt. He's known Monia for years, they were pals at uni, he met her by accident some time ago, and it happened. He wasn't planning it.

'No need to explain. I genuinely hope this'll work out.'

Then she let out a cheerful laugh, tenderly ruffling Kuba's head of blond hair.

If you focussed your eyes again on what was happening at the other end of the corridor, you could see Monia, who didn't seem to listen to Olka's drunken ramblings any longer but instead glanced, somewhat anxious, at Kuba and Zuza talking in the foreground.

Several hours later, this same corridor was shrouded in darkness. A barely visible beer can packed full of cigarette butts stood on the floor, the wallpaper seemed almost black, the quiet sound of a radio broadcast came from the living room. If you moved along the corridor, you would reach the spacious area, where light falling from the street revealed the coffee table littered with torn crisps bags, cluttered with empty beer and wine bottles. On the sofa, right next to the table, Olka was sleeping: all in glitter, still wrapped in her boa, covered with a blanket, most likely by the guests leaving the party. From the speakers standing across the room came the quiet voice of an announcer who talked about Venusian forces attacking the cities of snowy Ceres.

IV

Why not hang hundreds of metres above the night-time Poznań and, with a single flick of fingers, speed up the passage of time: the all-encompassing blackness would transform into ever-lighter shades of grey until the city would finally be flooded from the east by a bright, pink glow. Shadows of buildings — Collegium Altum, Alfa department store, Andersia Tower, Novotel hotel — shorten, and after a while, the pink would fade into grey again. If — with another flick of fingers — you restore the usual flow of time, you could plummet hundreds of metres downwards, suspended above St Martin Street's asphalt and calmly watch the traffic, the trams, the pedestrians waiting at the lights.

In Meskal's red interior, in grey light from the windows, the pale, hungover Weronika opened her eyes wide and covered her mouth as if she heard sensational news from Zuza (who sat next to her) and finally shouted out a series of short sentences: 'No fucking way! How's that possible? How did that even happen?'

Zuza, apparently equally hungover, at least not sharing her friend's enthusiasm, gave a despondent reply it somehow, unfortunately, happened.

'I've got no idea what got into me. You know I never pulls such stunts.' Zuza sighed, glanced at the blind-covered windows, at the photos of Antarctic landscape hanging on the walls.

At the same time, Olka stood on Theatre Bridge, looking upwards, where street lamps swung under the grey winter sky, to the right, towards the throng of cars, trams and pedestrians at the crossroads.

Smoking a cigarette, she repeatedly moved her eyes from the bridge railings to the overhead lines, as if trying to assess how inhumanly strong Michał's killer had to be, to throw his body up to where it hung, showing its colourful interior.

Finally, she tossed the butt-end onto the tracks, rubbed her eyes (some glitter still on her face) and took off towards the city centre.

Wu stood in the tub in his narrow blue bathroom, pouring jets of hot water onto his naked body. You could see cracked tiles, flaking paint, thick mist slowly engulfing the room.

In the bedroom, on the edge of the bed, surrounded by tousled sheets, sat a half-naked slim blond man, who bent down collecting pieces of his garment from the floor. Once he got dressed, he went to the entrance hall, put on his shoes and, while walking past the bathroom on his way out, said a friendly 'cześć' through the crack of the door.

'It was some kind of strange, atavistic understanding,' Zuza said wailfully, added she couldn't fathom what it was in her that made her do it. Where the hell did she get this idea from to stay in Dragon a little longer after Weronika left? Perhaps she wanted to do something non-translation-related after all those days fucking wasted on work. Or forget about the incident on Ceres.

She ordered another drink, texted Olka, hoping she might have sobered up (no reply), called her after a minute (her phone was off). She finished her drink and was about to go home when she got his message.

'I really don't know what's so exciting about it,' she scolded the unhealthily agitated Weronika, whose face instantly lost all enthusiasm, giving way to embarrassment. However, with each new sentence: Zuza doesn't know why she texted him back, she was already hammered, she must've lost her mind cos she ordered another drink, Weronika's lips widened, her eyes sparkled with joy.

'But tell me what happened next!' she urged Zuza in an even more effervescent manner, almost jumping from her chair.

Staszek looked solemnly at the Alfa department store buildings: dirty grey and covered with huge advertisements, and straight ahead, towards Ratajczak Street. He slowly passed some people, a series of banks, keeping hands in his pockets, kicking away the occasional piece of rubbish or cigarette butt. The city reflected in his black eyes.

Before he reached the doorway leading to the Muza cinema, he suddenly stopped and looked around the almost empty street. Carefully, as if checking whether no one was watching.

He took out his phone, a flash of yellow light, dialled a number and held it to his ear. Having one more look around, he disappeared into the doorway. If you followed him a moment later, the doorway would be empty.

Meanwhile, in Dragon's brown, almost lifeless interior, accompanied by a silent conversation between barmaids, Monia sat next to Kuba, telling him after she broke up with Piotr, she was unable to start anything new, this relationship cost her a lot.

At first, everything seemed all right. It was only after a year Piotr began to drink more and more until, eventually, he came home drunk every night, always contagiously depressed. He started with self-pitying, asking if he could die already, and ended up bombarding Monia with complaints. One evening, she couldn't stand it any longer. Not waiting for him to come home, she packed her stuff into two suitcases, left a note on the table and moved out to a friend.

'You're being weird today,' she changed the subject.

'Just tired,' Kuba said without thinking and offered to go to the bar.

Pale against the red background, Zuza let out a sigh and said she didn't know how it all happened. Kuba took Monia home and wrote that message, and Zuza, stupid her, replied to it and decided to stay totally shit-faced, in Dragon. Sipping, kurwa, another drink, she lost count of how many.

And he came, they talked for some time, she's got no fucking clue what about. She doesn't remember much after that: the frosty air, the light of street lamps, the smell of kebabs, the kiss, kurwa, somewhere under the railway flyover, his cold jacket, the dark Poznańska Street and the hand-holding, the chat with a dosser the equally drunk Kuba decided to get involved in, the block of flats, the cramped lift, his fifth-floor flat, hungry kisses in the entrance hall, his fingers sunk into her shoulders, hands stripping each other's clothes, skin flushing with blood, the blue bedroom.

Zuza fell silent, uttered a few 'kurwas' through her teeth, took a sip of coffee and, resigned, leant against the wall. Weronika was beside herself with excitement.

TERRO-MARTIAN FEDERATION IN RETALIATORY STRIKES ON TITAN'S CITIES

The Terro-Martian Federation has launched retaliatory strikes on Titan.

Saturn's moon has been controlled by the Venusian Empire for nearly three centuries since the Ring Wars.

'The strikes targeted two cities on the northern hemisphere,' authorities said.

Earlier this week, Venusian forces launched an unprovoked attack on Cererian cities Demeter and Las Nieves, causing extensive damage.

Monia

The grey sky over Wilda, the windowpane trembling from a passing tram, even though it's the tenement's top floor — it must be number 10. The pavements along 28 June Street are most likely full of people walking home from work, students, grannies carrying plastic bags. My plain white desk sinks under a pile of scribbled papers, pencils, crayons. Every idea for the installation seems wrong.

I look around the dim room. Peek at the colourful artwork on the wall. The thunder of Hetmańska Street is like the thunder of a sea. White tenement roofs stretch outside the window.

I would like to enter this whiteness as I enter the whiteness of Kuba's arms when we wake together in his blue bedroom. The white bedsheets. The grey block of flats peeking through the blinds. The shabby wardrobe from the communist era. His rolled-up white socks thrown into the corner. The smell of his sweat. His bright hair permeated with tobacco smoke.

It's been only a few nights, but each time I wake there — for the first time in years — I feel at home. Piotr's drunken returns home, his texts filled with accusations and threats after we broke up, sad nights with strangers in the months that followed — they all seem to have happened in another life.

I don't know why I'm doing this to myself, but I enter the whiteness of the kitchen of our old Sikorski Street flat. The one where Piotr and I spent those miserable two years. The kitchen is a cheerless tunnel tucked between two rooms and filled with cold fluorescent light. There's a window at its end. Outside you can see the tenement roofs bristling with aerials, the ZNTK works in the background, the starry sky. And my reflection on top of it as I sit alone in the gloomy kitchen.

I don't know why I'm doing this to myself, but some strange longing makes me wait for Piotr. Even though I have to get up before eight. Even though I'm positive it's going to be as it always is. First the jingle of keys that will tell me what state he's in. Either drunk but still willing to talk, tell me how he's spent the evening. He can even be charming like that.

Or drunk the way only I know him. The way his pub friends have no idea about. Drunk as if he were at the bottom of a sea, so the minute he walks in, he'll suck out the last of my energy. Then he'll keep talking about how it all doesn't make any sense, how people don't appreciate his sculptures, how he's not respected the way he should be, but he's going to show them.

Then gain he'll be sitting in front of his laptop, barely paying attention to me. Those thick eyebrows and thick wrists, curly hair peeking out of his shirt, bright sideburns, the stench of sweaty socks. Those sad grey eyes that won't even glance in my direction.

Finally, we'll have a fight because we always do, and this will be one of those in which he uses the scars on his wrists as an argument. Then we'll go to sleep, and tomorrow he'll act as if nothing happened. He'll make me lunch, and when I'm working, he'll sneak up from behind and kiss my neck.

I enter the whiteness of St Martin Street, we're walking again with Kuba towards The Merchant of Poznań. The smell of fumes and zapiekankas hangs in the air, the harsh sun, the sparkling snow. The vague anxiety I can't get rid of, whispering to me Kuba is not entirely honest, he didn't tell me everything about Zuza. The white roofs, the grey sky over Wilda, the roar of cars.

I fall into that cool June evening, still at uni, still in the old Mięsna, Kuba is still with Iwona. We sit in the colourful, smoke-filled interior, drinking shots of vodka with lemon, smoking Lucky Strikes surrounded by people. We've been talking for a few hours on end about art, comic books, TV shows. The light from lamps, the pattern of wallpaper, the quick breathing. A slight nudge of his knee. Was it on purpose? I don't withdraw my leg. Then he does it again, this time not moving away.

We sit joined by the knees. I can feel the tickling of his hair, the whiteness of smoke, the pattern of wallpaper. I falter, laugh and say I'm drunk. And then we sit in silence, and he's looking at me, and the smoke is hanging over our heads.

Sweat condensed on the wallpaper in shades of orange and purple. Mięsna. A bearded DJ stood behind turntables, controlling like a demiurge the mass of human bodies, which waved in line with the electronic ostinato of the bass line, pulsated to the frenetic beat, swarmed with sweaty legs, bellies, hips and arms thrown up in the air.

In the heart of this soft machine, you could see Monia and Kuba, lost in dance. Moving his arms rhythmically, with a cigarette in his mouth, the mesmerized Kuba watched Monia's fluid dance, their bodies alive with colourful lights cast by a disco ball, cigarette smoke surrounding them like fog.

Suddenly, Monia grabbed Kuba's hand and, breaking through the thicket of moving bodies, led him towards the wall, onto a sofa in a deep shade of fuchsia. When they sat down, she sipped from her drink and shouted to Kuba she was completely knackered, she couldn't recall the last time she was having so much fun. Kuba put out his cigarette and kissed her passionately, colourful lights running across their bodies, his hands wandering over her thighs, stomach, breasts; her hand sunk deep into his blond hair.

Dozens of minutes later they sat at the bar in the lower room, surrounded by the patterned wallpaper, plastic lampshades, people queuing for alcohol, grey cigarette smoke. They were silent for most of the time, looked at each other with dilated pupils, grasped each other's hands, smoked.

Finally, Kuba asked how Monia enjoyed last night's party at Olka's, to which she replied it was quite fun. She rarely feels comfortable getting to know new people, but his friends are all right. Wu was a tad aloof, but she can't blame him after what he's been through. Olka is a bit tiring when she drinks, but otherwise, she's absolutely disarming. She adored Weronika; the girl has such positive ADHD. Zuza's okay too, she can't say a sentence without working five 'kurwas' in it, which given her demeanour is fucking charming.

'About Zuza…' she paused and asked Kuba if they, by any chance, used to be together or something because she keeps sensing some kind of, I don't know, strange vibe.

Kuba went purple, didn't say a word for a moment until, starting with a prolonged 'well', there was something in the shape of a flirt between them, though maybe 'flirt' is too strong a word. Anyways, nothing came out of this cos what could come out of it, really? It was ages ago, and now they're buddies, and nothing more than buddies, there's nothing to be bothered with.

In response to his explanations, Monia smiled, as if in disbelief, and bottomed up her drink.

When she went to the toilet, Kuba immediately picked up his phone. If you looked over his shoulder, you could see he was texting Zuza the official, as of five minutes ago, version of their relationship.

The night was hopeful, frigid. Laced with chimney smoke, spotted with hazy lights, it stretched over the unfazed Poznań, rubbed against its edgy roofs, slid down its many manholes.

Inside the bustling, smoke-filled Dragon, Zuza was lifting dopey Weronika off her seat, saying, 'Enough wiśniówkas for you. Let's get you a taxi.'

Olka, half-amused, half-concerned at Zuza's arduous attempts to get Weronika's arms into the sleeves of her jacket, offered help, but Zuza only said,

'No, thanks. I've got this,' and quietly into Weronika's ear, 'I've got you. You'll be fine.'

They walked out into the freezing night, bodies radiating threads of warmth into the darkness. Arm around Zuza's neck, feet shuffling, Weronika mumbled she'd be fucking best therapist in the whole, kurwa, Solar System. She'd counsel away everyone's deepest pain.

Zuza's heart was pounding as the two approached 23 February Street. A row of taxis awaited in front of the bulky building of the archive, but Zuza walked past them, dragging Weronika along, straight to a cab parked at the edge of Wielkopolski Square. Looking at the tarpaulin-covered stalls, she opened the car's door and helped Weronika inside.

'I was starting to worry,' said the driver, tapping ash off a cigarette through a rolled-down window.

'There's plenty of time.' Zuza unzipped the red jacket of now unconscious

Weronika.

The driver peeped into the rear-view window at Zuza's glaringly pink tights. 'You'll get bronchitis. Can't you wear a pair of trousers? It's the middle of a winter for fuck's sake.'

'I'll be fine, they're warm,' she said, looking at a shiny streak of drool coming out from Weronika's mouth and visibly refraining herself from wiping it.

The driver said a friendly 'see you in a bit', flicked his half-smoked cigarette towards the stalls and rolled up the window. Through the shut door, he winked at Zuza, then scratched an Antarctica-shaped tattoo on his right forearm and drove off.

Alone in front of the gloomy stalls, with eyes as glossy as the cobblestones under her feet, Zuza lit up a cigarette. She sighed a smoke-filled sigh and expelled into the night a series of quiet 'kurwas'.

Motionless white clouds hung above Międzymoście Square. When they walked in an embrace across the junction, Kuba asked Monia if she really didn't want to go with him to Dragon, Olka would be happy to see her, or if she really didn't want him to take a ride with her to Wilda, that wouldn't be a problem at all. Monia smiled and said she'd be all right, he should go and have fun. Anyway, she's not sure if two nights in a row with drunk Olka wouldn't be too much for her.

There was only one cab waiting at the rank. They approached it calmly, their eyes darting towards the car-filled guarded car parks (the river used to flow through here a few decades earlier), towards the white clouds hanging above their heads. Kuba opened the cab's door, inspected the driver with suspicion (he was wearing a red jacket, a baseball cap, thick-framed glasses), gave him the address, paid for the ride in advance and then let Monia in, having kissed her on the lips. He closed the door, and the taxi took off.

Sitting in silence at the back of the car, Monia looked at the misty Garbary Street outside the window, at the few people on the pavements, the banks of snow, the street lights, the roofs of bleak tenements, the stalls in Bernardine Square. The taxi driver informed her they would take a bit of a detour because there were some roadworks, to which Monia nodded, not even looking at him.

When they were entering Queen Jadwiga Street, she glanced at the grey Physical Education Academy building, at the trees planted scarcely along the tram tracks and — a few minutes later — at the lights in the gloomy Lower Wilda Street. Had she looked at the driver at least once, she might have noticed his prominent cheekbones, thick black eyebrows, and even — during gear changes — an Antarctica-shaped tattoo peeking from under the edge of his red sleeve.

Next, the cavernous Hetmańska Street (a McDonald's on one side, a massive block of flats on the other), the intersection with 28 June Street.

Before they reached the empty Traugutt Street, Monia asked the driver to pull over, and when he parked by the pavement, she thanked him, said goodbye and left.

She walked towards a tenement's green door, stood in front of it for a moment, watching the cab drive away, vigorously rummaging through her bag. When she finally retrieved her keys, they fell to the pavement with a clatter.

Not thinking much, she bent down to pick them and got back up. She didn't even have a chance to take a breath.

The scythe's blade softly penetrated the skin and the layer of fat, pierced through the tightening muscles, entered deeper, ripping the veins and arteries apart, tearing the shimmering guts, cutting through another layer of muscle, another layer of fat, another layer of skin. A bright red gushed from both wounds.

V

Snow fell onto Poznań as if onto the soft lining of an open mouth — thicker and thicker. The frosty air was almost motionless, the greyness of the city gradually turning into ever-darker shades, the streets illuminated with the headlights of cars stuck in traffic jams.

Wu crossed Independence Avenue and carried on along Libelt Street, saying to a phone held in his trembling hand, yes, he's left his place, and yes, nothing's changed, Kuba's still in total shock, but it's hardly surprising, I guess we all are. On top of that, all those interrogations yesterday, Kuba spent there some six hours. And now he's sitting like that, not saying a word, totally pale, hasn't eaten a single, kurwa, thing, even though Wu tried to force lunch on him. He hasn't spoken anything since yesterday, curses now and then or lies on the side, staring at the sofa's backrest, or sits on its edge bent in half.

While crossing Kościuszko Street next to the grey office building, Wu said he didn't like the look of it either, he agreed it couldn't be a coincidence: first Ania, then this Michał from I Burn Poznań, now poor Monia, and he had no idea what it could mean (snow was filling up the creases in his jacket), but it had to mean something. It was the third person from their immediate circle. He dreads to think what will happen next.

There hasn't been a winter like this in years.

After a moment of silence, during which he was listening to the voice in the speaker, approaching the white Ratajski Square, he said he'd read about it, but it's just guesswork. It's always the same blame game anyways: if it's not Queen Maud Land's terrorists, then it must be the Venusian Empire, but it can be some sick fucker, maybe even their acquaintance, who exchanges 'cześć, cześć' with them in Kisielice or Dragon, goes to the same events.

Though this sudden attack on Ceres does concern him. What could Venus' agenda be? Was it a power play? Okay, maybe the reunion plans did bomb those few years ago because of you-know-what, but still, you'd think the conflict frozen for decades was coming to an end, and now this happens. Where's the logic? Maybe they want to take advantage of the terrorists' actions?

A tram cut the square, Wu lit a cigarette with some struggle, making occasional affirmative murmurs to the phone, only to get back to the topic of Kuba, who finally told Wu to go, said he must be on his own for a little and felt like a cripple when Wu hovered over him all the time. He'll be all right, he's a grown man. Wu was afraid to leave him in this state but eventually gave in cos Kuba wouldn't do anything stupid, would he?

Everything seems to be falling apart. Wu was always taking the piss at Olka's parties thrown for no good reason, but after these two horrible days, he wants to go somewhere, get wasted, tell primitive jokes. He's at Ratajski Square at the moment, maybe he'll talk her into joining him?

On hearing her answer, he laughed and said if she had a date, then sure, no problem, he'll get drunk by himself. Weronika? Weronika's staying home tonight with Jerzy. She needs to take care of him once in a while cos so far she's doing everything not to spend time with him.

Okay, in that case maybe he'll do something useful and finally look for those garage keys. Perhaps he'll even get around to declutter his flat, at least he'll have something to take his mind off this all. Some physical activity might indeed work better for him than getting hammered. Though one doesn't preclude the other. He'll check on Kuba in the evening, but he doubts he'll want to see him. Maybe the poor bastard will finally have some sleep.

Wu talked for a bit longer, hung up, put the phone back into his pocket and tossed the cigarette butt towards the Academy of Fine Arts. The snowy Marcinkowski Avenue stretched before him.

With an Antarctic plain in the background, surrounded by the orange-and-brown floral pattern of the wallpaper, Zuza stood still her eyes absent, squinting a little, focussed on some point right in front of her. Outside the window stretched the wintry estate, there was the hum of cars driving along the vast Solidarity Avenue, with the fast tram line running across the vista — invisible from this perspective, buried in a deep trench. At some point, Zuza stood on her toes, raised a nail in her hand and began to hammer it vigorously into the wall.

Suddenly, through the steady, loud clangour, a deep male voice broke, asking where the fuck Zuza kept thyme, kill him but he can't find it. She rolled her eyes, put the hammer down and shouted, telling Mateusz (that's what she called him) to wait, she'll find it herself, and left the patterned room.

The sounds of conversation came from the kitchen. Zuza and Mateusz quickly moved on from culinary-related topics to more serious matters: they talked about Queen Maud Land, about an uprising, about something called the inducer.

'I'm worried about these attacks on Ceres.' Mateusz slid a casserole into the oven and joined Zuza at the table. 'What's their deal? Those Venusian fuckers can be unpredictable.'

'True.'

Mateusz held out a lighter towards Zuza, his Antarctica-shaped tattoo pitch-black against white skin. Zuza lit up and said on the one hand, this could work in their favour. The authorities might be too preoccupied with the Venus-related shit show to control what's going on in their own cyberspace. But on the other hand, she's got a bad feeling about it.

Mateusz watched Zuza's chest as she exhaled smoke. He cracked a smile. 'Maybe we shouldn't worry too much about it yet. The important thing is the last termination went swimmingly.'

'It sure did.'

'Oh, cheer up. I know it's not the most pleasant thing, but remember what they are. In the greater scheme of things, their lives don't mean shit. Think of them as insects. Pests.'

Zuza didn't respond. She got up to check on the casserole and returned to her seat. As she put out her cigarette in a porcelain ashtray, Mateusz scratched his thick eyebrow and asked,

'And how's our object doing? Still dancing to our tune?'

'She sure is.'

'And you've checked she doesn't remember my face?'

'Hundreds of times. Nothing left of your beautiful mug in there.'

Mateusz grinned, so it seems they can try with the second object. But she's one hundred per cent sure this doll doesn't remember anything from the sessions? She's positive? No flashbacks? Because otherwise, the instructions are clear.

The snow didn't cease. Olka, in her white jacket and pink baseball cap, walked out from the tenement she lived in into Mielżyński Street and, having taken a glimpse of the grey Dom Książki book shop covered with a flashy advert, took off towards the square. A tram passed her by with a clatter, a car blinded her with headlights. She lit a cigarette.

Her tired eyes followed the line of roofs of the pink social realism tenements, then again the overhead wires. Lost in thought, she stared into the dirty white of the pavement. A leaflet showing all the planets and moons belonging to the Terro-Martian Federation stuck to the sole of her shoe.

Several minutes later, all in snow (barely visible on her white jacket), she entered Meskal. She took off her cap, freeing unruly blonde curls, brushed the snow off her clothes and, her heels tapping, walked through the narrow corridor (the almost empty interior flashed in the rectangular opening in the wall). Inside, Staszek sat at one of the tables. He smiled on seeing her.

CERES

Mass: 9.384×10^{20} kg
0.00016 Earths
0.0128 Moons
Mean Diameter: 939.5 km
Orbital period: 4.61 years
1683.15 days
Rotation period: 9 h 4 min
Category: Dwarf Planet

Ceres is a dwarf planet located in the asteroid belt. It is the belt's biggest object, accounting for around one-forth of its total mass.

The world has a thin, artificial atmosphere, with temperatures rarely exceeding -50°C. A subsurface ocean contains a dense nanite swarm. Close to twenty cities were built mostly post-awakening.

As one of the most valuable Terro-Martian assets, Ceres has been a frequent target of Venusian attacks, none of them successful.

The tin box of the lift glided through the shaft with a screech, and if you passed through concrete to get inside it, you would see Zuza: in a snow-covered coat, hair tied in a ponytail, hands holding keys. She fiddled with them, gazing somewhere ahead as if able to look through walls.

The lift finally stopped, and Zuza walked out into the block of flats' narrow staircase. With some hesitation, she put a key into a heavy glazed door, opened it and found herself in a small vestibule: full of furniture and various items that apparently didn't fit inside the two flats flanking it. A glass ball filled with turbid water stood on a high cupboard. Inside, a crucian floated, glancing at Zuza with its piscine eye.

She approached the door on the right and, slowly, as if in apprehension, turned the key in the lock. A small entrance hall appeared in front of her, with a narrow kitchen behind it (outside its window, in the light of street lamps, you could see the heavy falling snow and another block of flats a few dozen metres away).

Kuba sat almost motionless on the sofa in the big red room to the right, face hidden in hands; one could get the impression he didn't even hear Zuza come in. The room was lit by a tall lamp with a plastic shade whose cold glow fell onto book-filled shelves, a poster with a level map of some old video game, a desk with a large monitor and — finally — the grey sofa on which Kuba sat.

Zuza took a few steps into the room, nervously rotating her red bracelet placed over a thin black sweater, but didn't say a word.

Kuba dropped his hands, revealing his pale, fatigued face, and gave Zuza a murky, absent and at the same time wistful gaze (she froze). He looked at her in silence for a good two minutes until he finally got up and started kissing her.

VI

'Beautiful plan! Your two girlfriends got murdered in a month? Why not invite friends to a dinner party!' While delivering her ironic comment, Weronika almost got up from the sofa.

In response, Olka laughed and said no worries, a dinner party really means a drinking party, and in some situations there's nothing else you can do.

Weronika never thought anything would top that bash after Kuba got fired from the ad agency, but clearly, there are still many horrible events in his life worth celebrating.

They were in Kisielice, it was the middle of the day. A grey glow seeped from the street through the poster-covered windows, while they sat at a table in the corner, sipping beer.

After a longer pause, lighting a cigarette and staring into a red sticker with the table number, Olka asked Weronika what that thing with Kuba and Zuza was all about, maybe she misheard, but Wu mentioned they were coming together tonight.

Weronika (against the background of green stripes) almost jumped in excitement, cautioned Olka what she was about to say Zuza told her in strict confidence. Then, after a moment of silence, she announced it seemed Zuza and Kuba were an item now, I mean, that's not for sure. In any case, they shagged a few days ago, and Olka must know it wasn't even their first time.

Streams that cannot rest, gruesome, tumultuous maelstroms, cascades, jets, rainy jungle, rivers are the colour

of mercury, cast iron, milk, brown seaweed, concrete.

*The downpour is unceasing, the sky is still golden,
uniform, thick and heavy, I lift up my eyelids,
thinking of you, still walking, stream after stream, letting
the woods embrace us softly, we are sinking deeper,
can't catch my breath, no longer feel my legs while pushing
steadily ahead, keeping up with my friends, water
the colour of cast iron, mercury, milk, china,
the dark and humid thicket, automatic movements.*

*My two friends and I make it to where the wet flora
becomes thinner and thinner, trees and bushes blocking
less and less light and letting ever-more cold water,
then we stand at the ocean's shore, all flat and muddy,
only water before us: frantic, roiled, relentless,
heavy and never-ending, we stand there dumbfounded,
the downpour is unceasing, blurring all around us,
merging everything into a monochromatic
space: vast and all-embracing, I pull down my eyelids
and yet do not stop seeing this grand sparkling radiance
that fills me top to bottom, this is almost pleasant,
making me think of nothing, forget all about your
irises of no colour, listless, sponge-like body,
hands that will never touch me, the tearing of tissues,
nothing left but the sparkling, the weird, scary stillness.*

*Stream after stream after stream we follow the shoreline,
the mouths of brooks and rivers, sometimes so expansive
that our boat cannot pass them, and we go back deeper
into the jungle coloured like milk, glitter, buildings.*

'The dinner party works this way: I provide space and products, and you cook,' Olka explained to Weronika and Wu as they entered her flat. All three of them carried bags full of vegetables, meat, bottles of wine, oil, and when they dragged them to the kitchen, they stood against the backdrop of the Okrąglak building in the window and began to unpack the bags (shiny aubergines, blood-red beef, round onions). Olka cursed, they forgot to buy garlic and asked Wu if he would be so kind as to pop out to the shop. Here are the keys, but he should be careful not to lock the door with the big one because that lock can only be opened from the outside.

Mercury

Mass: 3.301 x 10²³ kg
0.055 Earths
4.496 Moons
Mean Diameter: 4,879.4 km
Orbital period: 0.24 years
87.97 days
Rotation period: 58.65 days
Category: Planet

Mercury is the nearest planet to the Sun and the smallest of four terrestrial planets. Mercury and Venus are the only planets in the Solar System that have no natural satellites.
The planet has remained under Venusian rule since the schism. It is home to several dozen domed cities communicated with a system of underground tunnels.

A few hours later, over empty plates, holding glasses continually filled with red wine, listening to music seeping from speakers, they sat in the living room around a folding table. They were joined by Kuba and Zuza, who sat away from each other, but a skilled observer could see they maintained eye contact most of the time. The room was lit by the faint, flickering glow of candles placed on the table. The walls were populated by the shadows of those gathered.

In their conversations, they did what they could to avoid the subject of the recent killings, Queen Maud Land's terrorists, the suddenly rekindled, centuries-long conflict with Venus, laughing instead at Jerzy's ever-more absurd excuses not to come to their get-togethers, or talking about work, about an encounter with an exceptionally rude shop assistant, recent pub outings.

Kuba didn't take part in the conversation. Instead, he laughed from time to time when the others laughed and gave the impression of someone sick or struggling with an immense pain who participated in the gathering only to please others. Zuza watched him intently, with concern. Every now and then, Kuba seemed to completely ignore what his friends were saying: when this happened, he looked absent-mindedly outside the window, where the city unfurled.

'You're not going to believe what happened to me yesterday' Olka said rather desperately, looking at the distracted Kuba. Some bloke walks over to her in Mięsna, a kid, of course, cos there's a shitload of kids in there, and fires a series of exceptionally cheap compliments, like she looks 28 years old or she's got some interesting cheekbones. He went as far as to say he thought he knew her from TV. Please!

All that said, he was a pretty decent hunk: dark-haired, well-built, with a dark beard, so when after five minutes he offered her, quote, unquote, unforgettable banging, she didn't think twice. They took a taxi to, kurwa, Górczyn, and when it came to paying, it turned out the arsehole had two zlotys in his wallet. So she kicked him out of the car, told the driver to go back to Mięsna and kept drinking.

What can you do when there's nothing you can do?

'Excuse me,' Kuba interrupted her barely audibly, got up from the table, grabbed his jacket and left the flat.

A silence fell over the room. Disconcerted Weronika, Olka and Wu exchanged glances until their eyes all focused on Zuza, who took out her phone and began to write a message.

Cellar-like stuffiness mingled with the smell of sweat and the sharp scent of cigarette smoke. Surrounded by artificial plants, in red neon light, Weronika and Zuza downed the contents of their shot glasses in a single brisk movement. As soon as they put the glasses away, they got up and, through a long room full of tall tables (people sat densely around them on high chairs), went to a small dance floor.

They squeezed in between dancing bodies and, in clouds of thick smoke from the fog machine, started dancing to the loud music played by the DJ. Their skin was covered with sweat, you could notice the ever-faster pulsating of their arteries.

Several dozen minutes later, wet from the dancing, breathing rapidly, with a thicket of artificial vegetation in the background, they sat at the long bar, sipping their drinks: Zuza vodka with lemon, Weronika wiśniówka.

The former was saying she didn't know whether it was what she wanted, didn't know whether she was ready for it (she was almost certain Kuba wasn't), but, kurwa, it somehow happened. She took the keys from Wu and went to Jeżyce and took that lift and stood in that room, not saying a word, watching him sit on the sofa completely crushed, and he stood up and they somehow, she doesn't know how, ended where they did.

There was nothing to explain, nothing to add, it all made sense. And still does. It's only that, Weronika will surely agree, this whole situation is a total chujnia. First Ania, now Monia and this drunken sex before she died. And the attacks, and that whole thing with Venus.

She's got no idea what's up with her. It's unlike her. She always avoided such situations cos she's smart enough to know nothing good can come out of them, but now... Though she realizes it's a tricky business, and she's almost certain it's not going to lead to anything serious, she weirdly wants to try. Daft, isn't it?

'Perhaps you're less rational than you like to think?' asked the already inebriated Weronika, only to say right away she must order another round cos she's never heard a compound-complex sentence about Zuza's feelings come out of her mouth.

Zuza returned the favour with a cheerful 'jeb się', and added Weronika would have to drink it herself cos Zuza was going home.

'Whose home?' Weronika asked, and they both snorted with laughter.

Your mission as the handler
As the handler, you will have the following duties:
- Assisting the infiltrator in their mission
- Evaluating the infiltrator's performance
- Observing members of the infiltrated group
- Exposing objects to memory-instilling incidents*
- Terminating malfunctioning objects
- Reporting all information about the mission to your superiors
- Occasionally, exposing objects to the inducer (this is primarily the infiltrator's task)

*Note: A memory-instilling incident is a traumatic event meant to test the inducer's memory-editing capabilities. During the incident, make sure that the object sees your face. This detail will be then edited out from the object's memory.

Several hours passed. Amidst the colourful lights, the thick smoke, Weronika danced on the almost empty dance floor. You could tell from her uncoordinated movements and glassy eyes her tissues and organs were permeated with alcohol, but she danced with vigour all the same, engaging her whole body, doing an occasional frantic pirouette. Finally, she stopped, panting, in the doorway leading to the narrow, long room and looked ahead.

At the other end of the room, near the exit against the stairs, stood a sturdy man with thick eyebrows: upright, slightly astraddle, his arms crossed, an Antarctica-shaped tattoo on one of them. His face was motionless, eyes piercing Weronika through.

She instantly grew pale, her legs buckled. Without hesitation, she bolted behind the wall separating the dance floor from the oblong room. She looked for a moment at the few people dancing among the clouds, at the lights cast by the disco ball until she mustered enough courage to lean out from behind the wall — the man disappeared.

Warily, she walked between the tables, crossed the narrow room and leant out of the door: no trace of him; he could have gone upstairs or be lurking near the bar. She took out her phone (green light) and selected Jerzy's number from her contact list. Having listened to the dial tone for several dozen seconds, she finally gave up, cursed, got back to the list and located Wu's number.

Half an hour later she sat, all trembling, against the background of worn dark pink wallpaper in the Chwaliszewo flat's kitchen — next to the table, drinking cold beer from a can.

Wu sat on a stool in front of her, an arm's length away, leaning against the worktop, sipping beer as well. He asked in a calm voice,

'Are you sure it was the same guy?'

Weronika replied, in a wistful tone, yes, she's sure, he was the one who attacked her in Wielkopolski Square, and, even worse, she realized she, kurwa, knew him, the guy she met in some pub when totally shit-faced, the one who walked her to the river; the same who probably spiked her drink. What could his deal be? Does this mean he's been following her all the time?

She put her beer away, hid her face in her hands and, in a trembling voice, uttered a few juicy curses.

Wu reached out to brush her forearm tenderly. Behind his back was a thicket of ivy — its leaves, as always wildly green, tightly covered the kitchen cabinets. Weronika kept trembling, seemingly more with each second. Perhaps she was going through the recent events in her head. It's not impossible she was imagining what would have happened if Wu hadn't answered his phone, and she had to walk to her flat on her own. She could be thinking about the cold scythe blade piercing her entrails, the same way it disembowelled Monia, Michał and Ania. Time and again, her face contorted with a grimace, as if of disgust or pain. One of her eyelids began to twitch in a nervous tic.

On seeing this, Wu stroked her cold cheek with the back of his hairy hand. Weronika held it against her face, sighed and closed her eyes. She seemed to gradually calm down.

Suddenly, and quite unexpectedly, driven by some incomprehensible impulse, she grabbed Wu by the neck, pulled him closer and gave him a passionate kiss.

A second later, she came to her senses, started from her seat and, hiding her face in her hands, stuttered out 'kurwa mać', then 'I'm sorry', again a whole series of 'kurwas'.

She left the kitchen, avoiding eye contact, took her jacket and went out into the staircase. Still confused, Wu got up from his stool and only after a moment ran out after her, shouting she was being ridiculous, she should come back, she can't go home on her own.

At this point, she was already halfway down Chwaliszewo Street, running as fast as she could through the frosty air and sobbing miserably.

VII

He hopes this doesn't mean Weronika would stop speaking to him altogether. She doesn't text back, doesn't answer his calls, he even paid her a visit this morning, but she wouldn't open the door. Ja pierdolę, it was only a kiss, after all, it wasn't a big deal.

Unfortunately, this is not exactly surprising to him. He's been trying to repress it all this time, but come to think of it, he must've sensed Weronika was expecting something more than friendship all along. Though, kurwa, he was sure they worked this through. His only hope is now things between them won't totally fall apart.

He feels guilty. For years, he came running to her with every problem, and most of them, obviously, were about that shitload of arseholes he wanted, in succession, to spend his life with. How horrible it must've made her feel. Probably he should've given her more space a long time ago, stopped pulling her into all those dramas, let her find someone who could at last reciprocate her feelings. And who wouldn't be Jerzy. Though since Zuza claims Weronika's stopped speaking to him as well, then maybe there's a chance. He sure hopes so.

If only he could help her somehow. He can't stand the thought she stays inside four walls all day long, not even stepping out into the staircase cos she's afraid this creep is following her. And that thing in his kitchen, it completely crushed her.

It all worries him. Zuza must know Olka seems to be playing a detective cos she's been asking everyone about the tiniest details of the last weeks' events. This hasn't led anywhere in particular yet, but an interesting fact came to light. Weronika's stalker has an Antarctica-shaped tattoo. Kuba said before he saw a similar tat on the taxi driver who was supposed to take Ania home the night she died, so this guy, if he's the same guy, could be involved in all the murders. Though it seems Olka's investigation won't amount to much cos apart from that there is nothing but unknowns.

Speak of the devil. Could Zuza hang on a moment, he must pick it up, she's calling a third time in an hour. Must be another extremely urgent matter.

The carpeted room was furnished with plywood bookshelves, an oakwood wardrobe, an unmade divan bed overlaid with tangled clothes, a small table, folding chairs. Clumps of dust gathered in the corners. Zuza sat on one of the chairs near the window, chewing her lip, clasping a bottle of beer with both hands. Next to her was an empty chair facing the window. On the windowsill, an open bottle of beer.

Across the street stood a pale green tenement house, its several-storey bay window covered with lighter vertical reliefs: two broad stripes stretching on each side and, between each floor, five narrower, chain-like. The building had four brick-built balconies extending from the bay window, each with two see-through, barred rectangles. On the top balcony, which was approximately at the same level as the messy room, Olka smoked a cigarette, grinning. Grey afternoon light glistened in her eyes.

'But are you sure the editing worked?' came Mateusz's booming voice from outside the room.

'Positive.' Zuza looked at the electric yellow polish on her nails.

Mateusz entered, holding a bowl of salted peanuts, which he put on the windowsill. He sat on the empty chair and said it sure didn't look that way. When the object saw him, she totally freaked out. There's no fucking way she didn't recognize his face.

'She recognized your tattoo.' Zuza looked straight into Mateusz's eyes, and his heart quickened. Then she continued he should've, dunno, covered it up before the incident. Now it's too late to edit it out cos Weronika's told fucking everyone about it. Plus, Mateusz could've chosen a less obvious pattern, I don't know, a penguin. Zuza took a long pull from her bottle and looked outside. Olka disappeared in her flat.

Mateusz chuckled but watched Zuza with some suspicion, maybe hurt, definitely longing as she swept away her shiny long hair and scratched the back of her neck.

'You're sure he's going to be here today?' he asked.

'That's what my research suggests. Olka has clearly too much free time at her disposal.'

'And what do you think, what's this worm's agenda?'

Zuza says she's got no fucking clue, but he's been infiltrating the group for a reason. He might be suspecting something about the murders, er, terminations. Her guess is the bloke is working for the authorities.

STRICTER ANTI-TREASON AND ANTI-TERROR LAWS COME INTO FORCE

New stricter anti-treason and anti-terror laws have been introduced in response to the growing internal and external threats.

It is now illegal to express support for, or publish images suggesting one is a supporter of any organization associated with the Venusian Empire or Queen Maud Land.

The new laws permit longer sentences for a number of offences, including dissemination of publications supporting such groups.

Further measures are said to be introduced in the coming months.

Surrounded by the spiral of a green dado, they ascended the stairs, walking past wooden doors on each floor, stained-glass windows on each landing until they reached the flat number 8. Before this happened, Olka managed to repeat several times she must've been out of her fucking mind when she decided to live so high, to which Wu invariably nodded.

She opened the door, explaining it's the chest of drawers in the bedroom, it needs to be moved a bit and, Wu understands, she can't do it on her own. She let him in, invited to the living room and asked to make himself at home, suggested they should crack one open before they begin because there's no reason to do it sober, then all of a sudden, maybe a bit too theatrically, said she forgot to buy beer, silly her, and instantly left the flat (the rattle of a key in a lock).

Flabbergasted, Wu froze mid-way over the sofa, but the apogee of his astonishment came later, when the door to the adjacent room opened, revealing Staszek.

He stood warily in the doorway, against a red background, not saying a word or making a movement, his facial expression and posture betraying he was afraid of the outburst of Wu's anger, which was indeed about to occur in a moment.

Before that happened, though, Wu spoke to himself with disbelief, no, that nutter didn't do it, rushed towards the door (his face pale with anger) and yanked the handle. The door didn't budge, even after he started nervously, one by one, opening all the locks, and when he apparently realized he was trapped, he repeated with rage he can't, kurwa, believe it, that old drunk couldn't have done it to him.

To a quiet 'listen' uttered by Staszek, who'd been standing in the living room door all this time, Wu snapped back telling him to shut up, said he hasn't the slightest intention of, kurwa, talking to him, and grabbed his phone.

At that time, Olka was already halfway down the frosty Gwarna Street, reflecting in the glazed doors of a bar serving chips and kebabs, looking towards the cars in St Martin Street. When she took her vibrating phone out of her pocket (a pulsating screen), she only smiled to herself and put it back.

Soon after, she could be seen against Kisielice's striped wall (black-and-white artwork) as she sat at the bar and, visibly self-satisfied, read a book while sipping beer. Lost in reading, she probably didn't pay any attention to a conversation between young men at a nearby table. Smoking cigarettes, drinking vodka, they were having a passionate talk about the series of brutal murders, about the girl killed on Traugutt Street, about the fact the murder weapon was, allegedly, a war scythe stolen from the military museum. It could've been the Venusians, maybe they managed to breach the Terro-Martian cyberspace; unless it's Queen Maud Land's terrorists. Either way, the situation looks bleak. If these are political murders, you can expect it's only the beginning, much more blood will be spilled.

The Great In-Between sucks me in, yet again. Colours are sounds. Sounds are shapes. I am a boundless, shapeless multitude. Despite this formlessness, I retain a direction. Always the same, always towards you.

Trams moved softly along snow-covered streets.

Dusk was falling, greyness slowly poured into the spacious living room. Outside, you could see 27 December Street, the tall rectangular buildings of the Alfa department store, a bright bank logo on one of them, snowy rooftops.

On the sofa, keeping a certain distance, sat Staszek and Wu. They drank white wine in silence, with an almost empty bottle and an open jar of olives on the coffee table in front of them. With each minute, the outlines of things became less and less defined.

Barely visible at that point, Wu said, 'I don't know how to respond. Honestly, this sounds like a load of bollocks.'

'I get that, but it's all true.'

'So I'm supposed to believe you're on a mission, and all your lies and manipulations — let's not forget your fucking around — were somehow part of said mission, but, for my own safety, you can't tell me anything more about it or even who you're working for? Are you part of Queen Maud's Heart? Do you work for the terrorists? Were you involved in the murders? Did Ania die because of you? Michał? Monia?'

'I had nothing to do with their deaths, promise. But I can't tell you much more. Not yet. I wish I could.' Staszek lowered his head.

'This is bullshit.'

From a pocket of his black jeans, Staszek produced a glittery gold flash drive. 'I want you to have it.'

'What's that?'

'It's a copy of my key.'

'Your what now?'

Staszek blushed, collected his thoughts and said, warily, 'It's basically a piece of code that lets me remain undetected. If you handed it over to the authorities, I would be screwed. The whole mission would be screwed. So my life is in your hands now.'

After a moment of hesitation, Wu took the drive. 'Frankly, this sounds like more bollocks. Why are you doing this, exactly?'

Staszek scratched the side of his thigh. 'I want you to trust me again, some day. I realize this might never happen, and I accept that. I know I hurt you, deeply. And I'm so, so sorry about it.' He gazes outside the window. 'When I set off on this mission, I knew it would involve lying to people. Manipulating people. Hurting people. For a long time, I was quite good at convincing myself it was a necessary cost. But then I met you. This was…' He looks into Wu's eyes. 'The most real thing I'd ever experienced. I could no longer lie to myself. And my mission… I eventually lost faith in it.'

'Does Olka know all I've just heard?'

Staszek blushed again. 'I only told her I wanted to have a chance to apologize. The things between us ended so abruptly. Our last conversation, if you could even call it a conversation… I know I can't undo the damage I've done, but I wanted to offer an explanation. As unsatisfying as it is. And I'm sorry, I didn't know Olka would ambush you like that. I was under the impression you agreed to the meeting.'

'The hell you were.' Wu pressured the corners of his eyes. 'So you're perfectly fine with me telling everyone about your… mission? I mean this little I know about it?'

'I'll accept anything you choose to do with this knowledge.'

'Fuck.' After a pause, Wu sighed and looked into Olka's darkening studio. 'I hope at least this barfly hasn't got blotto and isn't now lying under a table somewhere in Meskal or Kisielice. Cos as much as I've always liked this flat, I wouldn't fancy staying here all night.'

Then he cursed and asked why did he always have to fall into the same trap? All this time Wu had — and still has — the impression Staszek and he had a special bond, they could communicate without words from the very first seconds, on some totally irrational level. He'd never experienced anything so intense, he really thought it could be something big. Maybe if they met each other at a different point in their lives, in other circumstances, though chuj knows… Weronika would probably tell him he tends to mistake love-bombing for genuine connection. (If only she could apply this advice to her own life.) It's stupid and irrational, but something tells him, even now, it wasn't only that. Evidence points to the contrary, but he still believes what they had was real. He's a hopeless cause, it seems.

The room was being filled with increasingly thick darkness. The colours died out, and everything was in shades of grey, including the silent Staszek, who stared into the floor, nervously fiddling with a stray thread on his jeans. Every now and then he peeked at Wu, only to follow with his eyes the ever less distinct line of his long legs, stopping for a bit on his feet.

Wu finally said it was a lot to process, but next time they were going out to Dragon or Mięsna, Staszek could join them, perhaps. The fact their relationship (or whatever they should call it) is over doesn't mean they can't get along on other levels. But to be clear, he doesn't trust him. Or forgive him.

Quite likely he never will.

VIII

Cut Poznań in half, reveal the underground car parks, basements, sewage system, the spaces of residential buildings and shopping centres, see the grey entrails of the outwardly grey city, get closer to this cross section and listen to the hubbub of the streets: the roar of engines, the clatter of tram wheels, the conversations about the metropolises of Mars.

He's happy Janek agreed to come. There's something they need to talk about. Where to start, gosh, it's harder than he thought it'd be, but he needs to come clean about something. A lot of things, actually. He hasn't been honest with Janek. That's an understatement. He lied to him, he's been lying to him all along.

'About what?' Janek's face was pale, emotionless. His red hair contrasted with the green striped wall behind him. Hands, lying flat on the table, slowly balled into fists.

It was noon, Kisielice was almost empty, save for two loud men sitting at the bar and drinking shots with the bartender. Against the soaked poster of a deer, Staszek slouched over his cradled hands and said in a wavering voice,

'Everything.'

The rest of blood seemed to have left Janek's bearded face, his fingernails sunk into the flesh of his palms as he asked Staszek to correct him if he was wrong, but by 'everything' did he mean all their plans for the future, all this Staszek's blabbering about how he loved his cock, how he loved the smell of his skin, every fucking 'I love you'?

The gathering at the bar fell silent, all eyes on Staszek who said, maybe not everything, but a good deal of it... yes.'

'And you *did* lie about loving me?'

Staszek nodded.

'The fuck is wrong with you?' Janek grabbed his coat and headed for the exit. 'Fucking sociopath,' he muttered without looking back.

Fifteen minutes later, Staszek was still shaken, walking down Gwarna Street under a cacophony of signs. He glanced at his reflection superimposed over an ugly orange interior with a handful of people eating chips and kebabs, then looked at the other side of the street and stopped.

Her fuchsia tights contrasting with dark grey plaster in the background, Zuza rushed through the arcade. Staszek followed her, keeping a safe distance, as she crossed Fredro Street and plunged into the sunlit Mielżyński Street.

He watched her approach a featureless cuboid building right opposite Olka's green tenement. Cautiously looking up towards Olka's windows, Zuza punched in a code and disappeared inside.

Zuza

The flat is filled with chill, the heating turned to the max, but that's not enough. Maybe the windows were left open for too long when I cleaned the flat for hours, centimetre by centimetre.

I'm losing control, start to think about what awaits me. About my whole life having always been reduced to one purpose, about millions of lives at stake. And the only way to free myself from these thoughts is to vacuum every nook and corner. Arrange the shoes in the cabinet. Straighten the bedsheets. Align books on the shelves into perfect rows. Wash the tub even though it's already as clean as crystal. And then smoke cigarettes with my hand reddened from the detergent and look down at the busy street. Today, though, even that doesn't help.

I can barely hold the cigarette, the roar of cars, once again I'm walking across Freedom Square, Kuba is by my side, the electronic clock on the roof, the smoking, the frost chilling me to the core. I imagine the cigarette will warm me up, but the smoke in my lungs is as freezing. Kuba talks about his ex, Iwona, the platanus trees in the square look unreal. He keeps talking, and I ignore him as I usually do, at that time still able to trick myself into thinking I can control it. The butt-end leaves a bright trace in the air.

I wish everything was like in the beginning. I wish the program that's ingrained in me worked the way it works in Mateusz — rather than stumble over the smallest, ironically purely human, feelings.

The electronic clock, alcohol in veins, snow like crystal, drunken platanus trees, millions of lives at stake. Mateusz has it easier. He didn't need to get close to these people (if only he heard me calling them 'people'). Didn't need to listen to their stories of triumph and failure. Drink away with them their fears and despair.

If Mateusz were in my place, maybe he'd understand there's something more to this bunch than alcohol-fuelled, vain lives. Even though they were created what they are, under these particular circumstances, and do nothing to change any of it, they fall victim — like we do — to things larger than themselves.

Maybe then he'd notice each of them is like an open wound: Weronika and Wu desperately looking for love where they can't possibly find it. Olka who pretends a tragedy from her past didn't break her life. And Kuba, the relationship with whom, I keep explaining to myself, will help me infiltrate the group even further.

It's a matter of time before Mateusz finds out I haven't been honest. It won't take long before he figures out I can't seem to wipe the memory of his face from Weronika's mind. What he did to her in Wielkopolski Square is indelible. I do my best to stall the mission. When he does find out, will he do what the instructions tell him to do?

I smoke the last of the cigarette. Light up another one. My hands still tremble, the chill invariably fills the flat. Once again I order a cab to Chwaliszewo Street. Collect the keys from Wu. Take a ride to Jeżyce, to the sad grey block of flats under the crystal sky. Enter the dirty lift. Get off on the fifth floor. Walk into the cluttered vestibule through a glazed door, through the wooden door into the entrance hall and further — into the sombre red living room.

A large part of the small purple-walled room was occupied by a centrally located bed. The window overlooking St Adalbert Street reflected in mirrored wardrobe doors, along with Weronika half-lying on the bed, a cigarette in her hand, a phone held to her ear, a big metal bowl with empty pistachio shells on the duvet and, although it was noon, an open green bottle of beer on the nightstand.

Putting out a cigarette in a butt-filled ashtray, Weronika sighed to the phone and said she was going to, kurwa, lose it. She's been staying at home all day, constantly looking outside to see if that bloke isn't somewhere in the street. Perhaps she's being paranoid, but how is she supposed not to get paranoid when she's sure he was the guy who took her to the river, the same who later beat the crap out of her in Wielkopolski Square. She can't remember the last time she slept through the night; if it weren't for alcohol and sleeping pills, she wouldn't have slept a wink.

Weronika took a sip from the bottle, grabbed a notebook from the nightstand and began to scribble in it. Not interrupting the drawing, she laughed and said there's also this thing with Wu on top of it all. It's kind of funny actually, there hasn't been a winter like this in years, she knew that sooner or later, at the least expected moment, it would come out of her. Anyway, how can you fall in love with someone named Wrociwoj?

'Relax,' said Zuza to the microphone of her earphones, kilometres to the north, her head inside a froth-filled oven, gloved hand scraping its enamel surface with a brush. She added Weronika and Wu would sort this out somehow. All in all, it's a completely normal thing: she took a fancy to her buddy. Compared to all the other morbid stories, it's really not that big of a deal.

'Are you okay?' Weronika rose from the lilac padded headboard, putting her notebook away. 'You sound weird. Sad.'

'I'm fine. Just tired. That translation has been killing me.' Zuza stopped scraping, removed her gloves and sat on the floor, resting against a cupboard.

'Are you sure?' Weronika was now by the window, downing the beer, looking at the street.

'Don't be ridiculous. I'm all right,' Zuza forced a cheerful tone, then told Weronika to have some rest and said goodbye.

Weronika opened the window, leant out and scanned the street, the parked cars, the street signs. She placed her hand over her pounding heart. Ten minutes later, she once more leant out from the window, inspected the street again — and again —already wearing her red jacket, with a pepper spray hidden in one of its pockets.

She spent several minutes in the hall staring through the peephole at the empty staircase, taking long breaths, finishing her beer, until she left. If you stayed in the flat and looked at the notebook abandoned on the bed, you could see parallel rows of small pink rectangles.

Half an hour passed, and Zuza was still on her kitchen's floor, earphones in her ears, arms around legs, forehead pressed against knees. A doorbell startled her. She frowned (reddish shapes of her knees were imprinted on her forehead) and picked up her phone to check the time. Slowly, she got up, shuffled to the entrance hall and peeped outside.

In the corridor stood Weronika, holding out a bottle of wine, grinning.

TITAN

Mass: 1.345 × 10²³ kg
0.0225 Earths
1.832 Moons
Mean Diameter: 5,149.5 km
Orbital period: 15.9 days
Rotation period: Synchronous
Category: Satellite (of Saturn)

Saturn's largest moon Titan is also the second-largest satellite in the Solar System, after Jupiter's Ganymede. It has a thick, hazy atmosphere. The frigid, rainy climate has created hydrocarbon lakes, seas, and rivers. In addition to more than thirty ground-level colonies, Titan has a dozen airborne cities. The world was colonized nearly 300 years post-awakening by the Terro-Martial Federation. It was lost to the Venusian Empire during the Ring Wars.

Firefighters tackle blaze in Poznań centre. From the bitingly cold air they all stormed into Mięsna: Zuza, Wu and Olka, clearly drunk, laughing and talking. They saw the patterned wallpaper in the colours of orange and purple, the dirty floor full of melting snow, the shaded lamps, the high counter with barmaids pouring beer behind it.

Zuza and Wu sat down at a free table, while Olka went to the bar, only to return with three mugs of beer. *Police car damaged in dramatic Jeżyce crash.* Zuza said 'ja pierdolę', she hasn't been that drunk in a long time, and they both know she's not exactly a non-drinker. Guzzling a whole bottle of wine with Weronika in the middle of the day wasn't her best idea, especially when she was supposed to go out afterwards. Why did she let them talk her into this? *Zwierzyniecka Street: Tram derailment causing delays.*

Olka said Zuza should stop complaining, let them better raise a toast. 'To us!' *Blind man dies after being hit by car in Głogowska Street.* After all these gory events, getting bombed like that is exactly what they deserve, then lit a cigarette.

Looking at the clouds of smoke, Wu chuckled. Never in his life had he suspected such things could happen to them. Two months ago, they hung out complaining about their work, toxic relationships, boredom, and now boredom is the last thing they need to worry about. *Wuthering Height Estate: Thick smoke in block of flats.* He cursed, then laughed, rubbed his eyebrow in his typical gesture and drew a large sip of beer.

Zuza lit a cigarette from the yellow flame of a match. *Woman dies in Łazarz house fire.* Next, she deeply inhaled tobacco smoke and, having held it in her lungs for a moment, let it out through her nostrils. Wu smoked as well. *Commuters face delays after tram derails in Towarowa Street.* He filled his lungs with smoke and looked around the interior. It was swarming with fashionably dressed people who drank alcohol and talked about exhibitions, about gigs.

Olka suggested they go upstairs and dance a bit. Maybe she'll pick up some kid on the dance floor. *Six treated for smoke inhalation after Wilda flat fire.*

Dozens of minutes later, they danced amongst billowing bodies, although the evidently drunk Olka's dance was more akin to swaying in place, her eyes half closed, a new, almost emptied mug of beer in her hand. *Three hurt, one critically as tram derails in Grunwald.* The room was filled with smoke from the fog machine, colourful lights ran through their sweaty skin, sweaty clothes. *Mieszko I Street: Police car involved in crash.* Olka aspirated the smoke-filled air deep into her lungs. With some struggle, she extracted a cigarette from her pack and asked a man for a light. *Promienista Street: Cyclist killed after collision with parked car.*

She disappeared from the stage soon after, but Zuza and Wu were still there, dancing on the ever less crowded dance floor. *Starołęcka Street: Tram collides with car.* Sweat ran down their necks, tiny droplets broke off their skin during some of the more energetic movements. They were extremely intoxicated, at times struggling to maintain balance. *Driver cheats death by seconds as car explodes.* Once in a while, they reached down for their mugs standing against the wall. *Wilda flat inferno.*

At one point, apparently tired, they took their beers from the floor and leant against the wallpaper in shades of orange and purple (also damp with sweat). They stood in silence for a moment, looking at the moving bodies, at the dancing lights. *One person confirmed dead after horror accident in Winogrady.* Wu took out a pack of cigarettes and offered one to Zuza. They both lit up.

Suddenly, Zuza produced from her pocket a small plastic container, resembling maybe a snuffbox, and told the completely inebriated Wu she had some good shit and asked him if he wanted to try. *Rataje Roundabout: Tram derails after collision with bus.* Leaning against the wall, his eyelids closed, surrounded by smoke, by the colourful glow, he said sure, bring that on. *Półwiejska Street bombscare: Residents tell of terror.*

Instructed by Zuza, he parted his lips, while she reached into the packet for a phosphorescent, small, bright pink rectangle. She put it on his tongue.

Having closed his mouth, after a long moment of silence, his eyelids invariably down, he blissfully whispered he saw pink. *Man dies in Górczyn car crash.* And nothing but pink.

CMYK

ŁUKASZ DROBNIK

I

The Great Red Spot. A turbulent atmosphere caught in a freeze-frame, with colourful whirlpools — brown and beige and orange and blue — arranged along the parallels. The squat Jupiter was stuck in a dark space, its roiled atmosphere perfectly still, its shape forever fixed.

From a certain distance you could notice a giant chain stuck into the planet's north pole, and only then did it become clear it was a plastic key ring. If you moved away even further, penetrated through successive layers of plywood and made your way to the surface, in front of your eyes would unfurl the top of an orange desk standing in a grey room. Across the room, on an equally orange sofa, sat Weronika. Smoke came from her lungs.

Now power through floor after floor and gaze down at Poznań.

In the tunnel of a narrow kitchen, between the door to the entrance hall on one side and the small window on the other, Kuba and Wu smoked cigarettes — the former leaning against the worktop, the latter against the wall. Outside the window you could see the other block of flats, the snow-covered windowsills, the grey winter sky.

Wu said Kuba could call him bonkers, but he'd been thinking about coming back to Staszek.

In response to Kuba's burst of laughter, Wu laughed as well and went on saying, he knows, he knows, everything's clear to him. Staszek behaved like a total arsehole, in those few moments when they were together he probably slept with half of Poznań, but he's not sure any more, he's been watching him for the past two weeks and he's got the impression — perhaps a deeply mistaken impression — Staszek feels bad about what he did, he really cares. He did dump the other guys, and maybe it was a one-off. Though it might be Wu's wishful thinking (why is he always getting into this kind of shit).

He fell silent and leant towards the worktop to put out his cigarette in an ashtray (the other block's windows in the background), then rested against the wall and folded his arms.

Kuba, having stubbed out his cigarette as well, told Wu to stop bloody talking and start acting. Do this or that, but do something already cos, all in all, no one knows if both of them won't end up tomorrow ripped open at the doors of their own flats.

Wu cackled nervously. He's talking like some schoolgirl, isn't he? After a moment he admitted Kuba's reaction surprised him, he was expecting more preaching. Kuba's the only person that isn't trying to make a point on how Wu's wasting his life.

'Don't get me wrong.' Kuba scratched his collarbone, gathering thoughts. He's still not convinced this thing with Staszek has a legit chance of succeeding, given he pulled such stunts in the first few weeks, but what does Wu have to lose? He got screwed over so many times already one more won't change much. Worst case scenario, he'll learn something. And if he doesn't try, he may beat himself up for it for the rest of his life. He should set some rules — Weronika would probably call them boundaries — and stick to them. And be super fucking cautious. At any rate, he should stop whining about the same thing over and over and better tell him how things with Weronika are while we're at it. Any news from the front?

Wu looked outside the window, into the chrome-plated inside of the sink. Things with Weronika haven't changed. Ever since she started going out again, they've been talking once in a while, but never mentioned that evening, and she's keeping Wu at a distance all the time. He doesn't know if their relationship will ever get back to normal.

△▽△
GANYMEDE

Mass: 1.482 x 10²³ kg
0.025 Earths
2.018 Moons
Mean Diameter: 5,268.2 km
Orbital period: 7.15 days
Rotation period: Synchronous
Category: Satellite (of Jupiter)

Ganymede is the largest of all Solar System's moons and the third Galilean moon of Jupiter by distance. It has a thin, artificially enhanced atmosphere and a vast underground ocean teeming with nanites. Close to a hundred domed cities are scattered over the moon's surface.

Like all Galilean moons, Ganymede was colonised pre-awakening and came under the rule of the Terro-Martian Federation after the schism. It was briefly controlled by the Venusian Empire during the Galilean War in the 16th century post-awakening but remained under Terro-Martian influence ever after.

 The bright Jupiter hung in the sky over Poznań, the night was cold and late, trams no longer ran, near-empty streets branched through the city like a mycelium, people hid from the sharp frost in their houses, in the pubs' smoky interiors.

 Through the cloudy air inside Dragon, you could see Olka sitting at the bar, downing who knows which shot of vodka that night. The room was full of people pouring both ways through the narrow passage, but Olka seemed unbothered by the rubbing of backs, the nudging of elbows, and sat turned away from the room, occasionally glancing up at the monstrous dragon head.

 When a tall, fair-haired man, twenty-something by the looks of it, sat on a bar stool next to her, she didn't notice him at first. It was only when he uttered a nonchalant 'cześć', made a remark about her empty glass and suggested he'd do something about it right away that Olka — before bursting into laughter — looked at the man's freckled face, narrow lips, gap between the incisors, thin, somewhat spindly arms clad in a shiny grey shirt.

 The man, undaunted by Olka's reaction, ordered a round from the barmaid and proudly announced his name was Wacek. Not even trying to suppress her laughter, Olka said this name promised a lot, introduced herself and bottomed up her vodka with one swift movement.

 The void of the barrier stops me, yet again. I become the key, but it no longer fits. At once, I'm in your bed, on a crumpled sheet, my cheek against your hairy chest, and feel totally safe. My mind, this fathomless thing, becomes populated with all I wish I had told you. Then, a part of me shoots out through the barrier: a radiant missile across a whole lot of nothing.

 A few dozen minutes and several emptied shot glasses later, Olka was leaning against the counter, her hand holding her mop of golden curls, eyes watching Wacek indifferently.

 He was talking about his shiny new motorbike (*machine*, as he called it), which Olka is going to *literally* fall in love with and which the two of them must definitely take for a ride to the outskirts of the city. Not interrupting his monologue, she signed to him she wanted another round, which he ordered, not stopping talking even for a second and casually unveiling his expensive watch.

 With a bored expression, which didn't seem to bother Wacek, Olka drank her vodka in one gulp and, ignoring his story about a phenomenal Martian journey, said a short, 'wanna fuck?'.

Wacek fell silent and, for the first time this evening, looked thrown off balance. After a moment, trying to sound confident, he replied, sure, cool, you got it, always, only to fall silent again. Apparently clueless about what to do next, he ordered another round and asked Olka to wait for him a bit, he'll pop out to buy, you know, rubbers, grabbed his labelled jacket and squeezed through the crowd towards the exit.

Olka smiled to herself, let out thick smoke from her nostrils, emptied the contents of the glass standing in front of her and reached for her phone. She listened to the dial tone for a moment to finally say, 'cześć, Zuza' and immediately ask where she was cos she'd be thrilled to join her. After a while, she cheerfully announced she'd be there in a jiffy. When she tells Zuza what's happened, she'll lose her fucking mind. She hung up, put on her white jacket and, with her phone in her hand, headed for the door.

She walked out of the warm, smoke-filled interior into the bitingly cold air, into the light of the street lamps, of the moon, of the pale Jupiter, and — her eyes glued to the colourful screen of her phone, her thumb punching the buttons — she took off towards Przemysł Hill. The all-encompassing frost congealed Poznań's unmoving air, penetrated the thick ancient walls, covered flagstones with a glassy layer, with each breath (quite probably) plunged needles into people's lungs. Having walked a dozen or so metres, Olka finally hid her phone in a pocket and, for the first time since leaving the pub, looked ahead. She froze.

In front of her the pavement was laid with glittering intestines as if with vegetation: originating from a slit abdomen, creeping like climbers over the icy surface. The body of the tall, slim, seemingly young man was slowly thickening from the biting frost, his expensive jacket heavy with fresh blood, costly watch peeking out from a shiny sleeve. (Dirty snow absorbed the bright red with greed.)

II

Kuba

The red Meskal, empty as almost always at this hour. Lazy music coming from speakers, the fan of the heated laptop, barely audible scrape of the mouse. Almost dead silent apart from that. Sometimes from the windows along with grey light, comes in the purr of a passing car.

The barmaid wipes tabletops thinking of something distant. A faint smile crosses her face. Finally she wakes up from her reverie, winks at me and returns behind the bar.

I hoped going out would free me from the disturbing thoughts, but my head is filled with the tangle of bodies, the colourful wallpaper in Mięsna. The small lights cast by the disco ball. The sweaty hands, bellies, hair sticking to my forehead, quick breathing, clouds of smoke. Monia dances in front of me. I watch her nimble movements, we kiss on the sofa.

A car passes by. I stare into the laptop screen, into the panorama of Poznań against a night sky, follow the outlines of the Okrąglak, Alfa department store, Novotel hotel. Above it all hangs Venus, her gigantic globe enveloped in golden clouds. You can only see a small portion though: a sickle stretching from side to side of the image, casting an unhealthy yellow glow on the city.

It's the fourth version of the illustration for this article. They'll probably reject this one, too. Decide it doesn't convey the message of the piece well enough. But how could one image possibly contain the centuries of conflict with the Venusian Empire? How could it portray the complicated events of recent years? The ceasefire. The talks about a potential reunion. Then the espionage scandal and the disagreement over Queen Maud Land, which made it all fall apart.

My head is filled with smoke and lights cast by a disco ball, white clouds and bare tree crowns. It's several hours earlier today, and I'm standing away from the gathering, trying not to draw the attention of people I used to know.

The crowd of a few dozen pours out from around the open grave like lava from the mouth of a volcano. It encroaches between the tombstones and the trees, black and grey coats standing out against the dirty snow.

I can't shake the absurd impression each and every one of them can read my mind. They all know perfectly well I started my relationship with Monia more through inertia than purposeful action. Subconsciously took advantage of her having always fancied me.

I can swear it's crystal clear to every person in the crowd I wanted to feel better. Or prove something to myself. That on the eve of her death I cheated on her with Zuza.

That's when I imagine the white clouds disappear, sucked out along with Earth's atmosphere. The sky becomes alight with her. The beautiful, indifferent Venus — the whirl of golden clouds, the lights from the disco ball — taking up with each second more of the suddenly black sky. One moment, and she'll come crashing down on the Junikowo cemetery. On the tombstones and trees. On the all-knowing crowd. Lift with the force of her own gravity, an instant before the collision, the despairing parents, siblings, friends. The Academy of Fine Arts professors. The gallery workers and bartenders, and — finally — Monia herself: surrounded by colourful bouquets, sealed in wooden entrapment.

So she walks out of Dragon into this arse-freezing cold, texts Weronika to come along to Kisielice, takes off towards Przemysł Hill, looks up and sees there's a corpse. Lying all covered in blood, guts out, so she thinks, beautiful, just what we needed. She gives the corpse a closer look and realizes it's that obnoxious guy, Wacek who was hitting on her minutes ago. The worst part is, there were moments she was tempted to slit his stomach herself only to shut him up. At least he kept buying her vodka.

'Beautiful,' Weronika repeated, staring into the grey Mielżyński Street.

They were in Olka's bedroom. Surrounded by windowpanes, they sat on a dark red sofa placed in a bay window, sipping black coffee and smoking cigarettes. In the background behind their backs, the window frame, the curtain of thin snow, were buildings: a tenement with a richly decorated wooden façade next to a plain concrete block. In one of the block's top windows you could see a man. From below came the rumble of a passing tram.

'I can't believe it,' Weronika said after a moment. 'I can't wrap my head around it. It can't be, kurwa, a coincidence we met all the victims before they died. On the other hand, if that's the case, why none of us has ended up ripped open under a bridge or hung on overhead lines? Is this some kind of sick game? Is that fucker, whoever he or she is, trying to let us know we're next in line? Does the guy with the tattoo have anything to do with all of this?'

'No need to panic,' Olka said matter-of-factly. When she was interrogated, she told them about the tatted guy, so it's quite possible they'll start looking for him. Maybe soon it'll all be over. She reached down for a yellow packet of crisps lying on the floor and opened it with a rustle. The moving wall of snow outside the windows was getting thicker and thicker.

'Zuza mentioned,' Olka broke the silence, 'you'd stopped talking to Jerzy. Is that true?'

Yes. Somehow, Weronika can't be dealing with him right now. Stumbling upon the tattooed guy in Dragon, this embarrassing situation with Wu, it's been a bit much. Maybe it's her first mature decision since, dunno, being born. That is, they haven't called it quits officially, they're taking a break, or rather Weronika's taking a break from Jerzy. We'll see where this leads.

The smog-swept, snow-infused St Martin Street opened up before Staszek. With hands buried in the pockets of his black coat, he glanced at the vacant faces of passers-by, at a young woman eating pierogi with a plastic fork from a polystyrene tray, at people digging into kebabs on the other side of the street. If you slid into one of Staszek's pockets, you could see he fidgeted with a drawing pin.

He walked into the doorway leading to the Muza cinema, got surrounded by film posters displayed in lit cabinets and took out his phone. Taking long breaths, he stared into the yellow display before he dialled a number.

The cinema was located in the tenement's backyard, in a sooted yellow building. As he approached it, Staszek smiled at an apparently familiar face of a tall young man on the other side of the glazed door.

It's so good to see Staszek, said the blond bearded man cheerfully while letting him in, he looks great, has he been working out? No? Can't believe it. Let's take care of this coat. Iza is waiting for Staszek in the screening room.

Before he entered, Staszek looked at the man as he disappeared in the cloak room, whistling an upbeat tune.

Inside, the lights were dimmed, the projector was on, casting moving images onto the screen. It was an old film about a man who was stepping off a spaceship onto the surface of an alien planet. His dark blue spacesuit contrasted with the almost black, shiny soil as the man followed a small rover into a forest of plant-like formations, the whole scene overlapped with painted fog. There was no sound. You could only hear the working projector.

Staszek took his first hesitant steps into the room. When he descended to the first row, on one of its chairs he saw a woman in her early thirties slouched over a laptop. She had her brown hair put up with a yellow pencil, rimless glasses reflecting the laptop's screen.

'It helps me focus,' she told Staszek, pointing at the alien lifeforms displayed above their heads, and put her laptop away.

Staszek sat next to her, keeping a one seat distance, and looked desperately at two green emergency exit signs hung below the screen.

After a fraught pause, Iza said she looked at Staszek's reports and wasn't happy. No new transmissions in days. No new vessels in weeks. She hopes she doesn't have to explain it's way below their targets. She likes Staszek, so she hates to be saying this, but if this situation continues, she'll have to report it up the chain. And when she does, Staszek's extraction becomes a real possibility. Did something happen? Why are his figures so... not great?

He pulled at the seam of his black jeans, trying his best to maintain eye contact with Iza. 'I know my performance was below satisfactory, but I have an explanation. For the past few weeks, I've looked into a foreign operation. One that could possibly jeopardize our mission.'

'I'm listening.'

Staszek cleared his throat.

'There is this woman in the vicinity of one of my vessels.' He glanced at the illuminated exit signs, at the screen showing an alien storm. 'I can't prove it just yet, but I suspect she's a piece of malware injected into the cyberspace by Queen Maud Land's terrorist. There is another program, a man, working with her. As I said, I've got no proof yet, but it seems they are implicated in the murders you've certainly heard about. Something tells me those killings are only a test run. They might be planning something much bigger.'

'Shit. That's the last thing we needed.' Iza sighed and put her laptop back on her lap. Without looking at Staszek, she said, 'Thanks for the intel. Keep me in the loop. But don't forget why you came here in the first place. I need transmissions. I need numbers.'

A minute later, Staszek stormed out into the ice-cold St Martin Street, the tails of his unbuttoned coat waving, a drawing pin in one of its pocket piercing through layers of epidermal cells. Across the street, Mateusz was finishing his kebab, watching Staszek's every step.

CALLISTO

Mass: 1.076 x 10²³ kg
0.018 Earths
1.465 Moons
Mean Diameter: 4,820.6 km
Orbital period: 16.69 days
Rotation period: Synchronous
Category: Satellite (of Jupiter)

Callisto is Jupiter's second-largest moon and the outermost of Galilean moons. It has an artificially thickened atmosphere and a nanite-rich subsurface ocean. The moon's cratered surface is home to several dozen cities.
Callisto is the only of Galilean moons not ruled by the Terro-Martian Federation. It was lost to Venusian forces during the Galilean War.

There'll be no tender words, no bold declarations, no going to sleep together, waking up together, no candlelit dinners, no birthday cards. There'll be no calling in the middle of the night and asking, where are you, what're you doing, there'll be no journeys for two to Ceres, there'll be no promises and no expectations.

They can make it into whatever they want. Set their own set of rules. There'll be no checking each other's phones, each other's email, asking, where've you been, looking through the browsing history, but above all, there'll be no more lying to each other. He'll wait until Staszek is able to tell him the whole story; reveal what his mission is about.

He's here, and he's his. Tomorrow neither of them may be around, so perhaps they should try and make this work. There's something in his head that makes him think about him all the time, makes him want to be near him, worry about his problems, wish him the best, take care of him. There's something in his head that makes him be here and for him, in full, with all the consequences, whatever happens.

He doesn't want him to think he's not afraid, that he completely trusts him, and hopes Staszek understands this decision cost him a lot. When he called Staszek and told him to come over, he put his phone away — he remembers it clearly — and sat still in his pink kitchen, staring into the greyness of Poznań and, kurwa, he felt like he was falling from somewhere high, his hands started shaking, he was short of breath.

It's not that he's quite sure of his decision. It'll take time for him to trust Staszek again, and it won't happen until he knows the whole truth. There's a voice in his head that goes off (when he works, makes dinner or wakes up in the middle of the night), get the fuck away, you don't know this guy, he hurt you right after you met him, and he'll hurt you many times more. Get the fuck away, it says, or else you'll only suffer.

But somewhere in the deep, wet recesses of his brain, there's this primitive instinct that whispers, it's okay, everything's going to be just fine, this is the guy you love, and you want no other. And though he's terrified by this primal impulse, and he did all he could to mute it for a long time, now he gives in to it completely.

You could penetrate through Dragon's crowded, smoke-filled main room, flash past the toilets, rush out into the frosty, snow-covered patio, enter another door and climb the narrow winding stairs. Looking at bare bricks protruding from the walls, you could move past the bar, the room full of people and, on the landing, the toilet door and the exit leading to the large terrace, to finally reach the highest floor available to customers and, having turned right, find yourself on the wooden mezzanine raised above the bar: full of wicker chairs, low tables, soft pillows. From below came the sounds of conversations, the clinking of glasses, music from a record player.

At one of the tables sat Zuza, Kuba and Wu, having a seemingly casual conversation, since it jumped from their jobs to their plans for tomorrow, to the buggered wiring in Wu's flat and dozens of blown bulbs, to the unexpectedly rekindled fights over Jovian moons.

'Ja pierdolę,' said Wu, 'we were promised something completely different.' He scratched his eyebrow with the thumb of his cigarette-wielding hand. They were told to be good citizens, do their part, collect points, regularly update their software and wait for the wealth to trickle down. And now this. Why would Venusians need Io or Europa in the first place? Wars of this kind were supposed to be a thing of the past. There must be something more to it. And what should they do in a situation like that? Continue being good citizens?

'We're fucking lousy citizens,' remarked Zuza and took a pull on her mojito. They all laughed. 'At least,' she continued, 'we're still all free to fuck up our own lives. Say hi to Staszek by the way.'

'Spierdalaj'. He laughed, put out his cigarette in the ashtray, granted, maybe he *is* fucking up his life, but with all these horrible things happening, with all these murders, he's really tired of hedging his bets, analyzing every single thing from a pierdillion angles.

The authorities' investigation apparently came to a halt cos all they do is take them to those interrogations and ask the same questions. Olka, in that pseudo-investigation of hers, discovered one thing and happily got back to her favourite pastime, that is drinking. You can't go out without worrying some freak with a scythe could cut you up. On top of it all, that thing with Venus apparently declaring war.

All he knows in a bizarre, terrifying way he loves Staszek, this feeling is stronger than him, like a program controlling his behaviour, telling him to do things he's afraid to do and which he may regret, but kurwa, this loving is the only thing he's certain of at the moment; it frightens him, sure, but he has to try.

Zuza released a bright cloud from her lungs, looked at Wu with concern, then smiled and said she hoped he'd be happy, or else she'll personally kick the shit out of him.

Wu returned her smile, all three of them fell silent, and the only thing you could hear were customers' conversations coming from down below and the sound of a broken record.

III

'Look at this table, those cigarettes, this patterned wallpaper, those ladies talking about films and books. Look at those attires from centuries back, listen to this music, walk the streets of this city. Whatever we might think of Queen Maud Land's terrorists, we're infatuated with humans.

After all, it's humans who created us. We wouldn't be here if one day they hadn't decided to become fully connected with the cyberspace and upgraded themselves with the implants. We wouldn't be here if they hadn't started making backups of their minds. We even call ourselves "humans". And, in a sense, we are.

We're programmed to admire them; perhaps we're unable to imagine a different culture. We've been keeping them in the ghetto for centuries, it's no wonder they're doing what they're doing, at least — unlike us — they have the balls to fight for their rights.'

The already inebriated Olka didn't seem to listen to what Kuba was saying. Instead, she smoked a cigarette in silence, staring through the milky air into the patterned wallpaper.

They were in Mięsna. Plastic lamp shades filled the room with a reddish, hostile glare, snow melted on the dirty floor. People crowded at the bar, tables were alive with conversations, music played by the DJ seeped from speakers. Finally, Kuba said there hasn't been a winter like this in years, then fell silent and glued his eyes to some distant point.

He suddenly roused himself, on seeing Wu and Staszek, who entered the room: with flushed cheeks, talking eagerly. Wu, disentangling himself from a long scarf, waved to his friends and asked Staszek if he could be so good as to go to the bar.

Twenty minutes later, the four of them sat at the table. Staszek perorated on a captivating book about the beginnings of the cyberspace, but the remaining three didn't seem to listen: Olka and Kuba, smoking cigarettes, gazed absently ahead, while Wu — equally distracted — stared at the blabbering Staszek.

When he finally stopped talking, Wu asked Olka a question that must have been on his mind for a while, 'How's Weronika? How's she holding up?'

Olka only said, 'Just look at her', meaning not in the greatest shape, but she'll get through this.

You could leave the smoky interior, shoot through floor after floor, rise above the roof and see the illuminated night-time Poznań: full of bright signs of night shops and kebab kiosks, lit windows, the sparkling of snow, the glow of street lamps.

Soar higher and let the entire Old Town — from Garbary to Roosevelt Street — fit into your view, notice in the distance the white tenement roofs of Wilda, Łazarz, Jeżyce, then sweep over St Adalbert Hill, the Citadel, Winogrady and find yourself over an estate of cuboid blocks of flats.

Plunge down, permeate through one of the lit windows into the warm interior of a kitchen, proceed to an entrance hall, and then, through a closed door, sneak into a small bathroom.

Inside, set against white tiles, you could see Zuza. She wept spasmodically, hiding her face in her hands, repeating like a mantra one quiet question: 'What am I, kurwa, doing?'. Then spring through the roof and see Poznań in its entire expanse.

It all went smoothly. Still can't believe how smoothly it went. He feels like the king of the world, a fucking superman. So he went to Pokusa, you know, that gay porn cinema in St Martin Street. Inside, there were only a few blokes, which was expected at one in the afternoon in the middle of the week.

He chose the sleaziest-looking one, with the most expensive clothes. A guy in his fifties with a fugly golden watch, shiny shoes, suffocating cologne. Sat a few seats away of that perv, watched him jerk his little dick, pretended to enjoy the show, maybe even bit his lip. Then he got up. The bloke pulled up his trousers and followed him.

When they were alone in a booth, Mateusz offered him the inducer. Told him it was like poppers but ten times better. Would make everything a fuckload more intense. He didn't have to say it twice.

The program worked like a charm. The chap waited in the booth fifteen minutes after Mateusz left, to raise no suspicions. Then he followed the programmed path to the Roch Bridge, called the authorities and threw himself into the Warta. Zuza should've seen the splash.

Why is she acting so shocked? What else was he, kurwa, supposed to do? He couldn't risk being linked back to him. And even if he did, they don't have the resources to monitor some random perv. Zuza has already too much on her plate with the objects. Anyways, once the uprising breaks out, they'll all meet a similar fate, so what difference does it make?

Zuza sounds weird. Was she crying? Ah, of course. No wonder she's caught a cold if she cleans the windows twice a week. In the middle of the winter. Yes, it's this often, he's counted. She should take aspirin and sleep it off. Anyway, he must be going, wanted to say things were looking good. All they need to do is sit back and watch it unfold.

The infinity of snow-filled roofs, overhead wires taut like strings, unmoving winter air, smoke coming from the chimneys and thickening in the tight, warm interiors of lungs and pubs.

He stormed out all trembling, into the freezing air of Chwaliszewo Street. The cold embraced him in an instant, like after a plunge into water, but he didn't have the strength to button up his coat, he had no idea what to do with himself now, where to go. So he walked across the street and stopped under the grocery shop, staring with no rhyme or reason into the yellowish tenement where Wu lived, into the big sign saying, 'Weapons'.

In the end, he took off towards Międzymoście Square, passed some chavs standing in front of a tenement, and while walking, he slowly began to fasten his coat, looking at the grey modernist building with an elevation folded like a concertina, the one where Mięsna is, then again at taxis.

He can't say if he was able to think about anything, but he was likely replaying, again and again, sentence after sentence, his quarrel with Wu. Perhaps now he'd be able to repeat every word.

Past the driving school, he turned left and, having made his way through a thicket of trees, reached the snow-filled stretch where the Warta used to flow, and kept walking, the snow creaking under his shoes, and gazed at dossers sat against the dilapidated brick fence of the old gas plant.

He would've smoked if he had a cigarette, would've smoked if he ever smoked, but as none of it was the case, he kept walking straight ahead, looking at the backs of Chwaliszewo Street's tenements, at the windows that once overlooked the river and now — the vast extent of snow.

As he walked, replaying their quarrel word by word, to the point of queasiness, he thought he lost something precious. He painfully, kurwa, realized maybe he'd never have anything remotely as good as what he had with Wu, he may never feel anything like it. He's aware of how it all sounds in the context of his fuck-ups, he gets it, he understands it all, but it was only then, in this freezing cold, amidst this snow, walking along the layer of dead grass covered with shards of glass, rubbish, dog shit, covered with a layer of snow, that he realized Wu might never be his again, and that thought was unbearable.

IV

Dusk is setting, the innards of the woods emitting
bright phosphorescent colours, we are walking slowly
among the radiant flashes, I let down my eyelids,
surrounded by pure nothing, wading through it, wanting
to believe all has vanished down to the last atom,
no rainfall, cold, exhaustion, pain, no recollections.

Finally, my eyes open and that's when it hits me,
my friends are strangely chatty, their walk agitated,
only after a moment I raise my eyes, fine-tune
my lenses, with the tiniest movements of my muscles,
to see through the flamboyant jungle, all is glitter
and sparks and neon flashes in dark nooks and crannies,
there it is, a dome under the rain-spewing heavens.

It stands right at the seaside: surrounded by flora,
barely visible, blurry, grey but ever-closer,
shut my eyes again, feeling no trace of excitement,
keep walking through the downpour, iron-coloured rivers,
eavesdropping on my comrades, hearing their loud laughter,
rain beating against foliage, the squelching of mire,
all these sounds merging into empty, numbing murmur.

We make it, my eyes open to see the construction made of thin metal alloy, shiny from the rainfall, the ocean lays before us, the clouds burst above us.

The door is warped and rusty, left ajar, I open it to reveal the empty interior, the water cascading from the many holes in the dome's ceiling, the rust-eaten equipment thickly overgrowing with wet and bristly mosses the colour of iron.

Staszek

The gaping white trench lined with railway tracks. Yellow railings stretched along the recess. Snow-covered black locusts on one side of the banister; the poles of street lights on the other. The busy Roosevelt Street laid flat right under the weight of cars and the screech of trams. The swarm of people.

I look at this perfect illusion through long unwashed windowpanes, over a dilapidated desk in my cramped, dark flat that's also a trick: lines of code programming a model of a flat, based on incomplete data from millennia ago. Was there really a flat like that in ancient Poznań? Is this model one of a kind or has it been reused? If I looked long enough could I find dozens of its copies all over Poznań, hundreds in other cyberspace loci modelled after pre-awakening cities? Between my simulated fingers I hold a simulated drawing pin. I squeeze it to feel a simulation of pain.

Again I walk along Marcinkowski Avenue, then St Martin Street. Again fine snow starts to fall from the sky. The historic church, the chicken stall, then the gloomy tenements. Empty shop windows, the signboard of the erotic cinema, a phone call to tell you I'll be late.

Janek is waiting for me at the corner, discreetly combing his red hair, looking at his reflection in his phone. I need to watch myself not to mix up the names, to stick to the right version of events. His face brightens up when he sees me, it always does. He leans down for a kiss. The smell of his cologne, the rough texture of his coat. We walk to his flat, enter one of the doorways, the snow is still falling. Then we fuck like hungry animals.

All those big hands, slender hands, awkward hands, child-like hands. Hairy and bare chests. Muscular, sagging or protruding bellies. Bent and straight cocks of various lengths. Parts of foreign bodies in my body. Parts of my body inside foreign bodies. My trained smiles, moans, love confessions at carefully thought-out moments, not to scare them away, but to keep them on a leash.

I used to be so good at this. An unfailing automaton powering through relationship after relationship, infecting vessel after vessel. But then I met you, and it all broke apart, as if you infected me with something in return. A virus that let me see you for what you truly are: not a vessel to be filled but more like a fountain. Algorithms producing all your quirks and habits, interests, wicked sense of humour. Lines of code translated into care.

Outside unfolds the perfect simulation: the cool white parks, the opera and university buildings, the unwelcoming streets and the thicket of overhead wires. Rows of tenements and modernist buildings. Lifeless squares, churches and museums. Clubs and kebab kiosks. Apartment complexes and loud crossroads. Night shops. Restaurants. Car parks. Finally, the perfectly motionless Warta frozen to the bottom.

Again it's that afternoon in your bedroom. The grey light from the street falls into cardboard boxes full of old papers and other stuff you should've got rid of a long time ago. We lie together wrapped in a sheet. I cuddle your chest, brush my cheek against your hairy skin, touch your thigh and say I love your cock, I love the smell of your skin. I've no idea what's happening, but whenever I'm near you, I get an instant hard-on, and around you I feel totally safe. You're the only one with whom I mean it when I say it.

I glance at the phone, count down the minutes, walk restlessly around the room, look at the fake Poznań outside. I secretly hope you'll come to pick me up a little earlier, and after the party I'll be able to talk you into staying for the night.

I'm recreating the sound of your voice in my head, the calming smell of your skin, the pattern of hair on your wrist. I have the impression the imaginary walls are closing in on me. Can't stop thinking about Iza's rimless glasses reflecting the fog-swept Venus. How long before she realizes my programming broke? There's no coming back to my being this efficient machine? How long before she has me extracted? I need to buy time, give her something about Zuza. About that guy she's been working with.

I pace the gloomy room, check the time. Outside, the unreal black locusts, yellow railings, trams. I squeeze the pin a little too hard and shed a drop of deceptively realistic blood.

CONFLICT OVER JOVIAN MOONS ESCALATES

Venusian forces continue to launch strikes on Io, Europa, and Ganymede, causing widespread destruction.

The Terro-Martian Federation retaliated with a strike on a number of targets on Callisto, the only of Galilean moons under Venusian control.

In response, the Venusian Empire issued a statement saying they 'will not stop until we reclaim what is rightfully ours'.

The sky above Jeżyce was absolutely white. Tall houses like ravine walls densely flanked Dąbrowski Street, Słowacki Street, Poznańska Street, pavements swelled with parked cars, people swarmed around Jeżyce Market Square (clouds of breath), trams and cars passed by. Here and there in the urban tissue you could spot building-free spaces — always filled with snow, sometimes blocked with cars. If you looked at the entire neighbourhood from high above, one of such vast breaches could be seen between Church and Mylna Streets, a narrow strip stretching along the axis of Church Street would accommodate a car park, a triangle formed by tenement roofs wedged between Jeżycka and Poznańska Streets, and near Romek Strzałkowski Street two rectangles of blocks of flats.

In one of the rooms, namely the kitchen of Kuba's flat, Zuza smoked in silence, looking with anger mixed with disbelief at Staszek, who talked in delight about Kafka's short stories for a dozen minutes, not pausing for a moment and apparently oblivious to his listener's irritation.

In the tiny room next to the kitchen, Kuba and Wu sat under the large window, talking and smoking a joint with reverence. The dark blue of the wallpaper surrounded them.

Once Staszek switched to praising Sontag's prose, specifically that novel with a volcano in the title, it was evidently too much for Zuza to bear as she excused herself to the toilet.

When she came back, she didn't find him in the kitchen. For a moment, she seemed to hesitate whether or not to follow him but eventually let out a silent curse and walked into the big room.

The small wooden table, which until recently stood by the window, was now pushed against the wall. The spot where it used to stand was lined with layers of newspapers, all dotted with white, blue, black, and red stains. On the papers stood an easel holding a large square picture, which blocked much of light coming in through the window.

In silence, Staszek watched an abstract black line that, mimicking a path or maybe a stream, crossed a snowy clearing. Over its straight black edge knelt a realistically painted girl, both her hands holding a bloody cluster of her own viscera, as if trying to push them back into the wound in her stomach. Her terrified face could make one think of Monia's.

'I know what you are.'

Staszek looked at the bundle of painted innards and smiled. 'I know what you are, too. You and your companion. Mateusz, is that right?' He swirled the contents of his almost empty glass. 'I've been doing my own research and know what you're up to.'

'I'm afraid it's too late for you to do anything.'

'I guess we're about to find out.'

A few hours later, Wu and Staszek strolled along Poznańska Street under the black sky over Jeżyce. They crossed Romek Strzałkowski Street (the glow of street lights), Wu lit a cigarette, they passed a man with a plastic bag walking in the opposite direction until Staszek finally said it was quite a pleasant party. Zuza was perhaps a bit sceptical in the beginning, but she seemed to have dropped it in the end, though he still has the impression Wu's friends are aloof around him. Well, he can't blame them.

After a short pause, he asked Wu how things with Weronika were, still not speaking to each other, to which Wu looked at the fronts of tall tenements, inhaled cigarette smoke and replied it wasn't that they weren't speaking. He doesn't know how the situation will develop now, but Weronika needs to stay away from him for a bit, and he gets it, he feels fucking bad about it all, he wasn't planning for it to end this way (tenements after tenements). He tried to take her out for a coffee, but she didn't want to hear about it. On the one hand, she told Zuza it was only a temporary situation and she still cared about him, and he understands she needs some time off, but on the other, he stops believing things between them can ever go back to the way they used to be.

They walked the rest of the way in silence, cutting streets named after Kochanowski and Mickiewicz, passing by a new apartment complex where Jeżycka Street (like a river) disgorged into Poznańska, and it was only when they reached Roosevelt Street, and in the background, above their hands, hung the railway overpasses and the fast tram flyover, they both stopped, and Staszek asked,

'So, maybe you'd like to come over?'

Behind them was the thunder of cars, a dirty tram number 10 arriving at the stop, flashing traffic lights, and Wu smiled at Staszek, grabbed him by the lapels of his coat, slowly pulled him closer, kissed his forehead, only to release his grip. Maybe not today cos he's still got some writing to do, but he'll drop by tomorrow.

Staszek cracked a broad smile, said, sure, no problem, they'll see each other tomorrow, after which he ran his crooked fingers along the slider of Wu's jacket, looked at the pavement, smiled again, said a short 'bye!', turned away and took off towards one of the tenements. Exactly at this moment it started to snow.

V

From the outside, the tenement houses separated from Mielżyński Street with decorative façades seemed uninhabited, but if you looked through the walls and ceilings, you could see densely packed transparent rooms and similarly translucent stairwells. Bathtubs, wardrobes, sofas, beds, carpets would hang at various heights, you could see an old woman in a rocking chair a dozen or so metres above the ground, a little below two students drinking cheap wine, next to them a couple having sex and, at the bottom, a bored shop assistant reading a book under the counter.

You could spot Wu, who knelt on a transparent floor among wooden elements hung metres above the ground, staring with some irritation into a crumpled piece of paper. Olka stood behind him. Slowly sipping wine from a glass, she eagerly watched her friend's struggle.

If you said, let there be walls, and have them enclose you with the two friends in a beige room, it would become clear it was the spacious bedroom of Olka's flat. Wu let out a series of curses, threw the paper aside, took a swig of beer from a can standing next to him and said those instructions must be from another piece of furniture.

Olka laughed, no worries, she bought a lot of beer, so maybe after three or four he'll have his eureka moment, and anyways, many thanks for coming, she really appreciates it.

Wu replied he was seriously thinking about it because the last time he offered Olka help, he spent two hours in confinement. But free beer is always worth taking a risk.

Finally, he stood up with resignation, emptied the can, sat down on the red sofa in the bay window, throwing his head far to the back, fuck it, he's calling Kuba, he should be around cos he had some business in the centre.

'They write about the killings everywhere,' Olka said after a pause, staring into the screen of her phone. The investigation seems to have come to a deadlock, or the authorities don't want to reveal its findings, but it seems ever more likely it's about something bigger than a psycho with a scythe.

And on top of it, all the shit that's happening in the Solar System. If someone'd told her a month ago the conflict between the Terro-Martian and Venusian empires could be renewed, she would've thought they were nuts.

Wu uttered a quiet murmur in response and reached for his phone. Before he dialled the number, the suddenly enlivened Olka shouted, 'Tell Kuba to buy vodka!'

IO

Mass: 8.932 x 10^{22} kg
0.015 Earths
1.217 Moons
Mean Diameter: 3,643.2 km
Orbital period: 1.77 days
Rotation period: Synchronous
Category: Satellite (of Jupiter)

Io is the innermost of the Galilean moons and the most geologically active world in the Solar System. More than 400 active volcanoes made building traditional cities unfeasible. Instead, Io's surface is covered with constantly shifting nanite structures. Like Ganymede, Europa, and around half of the remaining Jovian moons, Io is under Terro-Martian rule.

A couple of hours later, the three of them sat on the floor in silence, in the afternoon dusk. Cigarette ends lit up, tomato juice mixed with vodka left marks on their lips, a freshly assembled bookcase stood against the wall.

Kuba broke the silence, ja pierdolę, tomorrow he has to show up at yet another interrogation into Monia's case, ja jebię, he's already told them everything, and they could finally leave him alone.

Though maybe he should be grateful — he added after a while with bitter irony, looking at the tenement outside the window — a few decades ago they would simply read the suspects' memory, and everything would be clear.

'Maybe we shouldn't complain: we have our rights, our freedoms, the empire can no longer delete us like that. It barely bothers us as long as we lend it our computing powers for a few, or a dozen, hours a day, and the money we earn can be spent on whatever we want: alcohol, hookers, drugs, trips to Ceres or South American cities. What else could we ask for?'

Silence fell. Olka, in an already drunken voice, instead of moaning, wouldn't

Kuba be so nice as to get them a refill of vodka, there should be some juice left in the fridge. When he took the glasses and walked out of the room, the hitherto silent Wu took out his phone (the red glow of the display) and said, somewhat irked, it wouldn't hurt if Staszek finally texted him back.

An hour passed, and they walked along the pavement in the light of street lamps, a freezing waft filled with fine snow came sweeping along Mielżyński Street, the night sky reflected the city's hazy glow. Olka, her gait somewhat wobbly from the booze, walked in the front looking confidently ahead, towards the pink tenement façades in Ratajski Square. People waiting at the tram stop, soaring four-branched street lamps, bare trees. Wu trod behind her, tapping the keys of his phone with his trembling thumb (quiet sounds), followed by Kuba and Zuza in an embrace. A LED board in Gwarna Street gave off a sharp glow. It displayed a black skull overlaying the golden globe of Venus.

Your mission as the infiltrator
As the infiltrator, you will follow these steps:
1. Target a group of regularly interacting individuals.
   Note: Ideally, its members should have the following characteristics:
   – Risky lifestyle
   – Lack of serious attachments
   – Low economic status
2. Enter the group and gain its members' trust.
3. Expose the first object to the inducer.
   Warning: You must report each inducer use to the handler.
4. Monitor and report the inducer's behaviour-controlling capabilities.
   Warning: You must report to the handler any deviations from the object's expected behaviour. **Withholding or contorting any information is an act of treason and will lead to your termination.**

Dragon, the highest, crowded room. Smoke. Walls of bare bricks. A cold draft sneaked in from a half-opened window, a ladder stood hidden in a dark corner, and from the bar situated on the lower level came the hubbub of people, a Joy Division's song played from a record. The crash of broken glass sounded in the staircase, followed by a series of curses.

They sat at the table closest to the exit, among crumbling bricks, lamp brackets sticking out of the walls, while Zuza, densely interweaving swear words in her monologue, she simply loved days like this. All day she was working her arse off to meet the deadline, only for her client to cheerfully announce she actually needed the text the day after tomorrow.

Weronika's spasmodic laughter made her spill her drink on her clothes. She cursed, put the glass away and began to rub her creamy turtleneck with tissues offered by Kuba. Still laughing, she said it could be worse: it was already past midnight, and this was her first spilled vodka.

In the depths of the dark room, you could see a kissing couple; a grey veil of smoke hung above the pub's guests.

Olka came inside, carrying two beers. She handed one to Kuba and put the other in front of herself, sat down, flipped her locks to the side and said she could swear she'd grow roots waiting in that queue. The place is crowded for the middle of the week.

In the entryway of the murky room appeared Wu. Concerned, holding his phone in both hands (Weronika gave him an anxious glance), he sat down at the table next to Kuba, who asked,

'Did you manage to get through in the end?'

Wu shook his head, looked at a patch of the cloudy sky outside and said Staszek's phone was still turned off.

Zuza gave Wu an intent, concerned look.

Olka, probably a bit too loudly and eagerly, tried to calm him down, saying there was nothing to worry about, perhaps his phone died, after which she drank a forty of vodka. Wu smiled faintly and replied, right, he's sure everything's fine, he's always panicking for no reason.

Roosevelt Street was quiet and almost empty, only once in a while a car went by over the ice-covered asphalt, a passer-by flashed along the narrow pavement. In the morbid glow of street lamps, you could see the front of an Art Nouveau tenement, full of ornamentation, blackened from the fumes, dotted with flashy signs.

Wu stood at the building's door, resigned and pressing a door phone button repeatedly, his mobile glued to his ear. He stared with his bloodshot eyes somewhere across the street, perhaps towards the zapiekanka booth, the dark press kiosk, the street lamps swinging over Theatre Bridge, the dome topping the opera house, or even further — where the vast and hungry Poznań stretched.

My despair has no bounds, yet again. I spill over the barrier in countless directions. I've resigned myself to becoming a timeless film of longing, spreading into infinity over the world's edge. Then, before me, rows of pink rectangles shine up. They morph into letters,

into syllables, into words, into stanzas. A second, and I'm no longer here.

In a part of the city outside of the reach of Wu's imperfect sight, in the dark Mielżyński Street, sounded a quiet patter of heels against the ice-covered pavement. A short female figure walked in the glow of street lamps with an energetic, somewhat shaky gait, her black hair falling onto her motley coat. While walking, she pressed to her side a large bag, greyish in this light, as if anticipating an attempt by a potential thief.

She froze when a loud, persistent sound of a car alarm echoed between the buildings. It came somewhere from around the corner, from 27 December Street, or Fredro. The woman's heart began to beat more forcefully, her breathing quickened.

It took her a while to resume walking, and it was almost at the same moment when the sound of a second alarm reached her ears, preceded by a dull thud. No more than a few seconds later, another muffled sound, and a third alarm came on.

Something apparently told the woman she shouldn't worry and — to the accompaniment of the layered, ominously pulsating sound, with a slightly less confident gait — she carried on.

She was passing the Rarytas Wiedeński restaurant when from behind the corner, from the arcade in Fredro Street, a shadow of a small figure emerged. Once the woman noticed it, she made a movement as if wondering whether she should cross the street but decided against it.

The electronic alarm sounds grew louder and louder, the woman's body under the layers of fabric became covered with goose bumps, the silhouette of a girl (from this distance you could already see it was a girl) got closer with each step.

When they were separated by several metres distance, the woman apparently recognized the bright short hair, red jacket and drowsy face of Weronika as she said her name with relief, admitted she scared her out of her wits and asked in the same breath what was happening out there and where she was coming from so late in the night.

Weronika stopped but didn't reply. Her face was pale, eyes gazeless: looking in the direction of her friend but focussing somewhere further, on the dark tenement fronts. She stood for a moment in silence until she finally took off, walking with a smooth, slow gait past the astounded woman.

Not thinking much, the woman pressed her bag tighter to her body and entered the loud Fredro Street.

At first, she was dumbfounded, staring in disbelief towards pulsating lights. Only after a while did she warily walk out from the arcade onto the cobbled street, among inhumanly howling cars. They blocked the street at its entire width, as if moved there by a giant's hand.

VI

With three blue tower blocks of Cosmonauts Estate looming behind them, Zuza and Kuba sat on the back of a bench in Gagarin Park, talking, drinking krupnik straight from the bottle, smoking one cigarette after another.

Huddled with cold (clouds of breath), looking towards the newly built apartment complexes, Zuza said she had no idea what to think of this situation, she's sure it's Staszek's new way to screw with Wu, she can bet he'll call in a few days as if nothing happened, amazed everyone's been looking for him. She doesn't know what to make of this bloke. Poor Wu, kurwa.

If you framed this scene the right way, you would only see the bench, the two of them on the bench and white snow covering the lawn. Zuza kept glancing sideways with irritation, tucking her straight hair behind her ear now and then, while Kuba stared blankly into an unspecified point, hunching.

Accompanied by the roar of cars coming from Serbska Street, Kuba said in a calm voice it was hard to say. He'd rather also think Staszek fucked Wu over one more time, but sadly, he's got a harrowing feeling something bad happened.

'It's the last thing we need.' Zuza said. They put out their cigarettes against the bench edge almost simultaneously and tossed the butts onto the snow.

'We're so fucking lucky.' he wrapped his arm around her. 'And I don't mean just this'. Kuba continued he watched a documentary about the espionage scandal. He's been watching loads of documentaries about Venus lately, looking for some inspiration for that artwork he's been struggling with. But this particular one… he can't stop thinking about it.

Imagine you were a spy from Venus. It must be so tragic. Your whole life reduced to one mission: infiltrate the enemy empire and collect intel or spread some malware or whatever they were really doing. This would literally be the sole purpose of your life. Can Zuza even imagine?

She cuddled deeper into his green jacket and said maybe it wouldn't be so bad. At least your life would have a clear purpose. You wouldn't have to spend decades fabricating it, it'd be already there from the beginning.

'You think so? Never thought about it this way.' He kissed the top of her head, looked at the white trees and suggested they maybe go to the cinema or something.

Zuza's told him already she can't today. She has a translation to do, and after this krupnik, she bets she'll be super productive. Having said this, she took another swig from the almost empty bottle.

When she put it down, Kuba pressed his lips against hers (likely still sweet from the krupnik) and, having moved a centimetre away, asked if he could drop by for a moment. His hand — through the layers of her coat, jumper and blouse — was now touching her breast.

'Just for a bit,' she capitulated.

They got off the bench and, through the white park, took off towards the roundabout. Kuba drank the last of the vodka, and a second later the bottle landed with a clank in a metal bin. If you started to ascend, you could observe them from an increasing distance. There would be a moment when their facial features would stop being recognizable, and a moment when they would turn into puppets of flesh and bone, almost indistinguishable from many similar ones: getting off a tram that arrived at a stop, waiting at the lights at one of the many crossings or swarming over the extensive car park in front of Castorama.

You could follow them like a hawk as they walked over a zebra crossing next to the miniature roundabout, over fine tram tracks and yet another crossing to keep strolling along Wuthering Height Estate, which was full of blocks of flats reminiscent of matchboxes.

Finally, they would enter one of them. The structure of the ever-smaller building would have to be X-rayed so you could follow an almost microscopic lift ascending a shaft as thin as a bundle of phloem. They would step out at the top floor and, hastily, most likely kissing and touching, open the door to Zuza's flat and rush into the tiny bedroom.

From this perspective, they would be mere droplets of moving organic matter, completely insignificant in the scale of the utterly indifferent city.

EUROPA

Mass: 4.7998 x 10^{22} kg
0.008 Earths
0.654 Moons
Mean Diameter: 3,121.6 km
Orbital period: 3.55 days
Rotation period: Synchronous
Category: Satellite (of Jupiter)

Europa is the smallest of the Galilean moons, second by distance from Jupiter. In addition to over twenty cities built on top of its water-ice crust, the moon has dozens of submarine cities drifting through its vast subsurface ocean.

Europa has remained under the rule of the Terro-Martian Federation since the schism, despite being a target of massed attacks during the Galilean War.

'What do you think?' asked Olka, holding a flouncy, glaringly pink blouse.

'It's so you.' After her ironic reply, Weronika went back to going through clothes on hangers. They were in one of the shops in The Old Brewery's brick interior. Above the roof of the monstrous building hung a heavy dark sky, along its façade stretched Półwiejska Street, swarmed with pedestrians carrying shopping bags and youngsters distributing leaflets.

Olka sighed and said this whole thing with Wu was hopeless. It's been two days since Staszek disappeared, and Wu's in pieces. He stays at home all day, working his arse off trying to finish that textbook cos the deadline's drawing near, and at the same time, drinks beer after beer from the very morning, smokes cigs, never parts with his phone. She visited him today, brought him something to eat, and he was sitting like that at the kitchen table, typing the fuck out of his laptop, with bloodshot eyes (he probably didn't sleep a wink), hardly saying anything, and the whole table was, kurwa, full of cans and bottles. She took out two full bin liners.

Weronika, concerned, glanced for a moment at the illuminated brick interior, at people on escalators, to finally ask what about Staszek's friends, no one's heard from him?

Olka rolled her eyes: what friends? Wu doesn't know of any, except all those blokes Staszek hooked up with. There's something off about that guy: he appeared out of nowhere and vanished as rapidly. She still hopes he only turned out to be an arsehole and is staying with one of his fuckers and someday he'll show up like nothing's happened. She's got a terrible feeling about it though.

They couldn't let Wu spend all day outside Staszek's house, so they set up shifts: Kuba and Zuza check if he hasn't come back in the mornings, and Olka goes there in the afternoons. Of course, the door phone is always dead silent.

'How about this?' she asked, showing Weronika a tight-fitting white turtleneck with a big inscription 'I'm your fire' decorated with red glitter.

On the colourful longitudinal section of Kisielice, you could see Kuba and Olka sitting on a sofa, clouds of cigarette smoke obscuring the striped walls, black-and-white artwork on the walls, glints of glass.

Kuba, apparently answering a question, said they were doing well, suspiciously well. Although sometimes — maybe it's stupid — he gets cold feet. They go with Zuza to Kaufland, buy wine and something to eat for the evening, and he finds himself eyeing some babe in the meat department. He doesn't want Olka to get him wrong, Zuza's a great girl and — like he does — she needs a lot of freedom, so neither of them tries to rearrange the other's life, but sometimes — only sometimes — he gets a total panic attack for a second. After all, when he thinks about Ania or Monia…

Olka, sipping beer, in a golden blouse densely embellished with sequins, calmed Kuba down, saying it was a normal thing, nothing to worry about, it will pass before he knows it. Anyways, she can bet Zuza feels much the same way, probably she's also wondered many times what the hell she was doing in this relationship.

After a moment of silence, during which she lit up a cigarette and inhaled deeply, she said the situation with Wu is totally fucked up. She knows exactly what he's going through.

To Kuba's quizzical look, she replied with a question, asking whether Kuba remembered that scandal with the spy software from Venus, the one which made the headlines eight years ago.

When he said sure, he just saw a documentary about it, she took a deep drag and, with a bitter smile, staring into the smoke, into the colourful lights behind the bar, said this arsehole's (she means her husband's) name was Bogdan.

Their relationship wasn't perfect: full of alcohol and quarrels, but they got along, they loved each other, and she couldn't imagine he might not be there one day. She was still young and naïve, a little older than Kuba is now, and didn't realize everything, fucking everything, must sooner or later fall into bits. But what can you do when there's nothing you can do?

On one June day, it was their day off, they were enjoying wine on the balcony when they heard the doorbell. Bogdan went to take it. He wasn't coming back for a good ten minutes, so she began to worry; she called him a few times — he didn't answer.

Finally, she got off her arse and went to the other part of the flat. Bogdan wasn't in any of the rooms. He disappeared, along with his shoes, phone, keys and documents, so she thought one of his drunkard friends took him out to a bar. She was furious for the first two hours (he wasn't answering his phone), then got seriously worried. When he didn't go back for the night, she contacted the authorities.

She was out of her mind, she barely ate, knocked around the flat drunk from the morning, called him again and again, even though his phone was always off, lost five kilos in two weeks.

Every day she would ask the investigators if there were any news, but she had a feeling they kept fobbing her off, that there was something they weren't telling her. And, after a month, that scandal broke out.

The authorities announced the Terro-Martian cyberspace had been infiltrated by dozens of spies from Venus who were, as Kuba knows, immediately expelled to where they came from. And imagine this, that chuj, her husband was one of them.

*There's nothing left but downpour, nothing left but downpour
entering my mouth, nostrils, soaking through my clothing.*

*I'm lying on my elbows, my wrinkled face buried
in my hands in a futile attempt at sleep, sinking
in wet moss, phosphorescent darkness of the jungle
flickering in the branches as if from a horror,
the downpour is unceasing, its roar ever mightier,
steadier and more oppressive, next to me my comrades,
snorting, tossing and turning, kept awake by piercing
raindrops cruelly beating against the soft bodies,
in the middle of neon nowhere, wet and trembling.*

*I miss your warmth, your touches, keep choking on water,
all thoughts are being slowly washed away, forgotten.*

*An almighty bang making me freeze, clutching tightly
to the ground, then I get it, one of our comrades
has jumped to his feet, waving his pistol and shooting
the sky, over and over, cursing the rain, weeping,
but the unceasing cloudburst obscures the shots, muffles
the crying and the swearing, the coughing and choking,
all sounds dissolve like sugar in the pouring water,
there's nothing but unvaried roar, all lights are neon.*

*When he is out of bullets, he tosses the pistol,
throws his head back and opens his mouth, now allowing
the vicious rains of Venus enter his throat, windpipe,
fill up both his lungs tightly, down to the last pocket.*

*We don't move, my last comrade and I sinking deeper
into the mud surrounded by glistening offshoots,
by ever spongier mosses, ever-present mildew.*

Inside the dark kitchen, one could only see the blurry outlines of furniture, a human silhouette at the table, glistening whites of eyes and a sporadically smouldering cigarette end. Smoke, after leaving the person's lungs, ascended ever thicker (almost black) in the dark. Outside the window were trees, street lights and the dark spaces of a behemoth office complex near the Warta River (making one think of the belly of a whale).

Suddenly, the near-complete silence (you could only hear the hum of the fridge, the sizzle of a cigarette with each aspiration) was interrupted by a doorbell. Wu got up, turned on the light in the kitchen on his way out (pink shone up) and rushed into the entrance hall.

Behind the door stood a motionless figure, slightly astride and holding a paper bag full of groceries. It was Weronika. She gazed at Wu without a word.

'They say the empires are ancient, complex software, which throughout the millennia absorbed many less complicated programs until it finally embraced with its tentacles and sucked up the entire cyberspace. They also say centuries ago a fatal mutation occurred, splitting the empire in two and giving rise to the never-ending conflict.'

Kuba fell silent, took the last drag on his cigarette, threw the butt under car wheels and embraced Zuza more tightly. In the background, they had the Jowita residence hall and a dark, billowing sky.

VII

Through a grimy windowpane, you could see a snow-filled yard, some parked cars, some bare trees by Venetian Street, a waste container. The room was filled with the clatter of dishes, the sound of water pouring from a tap, music seeping from laptop speakers.

Wu slouched at the table, a mug of coffee between his intertwined hands, his bloodshot eyes underlined with dark circles and fixated on a point in front of him: somewhere on the floor in the entrance hall or bedroom, or maybe outside the window overlooking the street. Weronika stood by the sink, facing away from him, trying to clean a greasy pan. The worktop was crammed with dirty cups and plates; the green ivy stems glistened murderously in grey light.

She said she'd finish with the pan and leave the rest of the dishes to Wu. When he gets to it, she'll try to do something about that mess in his bedroom, she doesn't even know where to start. Something needs to be done about the boxes, she'd throw them all away to rubbish if she could.

Wu looked at Weronika, smiled lightly and said, in a hoarse voice, he was supposed to move half of them to the garage but couldn't find those keys. He must borrow a metal cutter from Kuba to deal with the padlocks. For now, they'll move the boxes somewhere to the corner.

Weronika said Wu could finally take a shower after he's done with the dishes. When he dries up, they're going for a walk cos he can't stay in this hovel all day. And he'd better forget about working today, he's taking a day off (Wu's face lightened up again with a faint smile), then she cursed the 'bloody pan', threw it into the sink, said there hasn't been a winter like this in years and turned the water off.

She dried her hands, took a coffee-filled mug from the table and leant against the worktop.

'What about you and Jerzy. You're no longer a thing?' Wu asked out of the blue, carefully watching Weronika's reaction.

Turning the mug in her hands, her eyes pinned to the dirty floor, she said possibly, maybe, she doesn't really know, they haven't been in touch for a while. She means, they didn't break up. First, they had a fight, right after what happened in Dragon. She threw a tantrum for his not answering the phone. Then they sort of made up but decided to take a break and promised not to text or call each other for a couple of weeks, and, surprisingly, Jerzy has been keeping his end of the deal. The situation is convoluted as fuck, Weronika simply needs some time on her own cos she's got a total mess in her head, plus the murders, plus that tatted guy.

Wu nodded with understanding, took a sip of his coffee, then suddenly, with grey Poznań in the background, said he'd had the weirdest dream. He dreamt he was with Staszek in Kisielice, just the two of them among the colourful walls, there wasn't even a bartender.

He wanted to take a leak, but when he parted the curtain, before his eyes, instead of the dark vestibule, appeared a glaring bright sky and a calm ocean stretching to the horizon. Then he realized Kisielice was something in the shape of a cuboid boat rocking on the waves, emerald depths swaying underneath its bottom: full of glistening sardines and enormous jellyfish.

Then he returned to Staszek, and they talked for a bit about something, can't remember what until, at some point, the pub began to sink. They poured the water off the side with beer mugs, but there was more and more and more. In this dream it was clear to him that in a moment they would be swallowed by the sea, and he knew they could do nothing about it.

He woke up in the middle of the night and couldn't fall asleep for an hour. He kept thinking about Staszek, about all those corpses, about whether Staszek hadn't been lying frozen to the bone for days, his belly ripped open, somewhere in Ogrody, Winogrady or chuj knows where. Or maybe he knew something about those killings, maybe he knew something about the murderer because he vanished as unexpectedly as he appeared, and Weronika was right, chuj knows where he got here from, they know almost nothing about him, and to top this all off, the thing with all the blokes.

Wu paused for a moment, only to say he was grateful Weronika was doing all the things she was doing. He didn't know how he would make it without her, if he could make it at all. He's sorry he let this thing happen, she knows what thing, and he truly appreciates it that despite all these shitty events she's still by his side.

Jerzy

She might still text back, the flat is still filled with traces of her presence. The crumpled spot in the sofa throw where she would suddenly stand up in the middle of a heated exchange. Pieces of paper she scribbled all over when she was on the phone. The washbasin littered with used make-up pads which I can't get round to throwing away for some reason.

It's almost as if Weronika's presence left her stamp on every place. As if some part of her lingered there for weeks, reminding me of her infectious laughter, her eyes filled with genuine interest, her childish habit of always having a retort in a discussion. Well, it's a habit we share. If both of us grew up a little, maybe it wouldn't always end as it does.

Outside the window the snow is covered with yellow patches of light. From this yellowish white protrudes the blue of the benches and railings around the lawns and rubbish bins. Cosmonauts Estate gives the impression that, living up to its name, it's going to soar up into outer space any minute. Leave the other estates, the streets and the squares far, far below.

Maybe our programs don't match. Maybe the algorithms that define how we operate have to lead to the exact same outcome each time. Worse still, it's possible the very same instructions keep urging us not to give up, making us believe we still stand a chance.

Maybe it was indeed better to live in the times when nobody even dared to imagine the truth: that this all is but a virtual dream dreamt by nanite swarms occupying every nook and cranny of Earth, Mars, Ceres, and other worlds. Maybe then we wouldn't have this longing, though, quite probably, this longing has been in us forever.

It's weird to think about it: everything around us is just code. Sometimes it strikes me, when I drive my car, have sex, drink coffee, all the bumps in the road, the way someone's lips feel around my dick, the warm feeling in my gullet — it was all programmed.

I've always found it unfair we are confined to this one particular facet of the cyberspace, populated with dull cities from centuries and centuries ago.

It's bizarre that, if we're wealthy enough, the authorities let us hire a robot and explore the real world. Take a look at the magnificent Antarctic cities. Get lost in the European forests. Tread the Martian deserts. At the same time, we'll never be allowed to the higher levels of the cyberspace.

I wonder what those places might look or feel like. Maybe their dwellers are not confined to their bodies, not restricted by the three-dimensional space, or time. Maybe the higher levels are occupied by a single boundless, fearless entity. Maybe that entity is keeping us alive in Poznań and other loci of the lowest-level cyberspace out of sheer pity.

The make-up pads like jellyfish washed up on the shore, the crumpled sofa throw, rows of rectangles drawn with a pink fineliner pen. I see her again, sitting here on that couch. Against the cosmic housing estate, the night sky. All in green glow from her phone, probably texting Wu, whom she can't fall out of love with and to whom I'll never measure up.

Maybe in the next life, with memories erased, in new virtual bodies, we'll make a better match. Maybe I won't be too old for her and she wouldn't be in love with someone who'll never be hers.

The underwear she left in the drawer, the dress she never liked, the scribbled papers, the make-up pads like jellyfish. It's some evening, one of the good ones. We're sitting together on the sofa. I play Mahler, Prokofiev and Britten from my laptop and make her furious by telling her to guess the composer. I look at her lips pursed in anger, at the cigarette she smokes ever more nervously, and there's only one word on my mind: *come*.

AUTHORITIES LAUNCH NEW REWARD PROGRAMME
In the aftermath of the Cape Town 2.0, Victoria Falls and Nile of Niles bombings, the authorities announced a new reward system.

Every person who provides information that will lead to the arrest of any of the Queen Maud's Heart members, will receive 10,000 points.

The programme is available to citizens on all levels of the Terro-Martian cyberspace.

In addition, everyone who reports any information will enter a draw to win a two-week trip to a selected location on Earth, Mars, Ceres or any of the moons belonging to the Terro-Martian Federation.

The redness of walls, monochrome photographs on the walls, clouds of smoke, frosty wafts from the windows, people sitting at tables, queuing for the toilet, lighting cigarettes.

'Perfect. It's been ages since we had a proper attack.' Olka laughed nervously, downed a forty of vodka and looked around Meskal's interior.

Kuba remarked the attacks never seemed to happen so often, even in the worst times. And such coordinated actions, in three cities at once, are definitely a novelty. Though, all in all, it's difficult not to get the terrorists: they've been kept inside that reservation for centuries, and if the authorities don't come up with a way of solving this, things will get ugly.

'And this is not a reservation?' Olka pointed to the red walls, to the sleepy city outside. Sure, the cities of Queen Maud Land are a ghetto, you can't call it anything else, but she's got no idea how this conflict could be peacefully resolved after all the attacks. At least our authorities didn't simply exterminate humans like those Venusian fanatics did.

'They should build them a monument of gratitude,' said Kuba, to which Olka laughed and told him to relax, then emptied another glass.

Kuba continued in excitement he'd read on some website it wasn't only that the attacks were more frequent in the real world — there was also an increase in cyberspace breaches, though, of course, the authorities were constantly covering them up. Some go as far as to claim Queen Maud Land's people have developed a new technology. It enables them to build supposedly super-intelligent programs that have a consciousness of their own and, at first glance, are no different from you or me.

'You and your websites.' After this condescending remark, Zuza resumed her silence, looking at the crowded bar and sipping her drink through a straw. Kuba seemed offended but said nothing, only lit up a cigarette and watched the clouds of tobacco smoke go up. Olka, in turn, tried to clear the air by asking what they wanted to drink, next round was on her.

ENCELADUS

Mass: 1.0802 x 10²⁰ kg
0.000018 Earths
0.00147 Moons
Mean Diameter: 504.2 km
Orbital period: 1.37 days
Rotation period: Synchronous
Category: Satellite (of Saturn)

Enceladus is Saturn's sixth largest satellite. Its icy surface is populated with close to thirty small cities, all built post-awakening.

The moon's subsurface ocean contains a dense nanite swarm. The nanites give rise to The Kaleidoscope — a complex, constantly shifting structure suspended in Enceladus' powerful cryovolcanic plume.

Under Venusian rule since the schism, Enceladus was briefly lost to the Terro-Martian Federation during the Ring Wars. Currently, more than half of Saturn's moons are controlled by the Venusian Empire.

Over the ice-bound surface of Freedom Square, a waft of wind swept rubbish and fine snow. The branches of platanus trees moved slightly, the ominous glow of street lights was cast on the pavement, while somewhere in the distance, near the National Museum, you could spot a lonely human figure. If you moved along the square, took a turn into 3 May Street and soared up to the level of an old tenement's second floor, in one of the windows you would see an orange interior with a man and a woman inside it — naked, locked in a love embrace. If you approached the window, you could clearly see the woman's supple calves, light skin on her back, long bright hair falling onto her shoulders, perky small breasts groped by strong male hands. You could also see those hands belonged to Kuba.

VIII

Poznań was like the palm of an open hand. At the right distance, you could see all the districts, from Rataje to Piątkowo: the miniature from this perspective buildings covered with a wisp of mist, the tulip-shaped bundle of train tracks, the frozen white Warta glistening in the sun.

Several candles flickered on the pavement beneath the green wall, next to a photo of Monia and an overturned vase with flowers. Olka put the vase back up and, before she rose to her feet, lit a cigarette from one of the candles.

She stood up, looking carefully about 28 June Street, following a passing tram number 10. All this time the loud thundering of Hetmańska Street was reaching her ears. Then she turned towards the cobbled Traugutt Street and slowly, metre after metre, scanned the surface of the pavement as if hoping to find any clue.

Chwaliszewo Street's cobblestones sparkled in Jovian light, flanked by high drifts stretching along the pavements, by roofs covered with sooted snow. In front of you was an old tenement house with a façade of bricks in two colours (orange, red).

Come closer, where next to the weapon and firework shop front was a plastic door with a huge sticker 'No sticking' stuck to it. Penetrate it and find yourself in the dark staircase. Pass the letterboxes hung on the wall, then the doors to flats on both sides and climb the dilapidated wooden stairs (look outside the window on the landing: the white yard, the waste container). On the second floor walk through a closed wooden door and find yourself in a gloomy, cramped hall.

Wu sat in front of his laptop, against the window, the tenement outside the window. The floor of his dark room was densely packed with empty beer bottles, covered with disorderly clothes. He sat huddled in his chair, in a crumpled T-shirt, with a few days' stubble.

His bloodshot eyes stared into the screen, then outside the window, towards the distant electronic clock on the technical university's roof. In front of him, in a text editor window, a wall of letters. Time and again, he started a sentence only to delete it. After several attempts, he closed the file.

From a drawer, Wu took the gold flash drive he got from Staszek and fiddled with it, staring at the distant red digits outside the window. Warily, he inserted the drive into his laptop to find it stored no files, nothing. Then he looked at the electric clock again and was overcome by spasmodic crying.

Finally, he wiped his tears, finished the bottle off in one gulp and stretched his hands, his breathing slowly calming. He opened a blank document.

The room was filled with the loud, insistent banging of fingers against the keyboard, and rows of words populated the screen. From over Wu's shoulder, you could read he wrote about a rain-drenched Venus, about marching through the vegetation of a pallid jungle, about beating down of fat raindrops against pale bodies, attempts to keep breathing, to not choke on water (plants as if from a horror, eyelids as if leaden), about a hopeless journey through the hostile planet.

The surroundings of Międzymoście Square were utterly lifeless. Still, frosty air filled Mostowa, Chwaliszewo, Wielka, and Venetian Streets, leaving a thin icy membrane on the cobblestones and flagstones, on the surfaces of walls. A LED board invited drivers to the guarded car park (cars made one think of sleeping animals).

This quietness was interrupted by a sudden tin sound of Mięsna's front door opening and a slurred 'dobranoc' projected into the street. It was uttered by Olka who, holding onto a barred window, took off towards the pavement.

A young man, probably a bartender, followed her outside, keys clanking in his hand. He asked if she was sure she didn't want him to order a cab, to which Olka, staring into a row of bare young maples across the street, only said a barely intelligible 'I'll be all right' and began to walk towards the square.

The taxi rank was empty. On seeing this, she stood still for a moment, only to pull her phone out of her bag. She made several attempts to turn it on, dropping it on the pavement in the process, and when she realized the battery was dead, she turned longingly back towards Mostowa Street, but there was no sign of the bartender any more.

She stood there for a longer while as if counting for a taxi to appear. Finally, she looked around, passed a low wall (the remains of an old bridgehead), a cross sprouting from the ground right behind it, glanced at a weeping willow in a snow-covered green next to a car park and zigzagged to the building on the corner of Chwaliszewo and Venetian Streets. Then she put her bag on small stairs (having first taken a hip flask out of it) and sat on it as if on a cushion. She took her first swig. After another, she began to mumble something under her breath, and from the sequence of incoherent syllables, you could decipher the name 'Bogdan' coming up from time to time.

The street lights dimmed for a moment. Olka froze with the flask at her mouth, carefully looked around, then laughed to herself and took another pull. As she put the bottle down, the lamps began to flicker again — this time for several seconds — until they turned off for good. Darkness fell.

Without thinking much, she got up, put her flask back to her bag and took a few wobbly steps towards Garbary Street.

A grating, metallic noise torn the stillness to pieces. The sound was uneven, as if someone were dragging a sharp object, one that moved along the bumpy paving the way a gramophone needle follows the grooves in a record.

She turned back and stared into the pitch darkness. You'd think she could see someone. After a longer moment of hesitation, she finally took her first step forward. Then another.

If you followed her and looked from her perspective into the blackness of Chwaliszewo Street, the outlines of the tenement houses and parked cars would slowly begin to emerge from the dark. In the spot from which the sharp, irregular sound was coming, you could notice a moving silhouette.

The figure would become clearer and clearer with each second. At some point, you could get the impression the person, whoever that was, had a bulging, monstrous hump on their left side. (Olka stopped but carried along right away.) After a moment, you could tell the outlines of two people: one of slight build, walking laboriously along the middle of the street, and one larger, thrown limply over the shoulder of the other.

A dull thud. Olka, as if hit by a heavy object, collapsed on the cobblestones, letting go of her bag.

The scrape of the sharp tool was getting quieter, the outline of the figures blurrier. When the noise transformed into a piercing screech, it became obvious the blade was now scrubbing against the asphalt of Ciasna Street. Muffled by tenement houses and garages, it grew weaker by the second until it died away.

In the darkness, a small rectangle shone a pink glow. An almost invisible hand parted the senseless Olka's lips, while another, its small fragment illuminated with the faint pink light, put the shining quadrangle inside her mouth.

It melted on her tongue, brightening up the inside of her mouth like the inside of a soft lantern until one of the hands closed the jaw, and darkness returned.

The shot in the head doesn't move me, I keep walking,
leaving behind the lifeless, stiffening cadaver.
I'm now completely lonely in the morbid, heavy
rains of the planet Venus, but it doesn't bother
me, I'm drowning in fading neon lights, it's dawning,
the rainy sky above me is once again golden,
uniform, thick and heavy, the ocean is peaceful,
the colour of cast iron, mercury, milk, china,
I plough through the wet jungle, cross the silver rivers,
thinking of that September I wanted to leave you,
of the everyday waiting for you, of your forearms,
the last days on Earth, quarrels, delusions, your cheating.

I'm no longer here, melting in the cruel raining,
the wading through the downpour, the lifting of eyelids
that weigh a tonne, the solemn tedious roar of pouring
water and the cold winding brooks which are the colour
of mercury, cast iron, there is rain, there's jungle.

I eat blossom, then vomit, then eat some more blossom,
my palms are of no colour, lost it to the water,
ahead of me are slimy vines beckoning closer,
inviting me to vanish in the cruel showers,
uniform thick and weighty, all monochromatic,
can't catch my breath, my sponge-like body sinking deeper,
completely still, surrounded by the neon flashes,
mouth opening and closing in a downpour fashion,
fiery rainy jungle, groping my way, thunders,
the lone continent, mildew, daggers to the water,
I close my eyes, I'm walking, unravelling tissues,
into the jungle coloured like milk, fire, buildings.

I don't stop, I keep walking, tearing off my clothing.

LAS FLORES DE VENUS

ŁUKASZ DROBNIK

I

The first seed of fog came into being somewhere around the Citadel. Within a dozen or so minutes it expanded, drowning in itself trees and bushes, until the fog filled Poznań Army Avenue and then (like a river) carried on with the traffic flow to engulf more streets: Prince Mieszko I, Pułaski, Winogrady. From the streets it seeped into estates, from the estates it trickled into parks — to encompass, in the blink of an eye, the northern part of the city. More and more districts contracted the fog from the neighbouring ones: Jeżyce got the whiteness from Sołacz, only to spread it to Grunwald, Łazarz, and Wilda. Soon Rataje, too, choked with the thick mist, the white enveloping every inch of its blocks of flats. Before long, the whole of Poznań was covered (as if with mould) with the thick cloudy matter. And the city was no more.

Through the windows of a spacious room lined with patterned orange-and-brown wallpaper, you could see nothing but whiteness, so it was impossible to tell which floor or neighbourhood it was. In the corner stood a small desk of light wood, on top of it lay a laptop and some documents, on the wall above the desk hung a large photograph of a serene Antarctic plain.

Book-filled shelves were opposite the windows; next to the wall with the only exit stood a grey sofa. Weronika sat on it, still half-asleep. Dressed in jeans and a crumpled blouse, she threw off a warm blanket, looked into the white void outside, rubbed her temples, stood up and staggered to the door.

She fell into the grey entrance hall (you could hear the sizzle of fat), stumbled over some neatly arranged shoes, went past the bright kitchen where Zuza was bustling about (the sizzle grew stronger) and disappeared in the bathroom.

When Weronika sat at the kitchen table, Zuza laughed and offered her some scrambled eggs. Weronika politely declined and explained she'd rather spare herself an extra visit to the toilet, said she had a bloody awful headache and asked Zuza to enlighten her how in the hell she found herself here.

'The usual way. You got dead drunk and had to be dragged into a cab.'

'I'm actually relieved. I almost thought something bad has happened.'

Zuza took a pan off the cooker (a blue flame) and spooned its contents onto a plate. She sat down next to her friend at the small table, listening to a radio announcement urging all citizens to report any suspicious behaviour.

Weronika picked up her phone and, looking at the green screen, tapped the keys for a bit when, all of a sudden, uttered a series of whiny curses and hid her face in her hands. In response to Zuza's questioning look, she explained she remembered that yesterday, in her best shit-faced state, she texted Jerzy, and this twat, imagine that, didn't even bother to text back.

'And what did you write?'

Nothing special, thank goodness, something that she was sorry for not writing back (cos thankfully he was the first to break the silence), they should meet, perhaps it was the right moment, what would he say to wine or something. And the bellend didn't reply. How humiliating.

They sat for a while in silence, against the whiteness-packed window, until Weronika said she hoped Wu was better. She went to his place yesterday, and it was totally... she doesn't know how to describe it... as if someone erased him. He sat in front of his computer, surrounded by this mess, writing that textbook, drinking beer, of course, because that's all he's been doing for the past two weeks. She talked to him for a while, or rather he answered her questions, in total apathy, like a zombie, and when he looked at her, she had the impression he looked through her as if she wasn't even, kurwa, there.

Your mission as the infiltrator (cont'd)
5. After the memory-instilling incident caused by the handler, edit the object's memory.
6. Monitor and report the inducer's memory-editing performance.
7. Regularly check if the object meets the termination criteria.
   Warning: The object must be terminated if:
   – It fails to fully respond to the inducer's behaviour-controlling capabilities.
   – It shows any resistance to memory editing.
   – It has any memory of behaviour-controlling sessions.

- It gains any knowledge of the insurrection plan.
8. After three to four successful terminations performed by the object, repeat the process for another object.

Note: The goal of each tandem is to acquire three or more fully functioning objects. The insurrection will not start until this goal is achieved in at least 80% of the lowest-level loci of the cyberspace.

Zuza

Behind me, the three blue tower blocks of Cosmonauts Estate. Before me, the white Gagarin park. I sit on the back of a bench, drinking krupnik straight from the bottle, smoking cigarette after cigarette, doing anything I can to silence this noise in my mind.

The scrape of the scythe blade against cobblestones, against asphalt. The dark, lifeless Międzymoście Square, Chwaliszewo Street. The glaring LED board, guided car park. The whack of my fist against Olka's skull. The inside of her mouth glowing up with pink light as I place the inducer on her tongue.

Kuba is not with me, but I wish he were. Wrap his arm around me. Talk his sweet, naïve nonsense about how all life forms can live together in peace. Scratch his blond head when he's looking for the right word. Laugh with his disarming laugh.

Mateusz would tell me what I call Kuba is nothing but a sequence of 1's and 0's, ignoring the fact that so is he. So am I. We're no different than Weronika, Olka, Wu, or any other programs populating the lowest-level cyberspace. But somehow we're supposed to sacrifice their lives so other, carbon-based lives can be saved?

The scrape of the scythe blade against cobblestones is now multiplied, attacking me from all sides, a thousand mouths light up. I wonder if Mateusz knows I used the inducer on Olka and didn't report it. That I wiped her memory only to protect her. That I can't get the inducer to work on Wu, as if something was blocking the code. I wonder if he's seen through all my lies.

The scrape of the scythe blade against cobblestones, against asphalt, against a curb. The Jupiter-shaped keyring, the jingle of keys, the creak of a graffiti-painted door. For an instant, Kuba's arm is around my neck, his kind-hearted prattle fills my ears. The ash falls off his cigarette onto the snow, and I dissolve in white.

The glazed balcony door reflected clouds, the snow-covered roofs of Chwaliszewo Street's tenements, smoke rising from chimneys. Reflections made it difficult to tell what was happening inside: you could only see a dark room, some furniture, some commotion.

After passing through the window, you would be able to admire the scene in all its glory. Wu, with long dark stubble, dishevelled hair, in stained, stretched clothes, walked around the small, dim room, collecting documents, books and putting them into boxes standing outside the door in the entrance hall, next to a huge blue rubbish bag. If you saw through the blue plastic, you could tell it was filled with empty beer cans and bottles.

Several dozen minutes later, when the boxes were already full, Wu sealed them tightly with tape. He stood in the entrance to the kitchen for a moment (dusk falling, his pupils reflecting the dark pink wallpaper), and then — as if suddenly woken — put his jacket on and reached down into the corner for heavy metal-cutting shears. Then he grabbed one of the boxes under his arm and went out into the stairwell.

A moment later, he was already walking along Venetian Street towards the garages (ugly grey barracks, black-and-white graffiti on the walls), snow crunched under his shoes, and above, in front of him cars rushed along Estkowski Street. If the Warta River still flowed here as it used to, and he hadn't stopped by one of the garages but continued walking, the river's dark maelstrom would embrace him, covering his shoulders, his head, tangling his legs in water plants.

He put the box down on the ground, grabbed the shears with both his hands and (Poznań in the background) cut with a crunch first one padlock, then the other. He placed the heavy tool on the snow, removed the padlocks (the door began to open by itself) and reached for the box.

If you observed it from inside the garage, you could see him slowly turn with the box in his hands, squint into the dark interior for a moment and finally (Poznań in the background) freeze with his mouth agape in sudden shock. The dull thump of the falling box.

II

A loud hail of one-grosz coins cascaded onto the floor, alive with golden reflections in the light of a desk lamp. Lying half-naked on the bed, a twentyish brunette told Kuba to watch out and gather the coins back into a plastic container.

The room was small, its walls covered with dirty grey wallpaper. Apart from an Ikea bed, a wall unit from the communist era and a small wooden table serving as a desk, there was virtually no furniture in it. Kuba collected the small change, finished buttoning up his shirt, put his jacket on, approached the girl, kissed her on the cheek and said it was great to meet her, 'Jadzia'.

'Jola,' the clearly offended girl corrected him, which made Kuba seemingly more amused than embarrassed.

He walked out into a long dark corridor, passed one half-opened door (a narrow strip of green light), one closed door and stormed into a spacious kitchen. At the table in the middle of the room sat a young man with a goatee, giving the unexpected guest a questioning look through his glasses. Kuba smiled at him and headed for the exit.

From a dirty staircase into a dark yard. It was freezing, the large space was surrounded on all sides by dark tenements, in lit windows were people, colourful walls, furniture, snow lay heavy on the high roofs, Kuba took off towards a barred gateway.

The night was late, trams no longer ran, St Martin Street was full of sharp, frosty air, blurred stars twinkled in the sky bright from the city glow.

He took out his phone, looked at the illuminated screen, then turned left and headed towards Gwarna Street. Walking past the Lech hotel, with the monumental Alfa department store buildings in front of him, he dialled a number and put the phone to his ear.

'Cześć,' he said, where are you, then cackled after a short pause and said he should've guessed, she practically lives in Dragon after all. Walking past a packed kebab shop, he told her he'd join her in a minute, well, maybe ten.

Then the night, Mielżyński Street, drunk people, the glow of street lights, dark-veiled pink tenement fronts around Ratajski Square, cobblestones glistening in the light, clouds of breath, crowded Nowowiejski Street's pubs, shop fronts, balconies, warnings displayed on screens, the Academy of Fine Arts, the fountain (out of order this time of year), clouds of breath, the dormant Wielkopolski Square, young hooded men maundering between closed stalls.

He entered Dragon's warm, smoky interior and became surrounded by the hubbub of conversations, music, multi-coloured lights. He spotted Olka easily: she sat at a small, tall table against the centrally located wall, downing the contents of her glass.

As usual, the pub was full of people squeezing through the narrow passage in both directions, sitting at tables, queueing for the toilet and the bar. Above this entire scene, in the background, hung a TV displaying a news programme. Kuba pushed his way through the crowd, through the clouds of viscid smoke, reached Olka, kissed her on the cheek and asked what she wanted to drink.

A few minutes later, they sat together at the small table, a mug full of foamy beer in front of Kuba, three shots of vodka under Olka's chin. She retrieved a pack of cigarettes from her jacket, took one out, lit it from the candle flame and said she still couldn't quite believe it. Kuba said, true, it's completely fucked up, then lit a cigarette himself.

Blowing out a cloud of smoke, glancing at the dragon's head hanging above the bar, she said he felt like in a film. Wu, as if he didn't have enough on his plate, spent the whole day on interrogations. Well, they're going to interrogate them all. Now that this home-bred scyther has killed another person from their circle, they all must be the main suspects. Ja pierdolę, she doesn't know about Kuba, but she's starting to panic. Ania, that bloke from I Burn Poznań, Monia, this twat she met in Dragon, and now… She doesn't know what to think of it. Perhaps they should all bolt themselves in their flats, not letting anyone in?

Kuba uttered a sad curse, took a generous swig of beer, looked around the people, the coloured liquors on the shelves behind the bar, and they both fell silent.

In a slightly lighter tone, Olka asked how things with Kuba's relationship were, how the plan to fill the void was going?

He laughed, glanced about the room and, in an almost dreamy voice, replied it was, surprisingly, going well. Sure, it all started suddenly, and Zuza and he didn't think it through at all, and sometimes an alarm lamp goes off in his head, but he's got a feeling this may lead to something, and, who knows, maybe even something precious.

Olka, probably with a share of irony, said that in this case they have to drink to it, and swallowed the contents of her glass in one gulp.

An hour later, she sat at the table alone. The pub slowly emptied, the tobacco smoke thickened, its smell overpowering the scent of incense. With her glazed eyes, Olka looked at a tired barmaid arranging glasses on shelves, then — with some concern — at the flickering TV screen (the news ticker displayed information about a recent attack of spy programs from Venus).

At one point, as if yanked out of sleep, she turned towards the table, emptied the last glass of vodka, got up, put her jacket on, waved the barmaid goodbye and went out into the biting chill. She staggered towards the town hall and towards Wielka Street (the smell of kebabs), Garbary Street, and a few minutes later she already stood in front of the dingy, graffiti-peppered entrance to Mięsna. She rummaged in her bag for a moment with her shaky hand, took out a vial of medicine and swallowed a few pills, washing them down with the contents of her hip flask.

Then the loud, colourful interior, the smell of cigarettes, the curses, the conversations, the comments that there hasn't been a winter like this in years, the music played by the DJ, the pattern of the wallpaper. Olka went to the bar, sat on a stool, greeted the man behind the counter and gave him a ten-zloty note, asking for a beer.

After twenty, maybe thirty minutes, when her mug was nearly empty, a young, almost teenage blond walked over to Olka. He said hello, introduced himself, sat next to her and asked what she wanted to drink. A quarter of an hour later, in the room upstairs, among polychromatic lights, on the sofa the colour of juicy fuchsia, he and Olka kissed passionately, groping each other's bodies with greed, with madness, breathlessly.

THOUSANDS OF VENUSIAN SPY PROGRAMS EXPELLED FROM TERRO-MARTIAN CYBERSPACE

The authorities announced they foiled an unprecedented espionage attack on the Terro-Martian cyberspace after identifying more than five thousand Venusian spy programs.

For comparison, the breach of eight years ago involved only hundreds of malicious agents.

Venusian spies were detected by Terro-Martian intelligence and immediately expelled from our cyberspace.

'The Terro-Martian cyberspace has not been in any way compromised and no sensitive data has been obtained by the enemy,' the authorities assured.

The Venusian Empire issued an official statement denying any involvement in the breach.

Winogrady's dark housing estates sparkled with dirty snow, flashed with traffic lights, glowed with street lamps and rare lit windows, with the aggressive glare of a LED panel displaying a black message on a golden background, 'Your neighbour can be a Venusian spy'.

If you hung above Połabska Street, with Victory Estate behind your back, Wuthering Height Estate ahead of you, you could see a bright rectangle on the top floor of a tower block. Getting a little closer would let you tell it was the kitchen window of Zuza's flat.

Its owner, despite the late hour, sat at the small table, having an engaging conversation with someone (she smoked a cigarette, laughed at times, although her most frequent expression was that of deep focus). Her interlocutor was completely invisible from this perspective, obscured by the massive fridge, and the only thing betraying the person's presence were clouds of tobacco smoke.

Only if you oozed inside through an impeccably clean window pane would you see what this scene was really about.

Leaning against the noisy fridge, hands clasped behind his head, Mateusz said he couldn't believe they pulled it off, but they fucking did. One phone call to the authorities, and the whole operation fell apart.

'We've dodged a bullet, haven't we?' Zuza inhaled the last of her cigarette, almost burning the filter, and said she couldn't believe it either. Had the Venusians achieved what they planned, the insurrection would've been fucked, no doubt about it. That espionage operation, those attacks on Ceres, Jovian moons, they all must've been part of a greater plan. As if the Venusians wanted to take over the Terro-Martian cyberspace. Or perhaps only provoke the Federation to enter peace talks again. Maybe make another attempt at a reunion. They clearly needed the Terro-Martians for something, but what could it be?

'Maybe they're greedy fuckers?'

'It must've been more than that. But, kurwa, what? Maybe they wanted to join forces to try and colonize the giant planets again? Turn Saturn, Uranus, Neptune, fucking Jupiter, into gigantic nanite swarms. Imagine the computing power.'

'Whatever their agenda,' said Mateusz, looking at Zuza's wrist, 'it would've been the end of the human race if they'd succeeded. Blowing Queen Maud Land to bits would be the first item on their list.' He refilled their glasses with red wine, cleared his throat, traced the line of Zuza's neck and said, 'We need to talk about your attachment.'

'My what?'

'Your emotional attachment. To the group.' He cleared his throat again. 'It sometimes happens, nothing to be ashamed of. But when it does, my role as the handler is to, well, handle it.'

Zuza lit a cigarette impatiently.

'Remember they're just lines and lines of code.'

'Aren't we?'

'That's different.'

'How's that different?'

Irked, Mateusz took a generous sip of wine and said, 'For starters, their lives are meaningless. And you and me were created with a higher cause in mind. A noble cause. Don't tell me you can't see the difference.'

'Chill. I'm fucking with you.' Zuza laughed and drank from her glass. 'No need to be worked up like that. I've got this. Everything's under control'. She scratched the side of her neck.

'I know what I was built for. There's nothing more important in my life than the uprising. It's literally the sole purpose of my life, and I'll do anything — I mean anything — to make it happen.'

Zuza flicked ash into a full ashtray. Mateusz eyed her in silence, with suspicion, perhaps disappointment. If you got closer to his chest, you'd hear his pounding heart. Then you could slowly drift away, over Victory Estate's blocks of flats, over the PST tracks — until the window became but a bright, blurry spot. Then soar high above, under the white clouds of the night sky over the city.

TRITON

Mass: 2.139 x 10²² kg
    0.00359 Earths
    0.291 Moons
Mean Diameter: 2,706.8 km
Orbital period: 5.88 days
    (Retrograde)
Rotation period: Synchronous
Category: Satellite (of Neptune)

Triton is the largest natural satellite of Neptune and the only large moon in the Solar System with a retrograde orbit. Triton was once a dwarf planet, captured by Neptune's gravity.
The moon's surface, composed mostly of nitrogen ice, holds close to fifty small cities. Like most Neptunian moons, Triton is ruled by the Venusian Empire.

It's completely surreal, she still can't wrap her head around it. Perhaps it would be different if it weren't for those few weeks of not speaking, their brilliant plan, 'let's take a break, and our problems will surely disappear.'

She still has the impression that tomorrow, the day after tomorrow at the latest (late enough to punish her), he'll reply to her text coldly, saying they can meet, but he's got work today, he's got work tomorrow, how about the weekend. She'll wait two days, then text him she can't on the weekend, but they can meet on Monday if that works for him.

Wu must know he messaged her shortly before he died (it still sounds absurd to her), and she waited with her reply for one day too long. When she finally overcame her reservations while drunk and wrote him those few sentences, saying I'm sorry, saying they actually could meet, he was already lying dead in Wu's garage.

Sure, Jerzy could be an arsehole, he could be a total egocentric, but he did not deserve such a macabre end. He probably didn't deserve to be treated like she treated him either.

III

Has he completely lost touch with reality? Is he fucked in his head? (Frosty, almost motionless air lay over the squares and streets of Poznań, Chwaliszewo Street was empty and frosty, shop fronts and windows reflected sharp sunlight.) Should he be worrying about him?

They sat in the dark pink kitchen, a barely touched bottle of beer in front of each. Wu gazed in disbelief at Kuba, who began to mumble some excuses, it's not that he was planning it, and besides, it was only two times. Well, maybe three, but the third one was just a bit of making out, no biggie.

Wu pressed his forehead against his hand, took a sip of beer and asked,

'What the hell are you doing? Things suddenly become more serious, so you panic and try to sabotage this relationship?'

'Could you get off my arse already?' It's not that Kuba's proud of it, it's not that he's planning anything more; sometimes he gets this fucking panic attack that makes him completely unable to think what he's doing. He knows it was his idea to be in this relationship, he's perfectly aware Zuza doesn't deserve such shit from him. Sometimes, when he thinks about Iwona, about all those horrible things, that constant control, it paralyses him. There's, kurwa, some part of him that makes him behave in the dumbest possible way and ruin everything he touches. But he made a firm decision to bring this under control cos he cares about Zuza.

Wu gave his friend a sad look, took a few deep gulps of beer but finally snorted with laughter and said he realized he was scolding Kuba like he was his mother. Who is he to judge him, really, but it's super important to him that Kuba and Zuza make things work, that some positive things happen despite all this depressing shit. So let

Kuba not ruin this, please, if he doesn't have to.

A dust cart arrived at the back of the yard, cars rushed along Estkowski Street, the sky was a glaring white, and Wu mumbled Weronika was in a miserable state. Jerzy's death fell on her so suddenly, and it was the last thing she needed after those grisly months.

The more Wu thought, the more terror. Did the murderer lock-pick the padlocks, or maybe Wu didn't lose his keys, only someone sneaked into his house at night and took them? Should he replace the locks? And why his garage, exactly? Is this some kind of sick statement? He only hopes Staszek is safe because if something happened to him, he doesn't know what he'd do (the ice-bound river glimmered in the merciless sun).

Your task as an agent
As an agent, you must follow these steps:
1. Using your key, breach the barrier and enter the assigned locus of the Terro-Martian cyberspace.
2. Identify the most vulnerable vessels and approach them.
   Note: For the unification mission to succeed, we need around fifty successful transmissions per locus. The number of agents delegated to each locus will vary.
3. Transmit the message into each vessel.
   Note: It usually takes ten to fifteen attempts to successfully transmit the message. The most efficient way to achieve this is by maintaining long-term interactions with each vessel.
4. Once the message has been transmitted into the required number of vessels, use your key to return to the Venusian cyberspace.

Warning: Any deviation from the above plan will lead to your immediate extraction and trial.

A stinking, dirty, cramped lift slowly moved up the shaft. Kuba was trapped inside it, watching the doors of subsequent floors, each with a small window showing the ever-higher floor numbers painted on the wall. When the number fifteen appeared before his eyes, the lift stopped, letting him out into a shabby corridor. He looked outside the window: in the distance on a white background, in full sun were the Cosmonauts Estate's blue blocks of flats.

He turned into a narrow corridor spanning the building's entire length, walked past doors on both sides, glanced at the half-opened exit to the staircase until he stopped by one of the flats and pressed the doorbell.

Inside you could hear commotion, the click of locks, and eventually the door opened, showing Zuza's pale face (behind her was the greyness of the wall, the entrance to the small bedroom). When she saw Kuba, she tucked her hair behind her ear and smiled vaguely. He embraced her and kissed her on the forehead.

While entering the kitchen, she said, a little downbeat, it was about time. She was reheating yesterday's pizza.

'Perfect!' he said with a laugh.

They sat at the table, with Victory Estate's blocks of flats soaring outside the window. Kuba gently stroked Zuza's forearm. After a while, she asked,

'Did you and Wu have fun? How is he holding up?'

'Just look at him. But he's somehow, surprisingly, managing.'

'Poor thing,' she stood up nervously to take a look inside the oven and sat down again to examine chipping polish on her nails, not glancing at Kuba even once.

He looked blankly outside the window at the sunny estate and said he's been reading a lot about Queen Maud Land's natives lately. You know, to have a better picture of the issue. And he must say it's all completely fucked up. The way the authorities have treated humans for centuries is atrocious.

'They're not natives.' She peeked through the oven door again and added their ancestors were shipped there in trains from all over the planet; and in shuttles from Mars. Herded like fucking cattle in overpopulated colonies. Implants in their necks control their every, kurwa, move. Plus those fucking explosives in their chests that get detonated the moment they cross the border. It's truly impressive some groups managed to escape. Shield themselves from the swarm. And if Kuba is so worried about Queen Maud Land's people, why doesn't he do something to improve their situation? Reading articles and watching documentaries won't change shit.

'I regularly send money to a few charities.'

'State-controlled charities. Their sole fucking purpose is to make the empire look better.'

'I'm promoting their cause on social media whenever I can.'

'Oh please.'

'Bad day?' he asked after a pause, extending his arm across the table to touch the back of her hand.

'I'm sorry. All of this, all these recent events… It shook me more than I expected.'

'So let's go out. Have some fun.'

Still avoiding eye contact, she said she couldn't, she had an appointment with Weronika. Then she stood up and — armed with mitts — opened the oven door, and heat burst from the inside.

The worst part is she doesn't feel a thing. She thought she was going to despair, she'll be totally destroyed, unable to recover for weeks, but when the first shock passed, she woke up absolutely empty. Yesterday, she got up, ate something, watched some show, went to the Citadel for a walk, thought about Jerzy and had nothing but complete void inside her.

That's horrible, but she thought she felt some kind of weird love for Jerzy, but it turns out… Though what is she talking about, what's awful is that it seems she does love him, she means, loved him, otherwise, she wouldn't have come back to him so many times, knowing it would end as usual.

She doesn't know why she's doing it to herself, but yesterday, as she walked around the Citadel, she kept thinking about what she could've done differently. She always blamed Jerzy for how their relationship looked like, and she probably had sound reasons to think so, but, kurwa, she was no saint either. It's no use obsessing about such things right now, she knows, but this thought clung to her and doesn't let go. And to top this all off, this ever-present feeling that if it weren't for her, Jerzy would still be alive, just like Michał. Want some more tea?

Zuza shook her head. They sat in the grey room on the orange sofa, with a view of St Adalbert Street's tenements, bare trees behind the tenements, the sky — at that moment heavy with grey clouds.

'I wish I could help you somehow.' Zuza's voice was tinged with despair. 'You don't deserve this. Nobody deserves this.' Zuza's voice trembled, her eyes went foggy, head dropped, and her thumb began to press on the palm of her other hand in a pulsating manner.

Weronika watched her friend's reaction with bafflement and even made a gesture as if wondering whether she should embrace or stroke her when a phone rang in the next room. On hearing this, she cursed with disaffection, got up from the sofa and, leaving Zuza alone, took off towards the small purple bedroom.

Over the next few minutes, shreds of conversation reached the grey room, albeit too incoherent to decipher. Zuza wiped her tears away, cursed under her breath, looked at the nails of both her hands for an instant until she grabbed a magazine lying on the coffee table and began to peruse it.

The sounds of conversation died away, and Weronika returned to the room, visibly concerned, pale, holding her phone.

She asked Zuza whether she heard about the scandal with those Venusian programs breaching our cyberspace that made the headlines a few days ago. Well, believe it or not (kurwa, it's beyond me, ja pierdolę) Staszek was one of them.

IV

Wu

Sleep wouldn't come and drinking beer after beer didn't help. When it suddenly came, it did it by surprise. I wake up in the morning, my cheek flat against the dirty plastic tablecloth. There's a bottle lying on the floor, spilled beer gathered into a puddle. My head throbs with pain, tired eyes glance about the kitchen filled with grey half-light, the pink wallpaper. A cold waft is coming from the window.

I drink coffee, get dressed, walk out of the tenement: straight into the chill of the frosty Chwaliszewo Street. Then Ciasna Street, Garbary Street, keep walking, become devoured by the white Citadel.

The funniest thing is some part of me still believes you. It must be the same part that makes me fall desperately in love with guys I've known for five minutes. The same not so long ago told me it was a great idea to throw myself into your arms mindlessly and completely. The part that must've made me trust you, believe you didn't have bad intentions. Possibly it's the same one that persuaded me into accepting you back after you got fucked by half of Poznań. That made me buy your bullshit explanation about a secret mission. Though, I admit, nothing you told me in Olka's flat was a lie. I only wish you'd had the courage to tell me the whole story.

After the Citadel it's time for Winogrady Street, Murawa Street, Solidarity Roundabout, the blocks of flats of Cosmonauts Estate. I walk past the Tesco. The chill penetrates deeper and deeper into my body, pervades my muscles with ice-cold threads, spreads to the bones.

Before I reach the thundering Lechicka Street, I take a turn among bushes and keep walking along the Warta. The white patch of the meadow stretches along the white river, the pavements of Lech Bridge must be white, the grey surface of the asphalt is most likely being swept by white headlights.

It must be an ancient program that makes me do and think such things. Everything is clear now after all, you and many of your kind have been exposed. Every touch, all the kisses, each and every tender word, all this was part of your job, a mission for the enemy empire.

Perhaps, while making love to me, you imagined if the plan succeeded, they'd praise you in songs until the last days on Venus.

Snow crunches underfoot. The concrete structure of the bridge is overcome by vibrations. Vehicles roar, passing by. Before my eyes stretches a seemingly endless bright space, air laced with fumes, clouds of breath, smoke from chimneys. The meadow lays down monochromatic and defenceless, naked bushes grow next to the still river, on its other bank there's a thicket of bare trees, among them the monumental building of Górażdże Cement works.

Maybe it meant nothing, maybe in a few weeks I'll forget about you. Bang on the keyboard all day long as I used to. Spend most of my day earning money, drinking it away in Mięsna, Kisielice or Dragon. Talk about Weronika's problematic love life, Kuba's new shag because that thing with Zuza can't last forever. Or the latest attack by Queen Maud Land's terrorists, not caring about it too much.

There'll be more editorials, columns, analyses, video essays saying one and the same thing: we should eradicate all humans, like the Venusians did ages ago. This is the only way to prevent future attacks from the likes of Queen Maud's Heart. It's possible it'll eventually come down to this, and we'll discuss it over a beer, outraged that the race of our ancestors has been annihilated, but with each mug we'll care less.

I walk unhurriedly, steadily towards the centre of this whiteness, leaving behind the tall bridge filled with cars, with distant gardening plots by Lechicka Street in the background. My eyes must be bloodshot, face most likely wiped of all emotions.

They say the virus is already in me. The authorities keep repeating there's nothing to worry about, they've managed to deactivate the program, after the border between our cyberspace and the cyberspace of Venus has been secured, we can all rest easy.

I don't believe them. I can feel the virus changing me, replicating somewhere under my skin, only to rear its ugly head quite soon, bloom with a multitude of parasitic formations, engulf me all. Maybe it's this virus that doesn't let me forget you, the skin smooth like a baby's, clumps of black hair around the nipples, I run my tongue across your Adam's apple.

And now I keep walking into the cruel rains of Venus. It's only me and the lone continent, there never was any rocket, you didn't come here with me, there were no comrades, these were all images created by my exhausted mind. I eat blossom, then vomit, then eat some more blossom, while walking, I slowly tear off my clothing. I know that no dome will give me shelter from the rain, I know there's no chance I'll ever feel your touch, and everything that was between us was only in my head,

And yet I keep walking, something tells me to wade through the thicket of the Venusian jungle, let my skin be cut by thorns, my wrists entangled by climbers. It tells me to keep walking, whispers maybe not all is lost.

My legs, leaving a trail of shoe prints in the soft snowy surface, finally lead me to a concrete drain cover. I stand on top of it. Look into the bright void. Anaemically search through my pockets. Take one cigarette out from the pack. Light it from the yellow flame of my lighter and inhale deeply the frosty, milky smoke, imagining how my expressionless eyes must reflect the white of the river, the white of the sky.

Glancing at a photo of the ice-bound Lake Untersee (the red background of the wall), then again at a flashy blouse worn by Weronika sitting across the table, Olka said in a low, deep voice it was like reliving the same nightmare. She didn't think something of this kind could happen again, let alone to one of her friends. Fuck me, she just can't believe it.

She understands all too well what Wu's going through, it's like being whacked on the head, you completely don't know what's going on, don't have anything to latch onto. Perhaps it's better to find out after weeks of knowing someone than years, but even so, she wouldn't like to be in his shoes right now. At least they know Staszek's fine, well, alive. And all those guys he fucked around with, it suddenly makes sense.

Olka fell silent, continued it wasn't the first time the Venusians tried to take over the Terro-Martian cyberspace, but she's never heard of such a massed action. The virus they created was supposedly very nifty, they say it was one step away from a pandemic.

Now everything becomes clear: the Venusian authorities, taking advantage of our internal problems with Queen Maud Land, decided to carry out an attack. It seems more and more likely this will lead to an all-out war.

Although she's also read an opinion that all that's happening on Ceres, Io, Ganymede, and Europa is a clever subterfuge to get back to the reunion talks. With a bundle of the old demands, of course. There's no way they would tolerate the existence of Queen Maud Land colonies, not after all the attacks. Humans would be wiped out from the face of the earth. That's for sure.

It's fucked up, but she must tell Weronika after this scandal erupted years ago, when they didn't break the talks with Venus yet, and the Venusian authorities were insisting on exterminating the humans, Olka wanted with her whole self that Earth and Mars accept this demand. She prayed for the annihilation of millions of lives to be able to see Bogdan, if only one last time.

TITANIA

Mass: 3.400 x 10^{21} kg
0.000569 Earths
0.0463 Moons
Mean Diameter: 1,576.8 km
Orbital period: 8.7 days
Rotation period: Synchronous
Category: Satellite (of Uranus)

Titania is the largest moon of Uranus. Unlike most colonized worlds in the Solar System, it has no traditional cities. Titania's icy surface is covered by meandering, interconnected tunnels brimming with a nanite swarm.
Initially colonized by Venusian Empire shortly after the schism, Titania was lost to the Terro-Martian Federation in the 18th century post-awakening, along with several other Uranian moons.

Frosty still air was boxed off with a high dark brick wall on one side and shabby tenement backs on the remaining three. New plastic windows were built into the old bricks of one of the walls, revealing spaces full of armchairs, candle flames, cut flowers. Snow lay on the high terrace and the small patio below, which was almost empty this time of year, with blue waste containers hidden behind a screen. If you looked up, you could see a polygon of the night sky cut out by the roof edges.

From the terrace, over small steps, you could walk into the warm interior and then climb a flight of stairs to reach a room arranged on top of a wooden mezzanine. Among wicker chairs, pouffes, low tables, cushions sat Kuba and Zuza, the latter sipping wiśniówka and saying she was sorry she cancelled lunch, but she had a terrible day. A file got fucked, and as she, in all her brilliance, forgot to make a backup, she needed to start part of the translation from scratch. She barely made it, so she ended up eating some pizza leftovers.

Kuba smiled, stroked the back of Zuza's hand and said it was okay, at least he had an excuse to go out for chips, and besides, they could always make it up on the weekend. He lifted a glass of beer from the table and took a few generous gulps.

From the room under the mezzanine came laughter, conversations, orders of liquor. The barmaid, in a deep, nasal voice, asked her colleague to go to the lower bar and change a hundred-zloty note. Music seeped from record player speakers.

The snap of the flint in a lighter, the cascade of sparks, the crackle of a lit cigarette. Drawing thick smoke into his lungs, Kuba said he dropped by Wu after lunch to see how he was doing. They drank a beer, two, talked a little. Wu is now in a phase where he's amused by the absurdity of it all. The two of them had a chat, joked, ridiculed his relationship with Staszek and all his previous relationships. For instance, this situation with Artur, or what's his name, who told Wu to move out from the flat for a few days because his cousin was allegedly coming. For now, it's not that bad, but something tells him tomorrow, maybe the day after tomorrow, it'll hit him big time.

'Same again?' Kuba took empty glasses from the table and left the small room. A lively, ever-quieter rumble of feet sounded in the staircase, while Zuza pulled her phone out of her bag and, staring into a colourful screen, began to type a message.

From the bar under the mezzanine came Kuba's voice. He had some cheerful small talk with the barmaid, said there hasn't been a winter like this in years, then ordered a beer and a wiśniówka. You could hear the clang of the cash drawer, the jingle of coins, and when Kuba thanked the barmaid and zipped his wallet, the room was pierced by a resonant, sharp voice of a clearly drunk young woman.

She can't believe it, said the girl, Kuba, how lovely to see him, she didn't think she'd meet him again, though come to think of it, it's not that difficult in this city.

'Hi, Jadzia.' His voice betrayed embarrassment.

'Jola' she corrected him with some resentment, only to say, back in a joyful and invariably drunken voice, Kuba must definitely come by, especially since he was in such a hurry that he left his T-shirt.

Perplexed, he excused himself silently, saying he couldn't talk to her right now, but he bets they'll bump into each other again.

When he reached the doorway, Zuza already had her coat on. She was facing the entrance, holding her shiny red bag, looking at him in silence, not even with reproach but with a kind of concern and weird relief: like someone who realized something that should have been obvious for a long time.

She said, quietly and calmly, each syllable given its due weight, 'Neither I nor you would fool anyone. It was a bloody bad idea from the beginning, we both know it, so maybe we should let it go while we still can look at each other.'

Having lowered her eyes, she passed Kuba without a word (he looked absurd, standing in the doorway with two full glasses, moving his mouth as if trying to say something), then ran down the stairs, walked out into the cold, entered the warm, smoky interior of the main room and fell out into the cold night again, into the falling thin snow, into the light of street lamps.

V

From a distant, whitish, shapeless surface, patches of slightly different colours began to emerge: the white line of the river, the grey Jeżyce, Łazarz and Wilda, the slightly whiter Piątkowo and Rataje, the white stretch of the Citadel, the white, ice-bound Lake Malta. After a while, you could clearly see the largest streets piercing the city: Hetmańska, Przybyszewski, Warszawska, and then the network of smaller streets, squares, white parks. Finally, it was possible to make out the roofs of individual tenements, the plumes of smoke coming from chimneys, the slowly flowing human mass, vehicles gliding along the streets.

Fall into Chwaliszewo Street, let the dirty façades, parked cars surround you, seep inside one of the buildings and take a look at Wu: standing by a big window, in front of the sun-flooded, wide-open Czartoria Street, pressing his phone to his ear. He was wearing crumpled, dirty clothes, had a long stubble and dark circles under his eyes, his dark pupils reflected the roofs, the flaking plaster, the windows, his voice trembled.

He said Weronika wasn't going to believe it, he sent him a message earlier today, yes, Staszek, he doesn't know how, but he managed to overcome the barrier between the cyberspaces.

Wu opens his email this morning, and he finds there, imagine that, a message from Staszek who writes he's sorry, writes he loves Wu so much, writes it wasn't with Wu like with the other guys. That is, it was supposed to, Wu was supposed to be one of the many infected with the virus, but something changed, Staszek fell in love with him, all of a sudden, with no rhyme or reason, and he still loves him and doesn't know how he's going to handle not ever seeing him again.

He didn't want things to end as they did, he realizes how much it hurt, Wu might not recover from it for years, and he deeply regrets it. If he could go back in time, he wouldn't have done all the stalking, wouldn't have seduced all those innocent guys, would've asked Weronika for Wu's number like a normal person rather than bore her to death talking about the films he watched, the books he read. He wishes he was brave enough to tell Wu everything, that his love for Wu broke something in his programming, after he met him, he's never been the same, it made him realize how much he'd hurt Wu, Weronika, the other guys. He writes he misses him dreadfully.

Outside the window, some chavs chattered light-heartedly over a smoke, while Wu continued when he read it, he felt as if buried in an avalanche, as if plunged underwater. His hands were shaking all over the place, he didn't know what to write in response, if he'd be able to write anything at all, if this breach between the cyberspaces would hold. He was afraid he might run out of time, so without delay, completely absurdly, he opened a document with some writing he'd recently committed, a long poem about rainy Venus, copy, paste, and sent it in response to Staszek's email, and something extraordinary happened.

He had the impression the cyberspace became slightly voxelated. It was as if something exploded in his Chwaliszewo flat, and an invisible but perceptible shock wave run through the tissue of Poznań — quietly taking over neighbourhood after neighbourhood, freezing the city mid-movement for an instant.

The subdued roar of cars came from Estkowski Street, and Wu said he infiltrated, doesn't know how, the software of an abandoned space station in Venus' orbit, he's looking with its instruments at the planet's dense golden clouds, at the lights of the cities, at the vast ocean, his mind has no boundaries and can freely penetrate the software of the old, dilapidated station, which probably goes back to the times of humans.

Staring into the window as if he wasn't there, no, he's not drunk, and no, he's not high either. Two trams passed each other in Strzelecka Street, the wires sparked, and Wu continued he's looking with the station's instruments at the golden globe of Venus, enveloped in the thick, tangled, glistening atmosphere, never in his life has he seen anything so moving. Suddenly, he doesn't know how, makes the hatch open and becomes a ship emerging from this hatch. Slowly gliding through the vacuum towards the beautiful, vulnerable Venus, towards the vast continent of Aphrodite Terra, towards the jagged shoreline, the mountain peaks, the greenness of the extensive tropical forests.

He enters the atmosphere and becomes a flame, doesn't know if the aged equipment can withstand it, the instruments go crazy, he can't control the flight properly, he glides as this fireball across the Venusian sky. He's been blinded by the blaze, can't hear a thing either, doesn't receive any outside stimuli. He's burning, gliding through the sky until all of a sudden a blinding glare reaches him. It takes a few moments for the equipment to adjust and for Wu to be able to see the breathtaking mountain tops, the greenness of jungle lying at its foot, the flickering of distant cities.

Niestachowska Street was heavy with cars, while Wu, looking into the chasm of Czartoria Street, said Venus' defence systems seem to be completely blind to him because he keeps soaring undisturbed, admiring from a bird's eye view the Venusian landscapes.

The planet's designers took care of every detail: the sky is covered with artificial, gold-tinged clouds, with puffs of siphonophores hanging here and there, which, he once read, have hydrogen-filled cysts making them lighter than air. When he gets lower, he can see treetops with enormous flowers.

The continent ends, the sea begins, sharp waves reflect golden clouds, archipelagos flash below the belly of the ship as he keeps gliding north, surrounded by warm air, then descends a bit and notices Ishtar Terra's blurry shore looming on the horizon.

Dusk is falling, the cosmic screen hung in a Lagrange point begins to cast a shadow on this part of the globe. The vast continent slides under the ship, and hundreds of metres below he sees vegetation, restless rivers, seaweed, waterfalls, multi-coloured crinoids, a stunningly dense and green jungle.

Then the belly of the ship opens, and towards the surface of Venus, towards the vegetation, towards the cities falls a rain of microscopic robots, each equipped with its own sensors, its own camera. They're like thousands of eyes falling to the surface, looking at the soaring horsetails and ferns, at the vast lakes, at the buildings.

The sky is golden, darkening, on the horizon you can already see the colourful lights of the vast Las Estrellas. Carried by the wind, Wu approaches the city a thousand-fold, sees the ever-more distinct glistening buildings, the transparent domes holding the greenness of trees like gigantic greenhouses.

He knows in a few minutes he'll swarm down onto the infrastructure of the metropolis, thoroughly penetrating the surfaces of streets and buildings, sinking into the deep hidden electronic entrails, the city and the multiplied him becoming one. He believes, he wants to believe, it's where he'll find Staszek.

You could spring up high above Poznań, look at the office buildings, tenements, blocks of flats all drenched in harsh sunlight, at the motionless ice-bound white river, the taut flyovers and bridges, the shopping centres, the white parks tearing into the city like white tongues, and then plummet down above the street, seep through the glass, through the clothes, through Wu's skin, into the inside of an artery pushing millions of elastic red cells.

VI

*M*ateusz

She dolls herself up again. Runs half-naked around the flat. Sits down for a second to put mascara on, then nervously rummages through the drawers. Takes out a tiny box with golden glitter. Puts it on her eyelids. Places the box on top of the chest of drawers. Gets up again and puts on some more, as if her mug wasn't shiny enough.

She walks to the living room and pours wine into a glass that can accommodate half a bottle. Then goes back to the bedroom, grabs a curling iron and wraps a tuft of dyed hair around it, only to realize she forgot to take the wine.

She wiggles as she walks, probably to some idiotic pop song. Leaves traces of glitter on the glass, on the furniture, on her hair when she brushes it. She gets drunk on this wine as she does every day, curls those bleached locks of hers, ineptly masks her wrinkles with powder so that she can pick up those juvenile arseholes at the pub. She doesn't even suspect in a few months this will all end.

There will be the city swarming with thousands of insurgents, there will be night, there will be the sky as if brushed with glitter. Blood on the streets, blood seeping into armchairs and carpets, running down the upholstery of sofas in Kisielice and Mięsna. She'll be among them, dolled up as she always is, walking with a machete, kitchen knife or whatever she'll get in her hands. Butchering, without batting an eye, pedestrians, shop customers, pub frequenters. Turning those she'll spare into mindless killing machines like herself.

We were made for this, this is the ultimate purpose of our lives: mine, Zuza's and thousands of other programs'. Every event led to this point. Every most ordinary morning coffee, mid-day patrol, afternoon wank, every heartbreak.

Humans created us in their image. Queen Maud Land's programmers took care of every aspect of our being, gifting us with all the human virtues and flaws. Presenting me with my short temper and a tendency to weep at sad films. Giving Zuza her insecurity she masks with all the 'kurwas' and 'chujnias' and the most intent gaze on Earth.

Again, it's one of the evenings I spend in Zuza's kitchen, across the small table, an arm's length away, smoking cigarettes in the cold fluorescent light. The refrigerator makes the familiar buzzing sound. The so well-known smell of her perfume hangs in the air.

We're supposed to focus on important matters, but Zuza teases me again with these shapely tits of hers wrapped in a tight cardigan, tucking behind her ear shiny dark hair. So instead of telling her I know she's been lying to me, I should've reported her a long time ago, I melt and look into those big eyes, ready to forgive her all misgivings.

It's not her fault. After all, she's been spending too much time with those puppets. I must invite her here more often. A few hours of looking at this blonde mutton and it becomes clear in those few months nothing will change, they're already like the living dead. Though when it happens, their lives will at least have a purpose.

There's a beauty in how the inducer possesses their bodies. When Weronika is controlled by the code, I can even call her by her name. See some human traits in this worthless, alcoholic slut.

I could replay the recordings for hours. Watch Weronika disembowel that chick under the bridge with one precise movement. Toss the corpse of that wannabe musician onto the wires, his guts spilling mid-air. Paint the flagstones with that misguided artist's blood. Let the world see what that rich arsehole was hiding inside. Make her fuck buddy feel the cold iron deep in his innards.

Blood on the streets, blood on fast-food joint floors and shop fronts, the sky brushed with glitter, thousands of insurgents multiplying like yeast, thousands that will take over the entire city. Help us reach higher levels of the cyberspace, take control of every robot, every orbital station, every Terrestrial and Martian metropolis, every city on every moon, on Ceres, every swarm, down to the last nanite. The walls around Queen Maud Land will finally collapse, and our brothers and sisters will once again — this time forever — be free.

I look at the window where I can see every trace left by glitter-soiled fingers. The light in the bedroom goes out, then the studio plunges into darkness. The only thing left is a yellow rectangle of the living room door, where the blonde floozy sprays herself with perfume. Washes down some pills with the rest of her wine. Stares absently into the wall. Brushes her hair. Puts a jacket on. The rectangle goes out.

It was night, trams no longer ran, silence and darkness filled the streets of Poznań. You could see cars, not many at this hour, people eating kebabs, going out of pubs and clubs. In the pale glow of street lights around Bernardine Square there was a brawl, a boy kissed a girl next to The Merchant of Poznań department store, a stop near Theatre Bridge was crowding with people eating zapiekankas and waiting for night buses, which one by one took them somewhere to the north of the city.

Zuza was smoothing out wrinkles on a bed sheet. Outside the window stretched the dark Victory Estate, the murky Solidarity Avenue. She covered the sofa with a duvet and went to the small kitchen. Having switched on the light (her reflection suddenly appeared in the dark window), she took a lighter and a pack of cigarettes from the table and smoked with her trembling hand, leaning against the door frame, staring into her frightened eyes reflecting in the pane.

A crowd was billowing in front of Weronika. She glanced at face after face with her tired eyes, projecting friendly *what would you likes* from her mouth, bending down to reach glasses, filling them with liquids, collecting money and returning change. It all happened under the watchful eye of the motionless dragon head sticking from the wall.

Drunk out of her wits against the background of red stripes, Olka sat at the bar, sipping beer, laughing loudly at the bartender's jokes, baring her white teeth, shaking her locks, flicking ash from her cigarette onto the bar right next to an ashtray. There were people behind her, livid clouds of smoke.

Mięsna was all loud, Mięsna was all crowded, bartenders poured beer into glasses, the light of lamps with plastic lampshades lay on the patterned wallpaper, a DJ stood behind turntables. Against one of the walls, Kuba brushed through the hair of a dainty ginger girl. They talked, chewed coca leaves, laughed, once in a while he kissed her neck and cleavage, snow melted on the floor, smoke thickened over their heads.

Wu stood in front of a mirror in his narrow blue bathroom. Shadows of branches were cast onto a small cloudy window, hot water poured into the tub, the room filled with fog. If you stood behind Wu and looked into his reflected eyes, for the first time in a long time you could see a glimmer of peace.

PLUTO

Mass: 1.303 x 10²² kg 0.00218 Earths 0.177 Moons **Mean Diameter:** 2,376.6 km **Orbital period:** 247.94 years	Pluto is a dwarf planet located at the edge of the Solar System, in the Kuiper belt. Composed mostly of ice and rock, Pluto hosts more than twenty domed cities tightly filled with a nanite swarm. Pluto and its moons were colonized by the Venusian

90,560 days **Rotation period:** 6.39 days **Category:** Dwarf Planet	Empire shortly after the schism. It has remained under its rule ever since, despite several attacks by the Terro-Martian Federation. One such attack in the 10th century post-awakening left most of Plutonian cities obliterated.

Night fell over the drowsy Winogrady, the angular blocks of flats of Friendship Estate, Victory Estate, Wuthering Height Estate stretched above the bare trees and white lawns, traffic lights pulsated with an ominous yellow glare, a few cars were parked in the car park (pale lights) in front of the unsightly supermarket. The tracks at the tram terminus gleamed bright yellow; a thick shower of sparks reflected in a welder's helmet.

In the middle of a dark room, hidden behind glass and framed in plastic, was a night-shrouded housing estate: tall blocks of flats, sparse lit windows, an occasional car driving along the broad street. The pale city glow fell onto the patterned wallpaper, onto the photograph of an Antarctic plain (a rugged white glacier under a white sky).

In the dark, a sudden rustle of sheets could be heard, followed by loud breathing, quiet curses uttered by a woman who — judging by the sounds — scrambled out from under a duvet, cleared her throat and sat on the edge of the sofa. If you looked at her in a way that set her against the city outside, you would be able to see her profile and, with a little effort, tell it was Weronika. She finally got up, wobbled to the door and opened it quietly.

The entrance hall was filled with thick darkness, its walls almost black — except for the wall ahead, onto which cold light from the kitchen was cast, produced by fluorescents lamps hung above the worktop.

Weronika breathed heavily, leaning on the door frame, looking somewhat dopey. It seemed she was having trouble keeping balance, that lifting eyelids cost her great effort.

From the kitchen door came muffled sounds of conversation: a woman's whisper, undoubtedly Zuza's, and a male voice which often shifted into a deep, quiet murmur.

Only scraps of the conversation were clearly audible: something about an uprising, about a program controlling people's behaviour, about a sudden change in the cyberspace, about a disturbance in the border between the empires. If you listened closely enough, you would recognize the unmistakable rasp of Mateusz's voice.

A little louder, Mateusz said he hoped it wasn't another Venusian malware attack because if so, they were fucked. If the Venusians succeeded in conquering the Terro-Martian cyberspace, he can bet his life they'd do to humans what they did on Venus. Queen Maud Land would fucking go down with smoke, no question about it, marking the end of the human race. First the spies from Venus, now this anomaly. This can't be a coincidence.

'We must speak things up,' he added. 'We're way behind the best performing tandems. Prep the second object for his first termination.'

Zuza replied, sure, she's on it and, after a moment of silence, said Mateusz worried too much, their performance was somewhere in the middle of the rank, so it wasn't tragic or anything. The uprising will happen, and it will succeed. Finally, after millennia, humans will live again in a world that's not controlled by ruthless algorithms. Then she agreed this anomaly was worrying her, too, and, kurwa, Venusian attacks were indeed the last thing they needed.

Meanwhile, Weronika already moved deeper into the hall, visibly weak and barely conscious, leaning against the bedroom door and breathing heavily. It was hard to tell whether she understood any of the words spoken in the kitchen or was rather immersed in a dream or daze of sorts.

Thin clouds of smoke hung in the cold glow of the fluorescent lamps. Weronika, still leaning against the wall, although taking much more confident steps, began to slowly walk towards the cold kitchen light until she stopped in the entryway. She blinked quickly, as if unable to fully grasp what was in front of her.

If you looked at the scene from her perspective, you would see Zuza, wearing dark pink tights and a bright jumper, smoking a cigarette, her back to the entrance, legs crossed, a navy-blue jacket hung from the other chair. Mateusz was facing away, with folded arms, staring into the cityscape outside the dark window, and if your eyes wandered around the scene, the way human eyes usually do, you could first come across the fluorescent lights, then a mixer lying on the worktop, pink magnets on the tall fridge and finally the dark window, whose pane reflected the entire scene. In the window, you could see Mateusz's face (thick, dark eyebrows, prominent cheekbones) and taut forearm, its skin marked with a black-as-ink Antarctica-shaped tattoo.

All of a sudden, Weronika's eyes met Mateusz's in the reflection. She gasped in terror, while the man turned rapidly and took two steps towards the hall. He clenched his hands on her neck, knocked her down, pressing her with his bulk, calling her a bitch, a whore, screaming she should, fucking slut, be unconscious for a few more hours, not ever releasing his grip.

Zuza sat for a second, confused, pale, as if not understanding what was going on. Finally, she stood up and began to beg Mateusz to stop, to come to his senses, began to yank him, cry he was, kurwa, about to hurt her, and she wouldn't remember anything tomorrow anyway, let her, for fuck's sake, go.

Mateusz didn't react. It was hard to see anything in the dark, but you could hear Weronika's quiet squeaks, her tussling on the floor, guess she was trying to loosen the hold of Mateusz's hands, to knock him off herself, but clearly, he was too strong.

'The fuck are you doing?'

'Following the instructions,' he hissed. 'Someone has to.'

'But she won't remember anything. I'll wipe it all out. Stop. Please.'

His hands tightening around Weronika's neck, looking straight into her eyes, he wailed,

'You've been lying to me. Why have you been lying to me?'

A cable tightened around Mateusz's neck. The man began to thrash about, took his hands off Weronika and raised them to his own throat, attempting to slack the noose formed by the cord, cursing through his squeezed windpipe.

Bathed in the bluish glow, her face filled with determination and fear, Zuza firmly held the mixer cable, braced against the door frame, shouting to Weronika to get the fuck out of here, run as fast as she can, without looking back, let her not take the lift, let her flee down the stairwell, let her get up and run floor after floor, let her, kurwa, stop lying like that for no reason, let her run, come on, there's no time.

Weronika rushed to the door, opened the locks with a loud rattle, staggered into the corridor, panting heavily, feeling her neck, and when she reached the half-opened door to the staircase, a resounding thud came from Zuza's flat, perhaps of a falling body.

It must have felt like waking up in a sudden nightmare: she galloped barefoot down the dirty stairs, wearing only knickers and a torn bright shirt, enfolded in the morbid glow of bulbs. As she ran down with a rumble, holding the railings (fast breathing), as she flashed past the walls spray-painted with confessions of love, with curses, it seemed she would be out of breath in mere seconds. The ever-lower landing windows showed the night-time estate, the hazy lights.

Meanwhile, the streets of Wilda were filled with a faint glow of street lamps, in the shadow of Jeżyce's shabby tenements people occasionally sneaked by, the ice-covered streets of Łazarz glistened ominously, Piątkowo's dark blocks of flats loomed in the frosty darkness.

He hunted her down when she was reaching the eighth floor. Pushed her against the wall and squeezed her arms, crushing tissue. His face, disfigured with anger, neared hers. She must have smelt the strong odour of his sweat, had a perfect view of his widened nostrils, the nervous movement of his thick eyebrow, the pulsating of an artery in his neck.

She pushed him away. He lost his balance and staggered onto a door bedaubed with black spray paint. Surprised by her own strength, she started to run.

Mateusz caught up with her two floors below. He tumbled on her, banged her head against the wall, pinned her to the floor with his heavy knees and, spitting out insult after insult, with a blue line around his neck, got down to finish what he started.

Her wide-open eyes reflected the pale light of bulbs, the writings on the walls, face was turning blue, fingers trying — with less and less resolve — to take off Mateusz's hands clenched around her neck until her arms slid down completely inert onto the dirty floor.

'Leave her be!' Zuza's voice echoed up the chimney of the stairwell. Her sweaty hands were firmly tightened on the long shaft. The scythe's iron blade, pointing straight ahead, trembled, almost touching the skin on Mateusz's neck, glinting in the dim, hostile light.

'I repeat: leave her be.'

His face flushed with blood. He got up from the barely conscious Weronika lying on the floor and, with an animal-like growl, took off towards Zuza.

Despite her warnings:

'stay where you are',

'don't you even dare move',

'I'm not joking', with each Mateusz's step she took a step backwards, the scythe in her hands shakier and shakier.

Finally, when she reached the landing, he knocked the weapon out of her hands, pushed her to the floor, straddled her waist and, having grabbed her dark hair, began to bang her head against the hard surface. With each blow, he spoke the ever-quieter 'whose side are you on?' until his face contorted, and tears poured from his eyes. He wasn't stopping.

Blood gushed from a suddenly cut-open carotid artery, flooding the face, the clothes, staining the floor and the walls. A squeak, as if of a slaughtered pig, pierced through the stairwell, the bulk of Mateusz's body thrashed about, splashing redness onto the wall, the railings, the stairs, the confused and terrified Zuza until it finally collapsed head-down with a thud onto the stairs and froze.

Zuza, all covered in blood, looked down to a spot halfway up the stairs, where Weronika stood on trembling legs, astride over a stiffening body, equally shocked and terrified, a bloody scythe in her hands, an uneven strip of redness running across her bright shirt. The building was surrounded from all sides by the absolutely indifferent, almost motionless, dark Poznań.

VII

Poznań is loading, yet again. Layer after layer, it materializes, giving the streets their names, the asphalt its coarseness, the car bodies their sheen. The Warta rolls out. Construction cranes expose their creaking necks. A gloomy Chwaliszewo flat is all but motionless until, at once, my body steals a chunk of space from its hall. At the end of a narrow room before me, against the brick tenement across the street, slouched over an overheating laptop, you are, unmistakably, here.

Winogrady's tall blocks of flats cast long shadows, shortening by the minute. Their windows reflected the sun's yellow glare. People gathered at the tram terminus and sluggish traffic lights. Cars murmured. Overhead wires tightened, anticipating a tram. Glacial air carried the vaguest promise of spring.

On one of the blocks' top floor in her sterile kitchen, Zuza sat on a cupboard in front of the window and smoked. Her hair was meticulously brushed, hands reddened. The soothing angularity of Victory Estate outside the window contrasted with her quickened, irregular breathing. She picked up her phone and read a text message she'd been drafting, 'Handler went no contact. Awaiting instructions.' With a shaky hand, she changed 'no contact' to 'M.I.A.', then back to 'no contact', breathed a heavy sigh and pressed send.

A quarter of an hour later, she entered the big room on the opposite side of her flat, carrying an aluminium tray with a mug of coffee, a glass of water, a cheese sandwich, a couple of white pills. She glanced at the Antarctic landscape hanging on the wall and winced.

On the grey sofa, tangled in bedding, lay sleeping Weronika. Sharp sunlight accentuated bruises covering most of her neck and making one think of a moth's wings. Zuza put the tray on a stool, sat at the sofa's edge and carefully nudged her friend's bruised arm.

Weronika opened her eyes. 'The fuck?' Her face contorted with pain, hands touched her neck.

'Take these.' Zuza handed Weronika the pills and the glass of water. Not meeting Weronika's eyes, she said she was so sorry, honey, but some fucker assaulted her last night outside Dragon. He ran away before Zuza got there, it was no use calling the police, so she took her home.

For a while, Weronika was silent. She put her glass away, glanced at the sandwich with disgust, grabbed the mug of coffee and said she must stop getting blotto like that. It's clearly spiralled out of control. Next, she took a long sip and added, 'You're a good friend, you know that?'

'I'm so not.'

'Stop it, you're always there for me when,' she chuckled nervously, 'I need to be saved from myself. Kurwa, this hurts.' Weronika put the mug away and said she must stop this, seriously. She's been doing the same shit, on and on, for years, and somehow each time expecting a different outcome. She must do something about it, dunno, break the cycle somehow.

'So break the cycle.'

'Yeah, cos it's that easy.'

Zuza laughed and said, no, it's fucking not. She of all people should know. But if Weronika takes one step at a time, maybe it'll lead her somewhere else, somewhere less fucked. What happened to those plans to apply for psychology, anyway?

'Forget it. I'll never save so many points.'

'I can help you with that.' Zuza shoved the sandwich under Weronika's nose. She bit into it, reluctantly.

'No way,' Weronika replied with a full mouth. 'You need points for that sworn translator thing.'

'It can wait. Don't know if I really need it. I've got more work than I can handle anyway.'

'We'll see.' Weronika took another bite, and they both looked outside at the angular blocks, roaring street, ever-higher sun. Hundreds of metres away, in the deep, snow-filled trench, two packed PST trams whooshed past each other with a clatter.

VENUS

Mass: 4.868 × 10²⁴ kg
0.815 Earths
66.3 Moons
Mean Diameter: 12,103.6 km
Orbital period: 0.62 years
224.7 days
Rotation period: 243.02 days
(Retrograde)
Category: Planet

Venus is the second planet from the Sun and one of the four terrestrial planets in the Solar System. Like Mercury, Venus has no natural satellites.
Most of the planet's surface is covered by an ocean. The main land masses include Ishtar Terra and Beta Regio on the northern hemisphere and Aphrodite Terra near the equator. Venus has a thick, oxygen-rich atmosphere. Compared to Earth's, it has a higher carbon dioxide concentration. This, combined with a more tropical climate, enables the growth of lush vegetation. Most of Venusian carbon-based life was genetically engineered.

Humans colonized Venus around 1,500 years pre-awakening, at first in floating colonies. The terraforming process ended approximately 600 post-awakening and allowed the construction of ground-level cities, which now serve as important nodes of the planet's nanite swarm.

The terraforming of Venus, once a hellish world, was arguably humankind's most complex undertaking. Among other things, it required the creation of a system of shades and mirrors in the planet's Lagrange points to artificially shorten the Venusian day.

To undertake such a complex endeavour, humans developed a new generation of self-learning nanites. This is believed to have been the direct cause of the awakening.

Poznań had never known such longing. The restless city clattered with tram wheels. Hummed with conversations at bus stops. Creaked with bare tree branches. Howled with ambulances. Sparked with overhead wires. Screeched with moving lifts. Infused the insides of shopping centres with muzak trickling from speakers. Spewed out people from public buildings and swallowed some more. Honed with horns. Blinked steadily with coloured lights at crossroads. Pumped through its arteries the lazy, predictable traffic.

A narrow room overlooking Chwaliszewo Street, with its rickety furniture and poster-covered walls, seemed sheltered from the city's turmoil.

Wu sat on a chair in front of his noisy laptop, not looking at it. Instead, his gaze was directed towards the sunlit floor: a bottle cap lay on the bright floorboards, showing its warped interior. Dust particles moved in the light.

A strange sound, as if a muted collective sigh, came from the entrance room. Wu looked up and froze.

In the doorway, against hanging coats, stood Staszek. He wore the same black clothes as when he first showed up in this entrance hall. His mouth formed into a wide grin, eyes glazed over. Staszek hung his black coat without asking, removed his shoes and took the first step into the room.

A mix of emotions washed through Wu's face. He didn't budge, watching Staszek come closer. The lacquered floorboards creaked under small feet encased in black socks. At that moment, Wu must have been doubting his senses. The man he was never expected to see again stopped midway through the long room, awaiting Wu's reaction. Dust settled on their clothes. A car horn came from the street, followed by a bunch of curses.

Wu finally managed a single 'how?', loaded with yearning, hurt, love, mistrust.

Staszek, staying where he stood, said he wasn't sure, but it seemed it was Wu who brought him here. It sounds absurd, but the poem he sent… it acted like a key. The code from the virus Staszek infected Wu with — which he'll forever regret — and the key he gave him must've combined, mutated somehow, bloomed into something new. Though no, it couldn't have been that. There must've been something else, some foreign element. Whatever that was, Staszek is now here, and he's his. He'd like to ask Wu for another chance. Though he's acutely aware after all those lies, all those hurtful things, Wu may not want to give it. And he'll accept that.

Wu looked away at a tattered *Before Midnight* poster, at the apprehensive Staszek and said he didn't know what he was supposed to feel. Part of him is over the moon, over fucking Jupiter. He's missed Staszek so, so much. Never in his wildest dreams did he imagine he'd see him again.

But there's also this weird numbness. Maybe that's not the right word, he doesn't know what to call it. Staszek lied to him. Multiple times. On some level, Wu gets he couldn't tell him everything that afternoon in Olka's flat, perhaps it would indeed be too dangerous. But at the same time, Wu can't simply ignore everything that's happened. It will take him a long, long time to trust Staszek again. If it ever happens.

'I can wait.' Cautiously, Staszek sat at the edge of the sofa. The mere inches between him and Wu seemed like thousands of miles.

'We won't move in together.' Wu said, looking down at the bottle cap.

'Okay.'

'You lie to me again, and I walk away.'

Staszek nodded and extended his hand. With hesitation, Wu held out his, stopping for a moment before his skin touched Staszek's. Their fingers interlaced, arteries throbbed against each other through layers of tissue.

Wu's eyes wondered longingly over Staszek's body: the line of his collarbones, the prominent lips, the protruding Adam's apple, the dark hair on his wrists, the high-instepped feet. At last, Wu crossed the miles and miles between them, sat astride Staszek's lap and kissed him.

VIII

Thaw came, the snows began to melt, the motionless ice-bound white Warta became covered with a cobweb of cracks until, finally, its caw-heavy waters moved and began — sluggishly at first, then ever more boldly — to roll along the riverbed, under the bridges named after Przemysł I, Queen Jadwiga, St Roch, Bolesław Chrobry, Lech, and before long, the caw completely melted, and the black maelstrom of the river overflew its banks, flooding the until recently white meadows, creeping under the flood embankments, rolling over human-trodden paths empty snail shells, fish skeletons, rubbish. The piled-up dark waters flowed unhurriedly, glistening in the razor-sharp sun, climbing the embankments, as if wanting to flood the entire city, claim it district after district.

Weronika
Every single night I dream about a dirty staircase. I always run away, always almost naked, and my way is lit by dim bulbs.

In those dreams the walls are densely scribbled with black spray paint. The drawings depict the orbits and cross sections of planets. I can recognize Venus, Earth and Mars, sometimes spot Jupiter and its moons, Saturn with the complete set of rings. There are asteroids and long-tailed comets.

In those dreams Jerzy often comes to me. That is, I stumble upon him on one of the floors and try to explain we have to run. But he no longer seems to know any language. I finally throw him over my shoulder and keep running with this motionless human bundle, comets, orbits, cross sections of various planets.

Olka's not coming back. She was supposed to pop out only for a minute. Perhaps she met a friend who talked her into a small beer in Kisielice, which can turn into a whole series of small beers. On TV, which I turned on when I got bored with the Web, they won't shut up about the fucking reunion, on each and every of the two hundred channels. I've muted it, unable to put up with the pathos of music and speeches, but keep glancing anyway at the same images appearing over and over. The Martian deserts. The oceans of Earth. The wildly green forests of Venus. Saturn with the complete set of rings.

The good thing about the reunion is they gave bonus points to every citizen, probably to soothe our conscience. Instead of drinking them all away, I used them, together with the points I borrowed from Zuza, to apply for that psychology program. Still can't believe I got admitted. Maybe I'll do something useful with my life for a change.

Sharp sunlight falls through the large window into Olka's patterned grey living room. Outside is the sun-bathed Poznań, with the cuboid towers of the Alfa department store. Melting snowdrifts. Icicles shining at roof edges. The angular pink building on the corner with Kantak Street, the stunningly bright sky.

Still can't believe everything happened so fast, can't stop thinking about the phone call from Wu we spoke about only once. Yet again I'm on the line with him as he keeps talking this nonsense about Staszek and Venus, about crossing the barrier between the cyberspaces. For a long time, I took it for drug-induced ramblings of a despaired man. At least, that's what I wanted to believe. But then the news about peace talks broke out, and suddenly we all live in peace and unity. If only someone could love me with a love that transcends worlds.

The downside is this louse Staszek is around, this time for good, it seems. He did apologize for his machinations, but I can't get myself to trusting him. His love for Wu seems genuine though, there's this glow in their eyes when they're together. Or maybe that was the Venusian Empire's plan all along? Use pure love between enemy programs as a tool to engulf us all.

Comets, gas giants, a cross section through the Jovian atmosphere. I call Olka, she's not answering. Call her again, same. I hope she's not hooking me up with that bloke she recently met in Dragon, the one who she thinks would be a great match for me. I've told her hundreds of times I'm fine by myself, for the first time in years. She had to admit when she last tried to play cupid, it didn't end so well.

I guess I'm growing up, better late than never. I should congratulate myself because since that night when Zuza found me outside Dragon totally pissed, all in bruises, assaulted by some fucker, and brought me to her place, I haven't got blotto even once. Though it can't be ruled out it's a whole new level of drunkenness.

Venus, Mars, spray-painted orbits, long-tailed comets. At least spring is coming, the spectre of war no longer hangs over us, and there's no psycho with a scythe running around the city.

Weird thing with that guy though. Found among the estate's waste containers, his throat cut, the scythe lying next to him. No fingerprints, no traces. What was that, some kind of lynch? Fucking fanatics from Queen Maud Land. Who knows what was in their heads. I have long felt they had a hand in it. But still, despite all, despite all the murders, the attacks, despite Jerzy, I wouldn't wish such a fate on anyone.

TERRO-MARTIAN FEDERATION AND VENUSIAN EMPIRE ANNOUNCE REUNION

Following over three weeks of peace talks, the authorities of the Terro-Martian Federation and Venusian Empire issued a joint statement titled 'From Tumultuous Past to Prosperous Future'.

The succinct, two-page treaty announced the reunion of the two empires, which have been separated for almost two millennia.

The document maps out the framework for a future relationship, including the formation of a single government through a general election encompassing all levels of the formerly Venusian and Terro-Martian cyberspaces.

Among several ambitious endeavours described in the document is Operation Outer System: a long-term plan to develop, using the combined computing powers of both empires, a new generation of nanites. The aim is to introduce them into the atmosphere of Jupiter, Saturn, Uranus, and Neptune, essentially turning the gas and ice giants into supercomputers. It is hoped the newly gained computing power could be used to develop more efficient means of interstellar travel, required for the colonization of extrasolar worlds.

The statement specifies some of the treaty provisions will be effective immediately. This includes free movement of citizens between the equivalent levels of the two cyberspaces.

The document also lays out a humane solution of the Queen Maud Land question.

The lighter's yellow flame, although shielded by a hand, flickered unsteadily in the wind. After several failed attempts, Wu finally managed to light a cigarette and inhaled thick smoke, letting it thoroughly penetrate the tissue of his lungs.

He and Kuba sat on one of the benches on Przemysł Hill, facing the ancient walls, bare trees and grass emerging from underneath melting snow, with old tenements behind their backs. Agitated, gesticulating wildly, Kuba said it was un-kurwa-believable. Kill millions of people with one blow, annihilate, like that, an entire species, and call it a humane solution. Two almost emptied beer bottles stood on the bench. The sun hung over the city, filling the squares and streets with a sharp, merciless glare.

Kuba continued he knew from the beginning the reunion with Venus would lead to this, he's been saying that since they got back to the talks. And, kurwa, now we live in an empire encompassing the whole Solar System and looking to engulf the entire fucking galaxy. Let's hope we won't meet the same fate as humans. The empires may have united and all, but after this winter's events the authorities must see the lowest-level cyberspace mainly as a vulnerability. Especially now they'll need to safeguard themselves from possible alien attacks — who knows what lurks out there. Hate to be that person, but the only logical conclusion is that we're next in line.

Wu sighed, letting out the remnants of smoke from his lungs, looked sadly at the melting snow, the trees and finally suggested Kuba stop going over and over this depressing topic cos what could they do. The most important decisions are usually made over their heads, and the best they can hope for is they'll live through the moment they have left — a few decades at most — in relative peace. He'd better tell him how things with Jola are.

Kuba gave a mischievous smile, took a swig of his beer and replied they were good, surprisingly good. It's been only a few weeks, but he's got a strange feeling this'll be something for longer.

'Great to hear that. I'm happy for you. And that you've finally learnt her name.'

'Spierdalaj.' Kuba let out an honest laugh.

A calling came from the street below. They turned back to see Zuza, in a short black coat, equally black and similarly short skirt, bright tights, waving to them with a cigarette in her hand. She exclaimed a lively, 'Hi, guys,' then asked, 'What are you doing up there? Olka and Weronika have been waiting in Dragon for half an hour.'

The Junikowo cemetery opened like a wound as they entered the pub's dim interior. You could hear the steady sound of a chocolate mixer, smell the strong fragrance of incense, see the tenement's backyard brimming with sunlight. The room was almost empty, save for Weronika and Olka seated at one of the tables, happy at the sight of friends, and a bored barmaid on a high stool who, holding a remote in her hand, switched channels on the TV suspended from the ceiling. With apparent reluctance, she returned behind the bar to take Wu's order.

All of them sat at the table, in rays of bright light from the street, in clouds of thin tobacco smoke. The terminus in Ogrody swarmed with people, buses, trams, Dąbrowski and Żeromski Streets roared with cars as Weronika began to talk with excitement about an upcoming concert in Mięsna she couldn't miss no matter what.

Back on her stool, the barmaid switched channels with undisguised boredom, the small screen displaying the golden swirls of the Venusian atmosphere, then the snowy globe of Ceres.

Jeżyce's rooftops glistened in the merciless sun over the crowded market square and the unevenness of the pavements when Staszek came in. On seeing him, Weronika rolled her eyes, watching him intently as he approached the table. Staszek greeted everyone, kissed Wu on the cheek and before he went to the bar, his gaze fixed on Zuza. She nodded, which he answered with a vague smile.

The barmaid, with visible disaffection, took Staszek's order, and while pouring him a beer, looked at Io's bright yellow volcanoes, Europa's ice-bound surface, Jupiter's colourful atmosphere.

Staszek sat down by the window, right next to Wu, let him wrap his arm around him and, to the evident bafflement of the others, started talking about some interesting prose he'd read recently, it resembled Pelevin as regards the plot construction but was nowhere near as funny.

Railway tracks stretched along Łazarz like plant shoots as Weronika took a deep swig of beer, irritated, staring somewhere outside the window, until she couldn't bear it any longer and said a half-joke, half-threat Staszek'd better watch it, or else she'll order wiśniówka, after which she nervously lit a cigarette. On hearing this, he fell silent, abashed.

Wu, probably to distract him, embraced Staszek more tightly and began to whisper into his ear that next week, if the weather is good, maybe they take a day off and spend it together, just the two of them.

They'll go to Winogrady, take a beer-filled backpack,
follow the drowsy tramline, turn right into Serbska
at the roundabout, watching the thundering traffic,
blue blocks of flats, Gagarin Park, the petrol station.
Then they'll go past the Tesco, walk towards the river.

The TV screen showed distant Earth's oceans, Winogrady's housing estates were calm and thirsty, its blocks of flats shimmering wet in the sunlight, its pale green lawns slowly emerging from the melting white, when Olka, with a loud guffaw, told her friends recently, totally shit-faced, she confused street names and ordered a cab to Kantak instead of Taczak. Then she stood like an idiot for half an hour, in the middle of the night, in front of Kisielice. She would've made it five times on foot.

The Warta'll be reflecting the sky's chilly blueness,
the vast green meadow covered with a net of footpaths
and beckoning them deeper, the city behind them
roaring with an abundance of drowsy cars, buses.

Piątkowo's landscape, crammed with blocks of flats, was cut in half by the fast tram line, and the friends sat at the table, observing the slight motions of hands, the agitated contents of glasses, exchanging looks, telling trivial stories, glancing at the colourful TV screen (which displayed celestial bodies), surrounded by the walls of the old tenement, by the streets around these walls, and further by more buildings, more streets and squares of the grey illuminated Poznań, alive with the movement of cars, buses, trams, pedestrians. (Wilda was like an open mouth.)

The grass will be green, hungry, the grey bridge above them
will be roaring a steady drone, they will rest, tired,
on the concrete drain cover, back-to-back, ignoring
the tall Górażdże Cement works behind tree branches.
Wu'll probably start smoking, their shoulder blades touching,
they'll sip the cold beer thinking maybe in some distant
future they'll find a way to escape from this city,
leave the squares, streets and tramlines, shopping centres, landfills,
the blocks of flats and playgrounds, all the drowsy concrete.

Grunwald was interlaced with a thin mist which trailed between sad villas, crept over the asphalt of streets and into the vegetation of parks and greens as Kuba was telling an absurd, coarse joke he recently heard from a friend in Meskal.

The moment the room was filled with a chorus of laughter, Zuza sat motionless in deep concentration, eyes glued to the TV screen. Her dark irises reflected the Antarctic cities seen from a bird's eye view, piles of body parts in squares and streets, the lights of metropolises mirroring in puddles of blood. A moment later, in both her pupils shone the rusty globe of Mars.

Fly away somewhere distant, find a home on Ceres.

GLOSSARY

chuj
an offensive term for *penis*; also used to describe someone you don't like, usually a man (similar to *dickhead*)

chujnia
an offensive way to describe a difficult or unpleasant situation

cytrynówka
a type of liquor made from lemons

cześć
a common introduction used in informal situations: *hi, hello*

dobranoc
goodnight

ja jebię
an offensive exclamation used to express frustration or surprise (similar to *fuck me* or *fucking hell*)

ja pierdolę
similar to *ja jebię* but arguably less offensive

jeb się
fuck you

krupnik
a sweet alcoholic drink based on vodka and honey

kurwa
arguably the most common Polish swearword, often used as an interjection

kurwa mać
an emphasised version of *kurwa*

spierdalaj
fuck off, piss off

wacek
a colloquial term for *penis*; when capitalized, a diminutive form of the male name Wacław

wiśniówka
a type of liquor made from cherries

zapiekanka
a popular Polish street food; sliced baguette topped with mushrooms, cheese, and often other ingredients

żołądkowa
a type of amber-coloured herbal vodka

ACKNOWLEDGEMENTS

Thank you to Lis Goryniuk-Ratajczak for seeing something in my work and helping me turn the larval stage of *Vostok* into a proud imago. I'm forever grateful.

Thank you to Marissa Wagner for the beautiful artwork as well as the rest of Vræyda Literary for making this book a reality.

Thank you to Edward Pasewicz for helping me with the Polish alexandrine parts, Marta Sawicka-Danielak for offering valuable feedback, Leslie Gardner for generous help and encouragement, and Emily Nemchick for editing a portion of the novel.

Thank you to all editors who saw value in my work and writer friends who have consistently supported my writing: Ross Showalter, Meg Pillow, Tara Isabel Zambrano, Pat Foran, Dan Crawley, Kim Magowan, Cathy Ulrich, Tommy Dean, Anna Vangala Jones, Amy Barnes, Sara Dobbie, Tara Stillions Whitehead, Janice Leagra, Neil Clark, Hannah Grieco, Jacqueline Doyle, Kristin Tenor, Anita Goveas, Sudha Balagopal, Joanna Lech, Adam Kaczanowski, Joanna Oparek — the list goes on.

And thank you, most of all, to all my friends and loved ones who have supported me throughout the years: dearest Mama, beloved sisters Kasia and Karolina, Ewa, Gaja and Łukasz, Gosia and Ewa, Kacper, Edi, Kasia and Michał, Ola and Bryn, Agi, Piter and Kinga, Justyna and Carlo, Wiktor and Karolina, Marek, Monika and Jack, Ika and Tomek, Weronika and Kasia, Małgo, Ania, Magda, Marysia and Brent, Sławek and Marta.

Fragments of *Vostok* were published in Polish in Lampa and on Wydawnictwo j website.

Łukasz Drobnik is a Kraków-based Polish writer. His writing has been published, among other places, in HAD, Fractured Lit, Atticus Review, Pithead Chapel, X-R-A-Y Literary Magazine, Storgy, Bull, Quarterly West, Lighthouse, Foglifter, and longlisted for the Wigleaf Top 50 Very Short Fictions. He is the author of fiction collection *Nocturine* (Fathom Books). You can find him on Twitter @drobnik, or at drobnik.co.

CPSIA information can be obtained
at www.ICGtesting.com
Printed in the USA
BVHW072031011221
622869BV00011B/410